KINGDOM OF
BATS

Karlissa J.

KINGDOM OF BATS
Copyright © 2013 by Karlissa Martin

ISBN: 978-1-77069-690-7

Word Alive Press
131 Cordite Road, Winnipeg, MB R3W 1S1
www.wordalivepress.ca

 WORD ALIVE PRESS
Just Write!

Library and Archives Canada Cataloguing in Publication
Martin, Karlissa J., 1992-
    Kingdom of bats / Karlissa J. Martin.
ISBN 978-1-77069-690-7
    I. Title.
PS8626.A784K46 2012   jC813'.6   C2012-904698-1

To friends who inspire
And the One I desire

To Silvia,
Enjoy!
Karlissa J.

LIST OF CHARACTERS

Alécto (ah-layk-toh): giant Fox-Faced Bat from Scrubla

Bai'ic (bay-eek): ghostly white Flesh-Eating Bat

Bukinero (boo-kee-nair-oh): swallow, Chitolla's mate

Cattae (kat-ay): Flesh-Eating Bat, Spectral's priest

Chinaca (chee-nak-uh): Nectar-Drinking Bat, hopes to lead a war against Spectral

Chitolla (chee-toy-uh): swallow who loves stories and ends up in another world

Dreamer: One of the Guardian Princess' warriors

Eddie: Mouse-Eared Bat who supplies armour to the Big-Eared Bats

Flammeus (flam-ay-us): owl librarian who lives near Chitolla and Bukinero

Hermain: historian tortoise who visits with Chitolla

Higuero (ee-goo-air-oh): Stripe-Faced Bat who helps Patas across the Sea of Deception

Mano (man-oh): Vampire Bat, Patas' best friend

Maxéra Rea (mahz-ay-ruh ray-uh): the Guardian Princess of Sévéritas (say-vair-ee-tahz)

Péla (pay-lah): Vampire Bat, Patas' mother

Patas (paht-az): Vampire Bat who disobeys Spectral and has to flee from Thériava (thair-ee-ah-vah)

Savannah: friendly Big-Eared Bat from the Desert Mountains

Secha (say-chuh): Tent-Making Bat from the Iridescent Forests – small, white, and sweet

Spectral: Flesh-Eating Bat, lord of Thériava (thair-ee-ah-vah) – the Vampire Bats worship him as a god

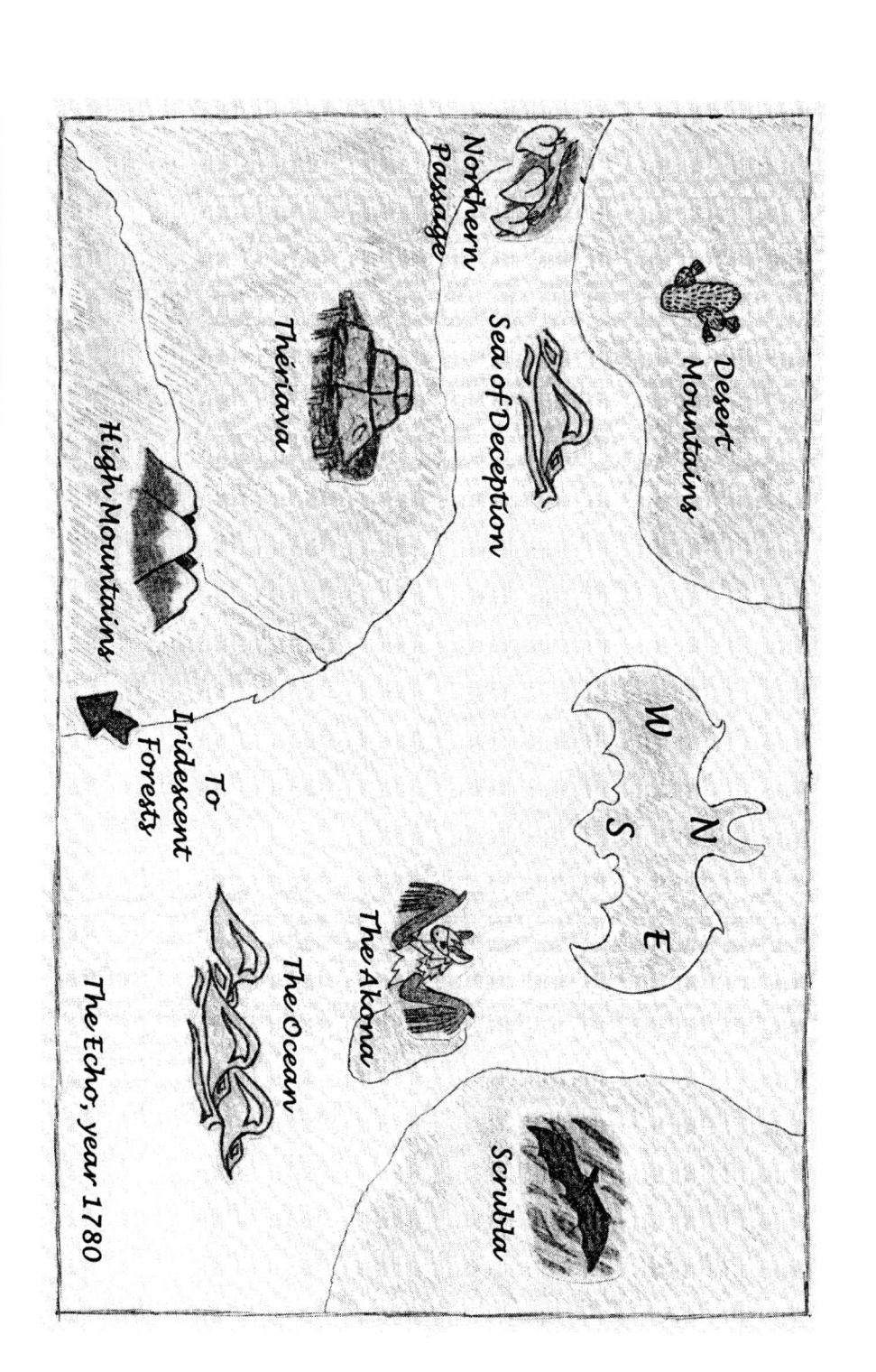

Desert Mountains

Northern Passage

Thériava

Sea of Deception

High Mountains

To Iridescent Forests

The Akona

The Ocean

Scrubla

The Echo, year 1780

 # ACKNOWLEDGEMENTS

I, KARLISSA, WILL START BY THANKING THE PERSON WHO SUGGESTED I should have an acknowledgements page: thank you, Daniel, for reading my multiple drafts, giving me advice, telling me what you thought would be cool to include, and insisting that (in regards to this book) I "soak it for all it's worth"! Thanks to Jason and Victoria, for your encouragement and enthusiasm for this story.

Thank you to the editor, for being honest about all the things that needed reworking. And thank you to Word Alive Press, for taking me through this process.

To God: thank You for giving me this opportunity, and the courage to take it. I'm looking forwards to the next adventure I'll be going on with You!

Do any remember when the worlds came to be?
Do images of ages past still live in memory?
When our two worlds were placed in Time's grasp,
And connected through a Bridge designed to last?

The Veil held animals of every form;
Together, they spoke and invented and explored.
The Echo had bats of every shape and size,
And on it the day was shorter than the night.

The worlds welcomed each other with music and cheers,
And all lived in peace for many painless years.
But Traitor looked at the worlds through covetous eyes,
And he made up his mind to end their deep ties.

With flames, he covered the Bridge between worlds,
And with time, the creatures forgot where it was.

So the Bridge has been lost, but it was not always this way,
And someday the worlds will meet each other again.

—from "The Story of Worlds," first written in the Veil, 1102.

PROLOGUE: THE ECHO

YEAR 1784

A PAIR OF ROUND EYES, BLACK LIKE OBSIDIAN, PEEKED UP AT THE STARS and sparkled for a moment with their light.

The young bat quickly closed his eyes again, pretending to be asleep. He snuggled under one of his mother's wings, her furry body and elegant face pressing gently against his side as she kissed her young son. Ignoring her affectionate nuzzling, he listened and waited. He could hear his mother humming a tune she had been humming to him since he was a newborn pup.

His ears perked slightly as her hum gave way to pleasant singing, the familiar melody replaced with well-known lyrics.

Tell me that you love me,
Tell me that it's true.
Tell me, 'cause my love,
You know I love you too.

As the stars fade into day,
If you're lost and can't find your way,
Sing out, sing my name;
Let the sound guide you to your dwelling place.

Satisfied, the young bat opened his eyes again, pushing his mother's wing away so he could look out at the deep blues of the sky and deep greens and reds and browns of the forest.

"Well," his mother chuckled, smiling at her son, "good evening, Patas. I was afraid you might be thinking of sleeping all night."

Patas shook his head fervently, grinning boyishly as he spread his little wings and dropped from the branch where he had been hanging. He flew in circles a couple times, relishing the feel of air rushing around his wings, his body seemingly weightless as he glided around outstretched tree limbs and hanging vines.

Péla watched her son's antics and sighed. "Dear, it took weeks before you finally learned to fly. And now it seems like you never want to stop!"

Patas giggled as he flew in loops around his mother, doing his best to prove her point. His circles quickly became warped and wobbly, and he collapsed onto a nearby branch, panting as he gripped the branch tightly with his two thumb-claws, trying to steady himself.

"Mommy, why is the world spinning?"

Péla laughed as her son, disorientated, clumsily attempted to crawl along the branch. "You shouldn't make yourself dizzy, Patas."

Péla suddenly gasped in fright.

Hearing her, Patas turned to look in the direction she was facing. He soon caught sight of another creature, hiding within the dense shadows cast by outstretched tree limbs. He watched with curiosity and alarm as its two dark eyes stared back at him through the thick green leaves of the canopy. Hesitantly, Patas began to sing one of the songs his mother had taught him for seeing through vegetation.

He stopped short as the form grew, spreading enormous wings to either side of its already massive body. Its leathery wings snapped against still air as it approached the fearful duo. Within moments, it landed near Patas, hanging from a branch not far above the little bat.

It smiled down on him in a friendly manner. "Hello."

Patas' eyes widened in wonder as he looked up at the giant. It was twice as big as his mother. Its lengthy ears and round black eyes focused on him. The bat's jaws were long and well-formed, and it had a tall, leaf-like projection at the tip of its snout. Its body, a single, dusky grey, was quite muscular.

"Hello." Patas responded in a small voice, shrinking back as the intimidating creature eyed him carefully.

"Have we been introduced, young bat?" the giant asked in a grating voice.

Patas nodded. "Yes. You are Cattae, the priest, the right-wing assistant to our god, Spectral."

"Good child." The grey bat nodded in approval. "Did your mother tell you I would be coming?"

Patas glanced in Péla's direction. She trembling on a nearby branch.

"Cattae," she spoke up timidly, "I hadn't told him yet. I didn't expect you to come when he was so young…"

The large creature's dark eyes turned to her. "Are you questioning my judgement, servant?"

Péla shook her head fervently. "No, no, of course not." She looked at her small son again, who waited expectantly. She tried to keep her voice from shaking as she addressed him. "Patas, go with Cattae. D—do whatever he tells you, alright?"

Patas nodded as Cattae ushered him on with an outstretched wing. "You know where to go, little bat?"

Patas could only think of one place the priest would want to take him. As the little bat flew off, Cattae cast one last glance at Péla before spreading his own wings and following the young pup through the shady forest.

Péla watched as he left, her heart beating fearfully. She tried to swallow. "Spectral, please, let my son return to me. Let him live."

* * *

Patas did not speak as he flew alongside Cattae. He kept his eyes on the dark leaves and reddish branches as he fluttered through the upper canopy of the rainforest, breathing deeply of the faintly flowery air. He sang a song his mother had taught him for flying through the forest, the first song he had ever learned. He thought back to the night she had taught it to him.

"Songs are important to bats, Patas," she had told him. "They change how we see the world around us."

Despite his desire to concentrate, Patas found it nearly impossible to resist sneaking glances at the brawny bat flying alongside him. His eyes were drawn to the creature's massive wings rhythmically beating the air, driven downwards by burly chest muscles and upwards by powerful shoulder muscles.

He tried even harder not to look at Cattae's large jaws, thickly built and filled with strong, sharp teeth. But again, he found it hard to avert his eyes. *His jaws really do look like they're made for crushing heads...*

Cattae glanced at the young bat and Patas turned away, pretending to have been looking at the path ahead.

The larger bat let his gaze linger. "Are you afraid?"

Patas shook his head, not daring to look into Cattae's face. He heard harsh chuckling next to him.

"Well, little *fleshling*, you should be."

Patas quivered, his wings breaking out of their rhythmic pattern for a split second. He hoped Cattae hadn't noticed.

"We're here." Cattae's hoarse voice brought Patas' attention back to the path ahead.

He could see in the distance a clearing where tall trees had been removed to make room for a large stone structure. The structure, situated at the highest point on the forested mountain, rose above the trees. Patas' heart raced as he recognized the artificial cavern.

Spectral's Temple.

"Get inside," Cattae ordered, abandoning the other bat as he flew off into another part of the forest.

Patas, refusing to look back despite his desire to watch Cattae's impressive and frightening form fade into the jungle, focused ahead, searching for the entrance to the pale stone building.

* * *

Patas clung to the rough stone wall, his body vertical to the ground. His eyes journeyed the interior of Spectral's Temple, memorizing every detail.

There wasn't much to it. The roof and three of the four walls had been left coarse and bumpy so that bats could more easily cling to them. The remaining wall, across from where Patas currently perched, was a dark crimson, unlike the monotone grey that filled the rest of the building. This wall had been smoothed down, with little grooves carved into it, and in the upper left corner was a large round hole, the temple's entrance. The floor was covered in rocks and small pebbles, aside from one cleared area where bats were permitted to stand if the walls were too crowded. There was a small platform of sorts, also made of stone, situated between the cleared and rocky areas.

That's where traitors stand when they're on trial, Patas thought. *Or where the sacrifices...*

Patas heard a small sneeze to his left. He looked over to see another pup, rubbing his nose, his body shaking slightly. There were about a dozen pups in the temple, young bats both male and female, waiting quietly for Cattae's return.

Patas smiled warmly. "Hi. I'm Patas."

The pup tried to smile back, nervousness threatening to twist his face into awkward positions. "My name is Mano. Do you know why we're here?"

Patas shook his head.

Mano let out a weak laugh. "Lucky. Mom says the anticipation of something bad is always worse than the actual thing."

Patas considered whether to ask Mano what he meant when a whooshing sound from across the room announced Cattae's arrival. All small talk stopped as he glided to the group of young bats, a wide grin revealing pearly white fangs.

"Welcome," Cattae began, his voice echoing around the stone building. He landed on the ground below the young bats. "Today is a day you will recall clearly for the rest of your lives."

A smirk broke out across his face, and his eyes bored into a small girl pup. He continued speaking as she quivered. "You are here to learn more about what your god, Spectral, requires of you, and what gifts he has given you in return for your loyalty. And maybe," his voice betrayed his pleasure at this thought, "maybe you'll even get to meet him for the first—and last—time."

He allowed his words to hang in the air before continuing. "As your parents should have told you, you have been blessed by Spectral in many ways. He has offered you guidance. A home. Protection. He has built this kingdom for you to feel safe and sheltered, pushing out the other, more pathetic bats that once colonized this mountain. You know the ones I speak of: the Nectar-Drinkers and Stripe-Faces who act like they're so high above us. Truly, their contempt for you is nothing more than fear. And what is it that sets you apart from them? What sustenance did Spectral teach your ancestors to collect, in order that you may become higher and stronger than the other races?"

Everyone thought of the answer, yet no one made a sound. Their eyes focused on the crimson-coloured wall.

Cattae nodded, satisfied that they had understood. "Spectral, your god, is the god of shadows and the king of the Underworld." Cattae backed away as he spoke, all eyes following him. "And today, you are going to experience the Underworld for yourselves."

Cattae motioned with his right claw to a strange, perfectly circular hole carved into the stone floor, big enough that even a giant such as himself could fit through.

Patas repositioned himself so he could look deeper into the opening. Seeing what lay inside it, he shuddered.

Floating around the hole were seemingly random patterns of wavy blue lights, each one snaking through the air as if containing a life of its own. The lights cast an unnatural glow. Despite this, Patas couldn't see past them to what lay deeper. As he observed the dancing lights, his eyes began to pick up their pattern; he watched as they formed the unmistakable shape of a flawless spider web.

Cattae cleared his throat, and the little bats drew their eyes away from the blue lights to look at him with apprehension. He smiled at them and tilted his head towards the hole. "Go in."

For the first few seconds, no one made a move.

Cattae grunted angrily. "Might I remind you that your god has given me the authority to take anyone I want as a personal... sacrifice?" His voice became icy. "Remember: that is *my* sustenance."

Cattae smiled smugly as the little pups became a flurry of wings and squeaking voices, all jostling for position as they rushed towards the circular hole.

Finding himself near the back of the group, Patas stuck as closely to the other bats as possible, ignoring the wings that slapped against him. Catching sight of Mano in the confusion of small bodies, Patas rushed to keep up. When Mano's form disappeared into the hole, Patas didn't think twice before following.

The moment his body made contact with the lights, a ringing sound shot through his ears and reverberated in his head. His vision faded and he gasped, wondering if this had been a good idea. The air hardened and became almost stiff. His wings, suddenly weary, fought the thickening air, beating against it with slow, tedious strokes.

It felt like the world had shifted away from him. The temple and the forest where his mother waited were gone—and a new world had taken its place.

Patas coughed, choking on the strange air. His eyes burned as an unfamiliar chemical touched them, filling them with tears. An overwhelming red and orange glow filled his vision. The glow itself radiated heat, a sweltering wave that reached up from below, enveloping him.

Fire, he thought. He had never before seen it, but he was positive. *This is fire.* At first, Patas saw no one. But soon, he noticed an unmistakable grey shape below him. *Cattae!*

Patas folded his wings and dropped as fast as the dense air would allow, down towards Cattae, never before so thankful to see the giant bat. He spread his wings again and followed Cattae through the fiery world, manoeuvring around the many monstrous flames reaching up to lick at his fur.

Cattae appeared to ignore the heat, smoke, and burning brightness, his flight just as casual and steady as it had been traveling through the trees in the upper world. Patas tried to do as his guide and ignore the pain, but his eyes dripped tears, closing every time a flame rose from below, stretching out wispy arms as if to grab him.

Dizzy and frightened, Patas hadn't noticed until that moment that the air slowly thinned the further Cattae led them from the entrance to this world. Still, his wings ached from fighting the thick air. He panted heavily, trying to get enough oxygen to stop the throbbing in his head.

Patas wasn't sure if he had passed out or if the deadly air was playing tricks on him, but the next thing he noticed was his feet gripping tightly to a stone surface that reminded him of the roof of a cave. He found Mano beside him, watching the scene through blurry eyes. All the pups were lined up in a row.

Cattae flew in steady circles below them, yelling to ensure that all could hear him. "This, young fleshlings, is the home of your god, Spectral. Don't bother trying to use songs to see around this world— they will do you no good. Only Spectral and I, his dearest servant, have eyes that can pierce the flames. I am the only one he brings down here frequently, because I am his chosen one. He has taught me the secrets of thriving in this world."

Cattae released another one of his maniacal laughs. "I say thriving, not surviving, because surviving is easy: the very air of this world forces one to become immortal. Immortally agonized, if you do not know its secrets. If you did—well, you would be a god, like Spectral. Bigger, darker, more powerful, immortal... a craver of flesh..."

Patas shivered.

"Any questions about this place or your god?"

A moment of silence followed, eventually broken by a small, hesitant voice.

"Aren't you a god, too, then? Why is Spectral called a god, and you're just his priest?"

Patas sighed gratefully when he heard the other pup ask the question he was too afraid to speak aloud.

"I am not yet immortal in the outside world," Cattae replied, not bothered by the question. "But I am on my way to becoming a god, because Spectral has chosen me. You, as well, have taken the first steps to godhood by giving yourselves to Spectral as his servants and accepting the sustenance he gave your ancestors. Any other questions?"

"When can we leave?" one of the girl pups spoke in a quivering, desperate voice. "I want to see my family again. Daddy—"

"None of you will leave until *after* Spectral has chosen his sacrifice!" Cattae roared. "One hour is all you have to stand, fleshlings. One hour in the Underworld."

Patas closed his eyes and thought back to his mother, who waited for him back home in the forest, back in the "real" world. He envisioned her as he had last seen her: eyes filled with fear.

He heard wheezing breaths beside him and opened his eyes. Mano was shaking violently, whispering to himself, "One hour… one hour… I can't take this…"

Patas reached out a claw to touch Mano on the shoulder. The other pup's eyes drew to him, and Patas smiled reassuringly. "We'll be okay," Patas said. "This is our initiation, right? Our parents went through this, and they're alright. If they can do it, so can we."

Mano nodded, allowing a small smile as he reached out his own wing and wrapped it around Patas' shoulders.

"Let go of your friends and let them be!" Cattae barked, suddenly appearing below Patas and Mano. "Allow Spectral to choose whomever he pleases. The one who is chosen should consider it an honour, not a burden."

Mano pulled back his wing, and Patas obediently withdrew his claw.

Patas swallowed, then blinked back regretful tears as a horrible burning sensation ran down his throat and into his chest.

One hour.

* * *

Patas was sure he heard other questions, pups whispering to each other fearfully, but perhaps they were just in his imagination. The brilliant dancing flames and painfully toxic smoke and harshly boiling heat continued to confuse and overwhelm his senses.

Strange voices, faint whispers, bounced around this forbidding world.

At first, they were all frightened screams and cries of agony, but slowly, as he closed his eyes and listened more intently, he picked up echoes of sweet songs, soft and comforting voices, and friendly chitchat. He became convinced that, if he opened his eyes, he would see lovely, welcoming faces smiling and leaning over to greet him…

Then he recalled where he was. *Am I going insane?* he wondered. *What's going on?*

A chill ran down his spine as he heard other bats gasping, whimpering in fright.

"He's here," Cattae announced, though he certainly didn't need to; everyone could feel the new presence approaching them, hiding from their sight within the many flames. "Spectral is here to choose his sacrifice."

Patas shuddered, his heart racing. Mano's breathing again became rapid, and he mumbled incoherently.

Patas closed his eyes and tried to shut out the sounds and sensations around him. He remembered his mother, her gentle touch and beautiful face, her voice singing lullabies as the stars began to fade from the sky.

> Tell me that you love me,
> Tell me that it's true.

A blood-curdling scream echoed through the strange world, and Patas unwillingly opened his eyes, just in time to see a large, dark shape rise up from the flames below. Jaws even larger and stronger than Cattae's reached towards a screaming, flailing pup.

Patas shut his eyes, turning away, trying to close out the pup's horrible screams as she was pulled into the flames. The screaming stopped abruptly, and Cattae's voice rang out again.

"A sacrifice has been chosen. Say a prayer to your god and return with me to the upper world."

* * *

Patas drew a deep, painless breath as he felt himself leave the other world and return to his own. He again surveyed the inside of Spectral's Temple, gratefully soaking in the plain grey stones, his vision no longer clouded by wisps of noxious smoke.

Mano pulled up beside him, panting heavily as he pumped the air with his wings. A wide grin engulfed his face. "We did it!" he said excitedly. "We made it out alive!"

Patas turned to see the other pups, some fluttering joyfully, others choking back tears as they tried to put on a happy face. A pang hit his heart as he looked into one young girl's eyes, red-rimmed and stained with drops of water.

Someone didn't make it out alive...

Cattae was the last to appear out of the hole. Patas watched as the large bat collapsed on the floor, chest heaving. Cattae grunted and gritted his teeth, as if in pain, and for a moment he held his wing over his eyes to shield them.

Finally, Cattae pulled back his wing and took a big breath, his body relaxing as he released it slowly.

Patas' heart skipped a beat as he found himself again staring into the dark eyes of the giant. Cattae watched him unblinkingly.

The giant averted his eyes, and Patas breathed a sigh of relief.

Cattae cleared his throat. All the pups stopped chattering, mouths closing and eyes turning to him.

For a few seconds, Cattae simply stared at the ground. "Your priest is hungry," he announced coolly. "The last fleshling to exit the temple—"

No one waited for him to finish the sentence. Patas found himself fighting against the other bats crowding around him in their mad dash towards freedom. All his mind and energy focused on the hole in the crimson-stained wall.

When he felt fresh rainforest air envelope him and saw the stars sparkling above, he didn't even think to look back. He immediately began to sing, the words meaningless as he tried to find his way back to his mother's loving wings.

Kingdom of Bats

As the stars fade into day,
If you're lost and can't find your way,
Sing out, sing my name;
Let the sound guide you to your dwelling place.

THE VEIL

1

BUKINERO RAN HIS BEAK THROUGH THE FEATHERS LINING HIS CHEST, puffing them out as he preened them. Pausing from his work, he spread his wings and released his grip on the thin branch to which he held. He glided down from his perch, flapping only occasionally as his streamlined wings carried him through the steamy rainforest air to a clear pool.

Staring for a moment at his reflection in the still waters, he admired his new coat of fine feathers: iridescent blue, with patches of orange on his face and snowy white covering his chest and belly.

Finally, he thought to himself, *I don't look like a fledgling anymore.* No more dull-brown and off-coloured feathers for him.

"Big brother!"

Bukinero caught the loud, plaintive cry as it travelled through the heavy air.

"Mommy says you need ta bring me somethin' ta eat!"

His eyes scanned the pond for signs of insect life. Fluttering silver wings caught his attention and he darted across the surface of the water. Grasping the flying insect in his beak, he swerved upwards, the air rushing under his wings as he turned towards the sound of his younger brother's call.

Not far from him, a tall cliff of red clay rose above the muddy, chocolate brown earth below. Lining the cliff were round, mud-made nests in which busy swallows darted to and fro, greeting each other and chatting warmly as they tended to their needy chicks.

Bukinero darted towards the cliff, following a familiar path through the well-travelled sky until he made it to the nest where his little brother waited eagerly for his arrival. Bukinero landed on the edge of the nest, his claws gripping the dried mud, and lowered the captured insect towards his brother's open mouth.

Gulping it down, the chick smiled gratefully. "Big brother, are you mad at us?"

"No. Why do you ask?"

"'Cause you're leavin'."

"Not because I'm mad at you," Bukinero explained. "There's more space to build nests at the Stone Place, higher up the mountain."

Bukinero surveyed the mud nest, investigating its cupped form for anything that might need repair.

"Are you old enough ta build a nest an' marry a girl?" his brother asked.

"Yes, I am."

"Then why don't you have one?"

"A nest?"

"No! A girl!"

Bukinero sighed, slightly irritated. "Criol, do you want anything else to eat?"

Criol ignored his brother's question, staring up and to the right of his comfy clay nest. "Gradly has a girl."

"Gradly's always has a girl. He's… a bit crazy. Criol, do you want anything?"

Criol shook his head, eyes fixed upwards. Bukinero looked up to where his little brother was staring. A short distance away, perched along a ledge, was a group of young swallows, some bluish or purplish in colour, others a solid or dappled shade of brown.

Bukinero glanced back at his brother, who appeared quite enthralled with the group of swallows. "What?"

"Will you marry one o' them?" Criol questioned. "They're all goin' up the mountain, just like you. An' they're all girls. Are you gonna intaduce me to your mate after you meet her?"

Bukinero failed at holding back a smile. He allowed his gaze to return to the group of young swallows, who chitchatted excitedly, joyous laughs escaping every few moments.

"Which one will you marry?" Criol peeped up excitedly, apparently getting the wrong message from his brother's reaction.

"How should I know? I might not marry any of them." Bukinero scanned the nest again. "Do you need any more feathers?"

"No! I need ta know who you gonna marry, so I can apoove!"

"You mean, approve?"

"Yeah! I *need* ta know!" Criol turned his attention back to the group of young swallows. "Marry da bright blue one. She's funny, an' she talks a lot, so you would always have someone ta listen to."

"Uh, no, Criol. If you're going to pick for me, try someone quieter."

Criol stretched out his skinny neck so his large, round eyes could get a closer look at the young females. "Da lil' brown one doesn't talk much. But she's a runt or somethin'."

"Criol, that's rude."

"Why? I'm a runt."

"Who told you that?"

"Dat's why I'm the only one left in da nest. Bukinero, do you like the lil' brown one?"

Bukinero turned his eyes back to the young birds. It didn't take long to recognize the one his brother meant. She was notably small. The majority of her feathers were a soft shade of brown, but her belly, chest, and throat were pure white. Unlike the others, who spoke in raucous voices, her words were soft, barely audible.

He observed her for a moment, surprised at himself for going along with his brother's game.

Actually, he thought, *she is rather pretty...*

Suddenly, the young female turned and looked in Bukinero's direction, apparently aware of the fact he was watching her.

Embarrassed, Bukinero returned his gaze to his little brother. "Is there anything else you would like, Criol?"

Criol giggled impishly. "She likes you."

"We haven't even met! Now, is there anything else Mom and Dad wanted me to do for you?"

"They said you have ta say goodbye ta dem bafore you leave."

"Of course I will," Bukinero assured his little brother. "And I'll say goodbye to you too."

Criol's mouth widened into a gaping yawn. He blinked sleepily. "Okay, big brother. I'll say goodbye now. Goodbye."

"I'm not leaving yet," Bukinero replied, chuckling. He watched for a moment as Criol snuggled into the soft down feathers lining the clay nest. As Criol's breathing became steady and deep, Bukinero's gaze returned to the group of young swallows.

He was surprised to see the small brown one alone, the others having flown off. She turned her head slowly in all directions, staring at the cliff and the many nests covering it, then out at the rainforest. Finally, her gaze lifted to the pale sky blanketing it all. Bukinero was sure he saw her release a small sigh.

His thoughts returned to what Criol had said: "They're all goin' up the mountain, just like you." How his brother knew that, Bukinero couldn't even begin to guess.

Go talk to her.

The moment the thought came, Bukinero shrugged it off. It only came back stronger.

Go talk to her!

Nervously, he spread his wings and threw his body into the faint breeze. Shaping the air with his wings, he pulled himself back up the cliff face, towards the ledge where the swallow sat.

Her dark eyes turned to him as he landed. He cleared his throat, speaking hesitantly. "Um—hi, I'm Bukinero. I heard you're travelling up the mountain, to the Stone Place."

She nodded, but remained silent, as if expecting him to say something else.

"I'm also moving to the Stone Place," he continued. "This will be my first nesting season."

"Mine too," she responded, a pleasant tone in her gentle but clear voice. "I'm Chitolla. My family has been planning to move up the mountain for some time. We've been waiting for my youngest siblings to fledge."

"Really?" Bukinero glanced back towards the nest where his little brother slept peacefully. "My family isn't coming with me. I'm going on my own."

"You don't have a mate yet?"

He shook his head.

"Me neither," Chitolla said, nodding slightly. "I was hoping to find someone when I got there." For a moment, her gaze travelled around the cliff and the nearby jungle. "I'm really going to miss it here."

Bukinero nodded in agreement, his heartbeat skipping strangely. Her black eyes, barely tinted with blue, scanned the world. A hint of iridescent indigo flickered along the top of her head and back, silvery patches running across the side of her face. What from a distance had seemed to be a simple shade of brown was a complex pattern of coloured feathers.

"So, when are you leaving for the mountain?" he asked. *And can I travel with you, by any chance?*

"Actually," Chitolla said, looking down at a nearby nest, which Bukinero assumed was her family's, "I think we're leaving right now."

Bukinero's heart dropped in disappointment. "Oh. Well, have a safe trip. Maybe I'll see you again."

"Of course you will." There was a tone of slight puzzlement in Chitolla's voice. "Aren't we moving to the same place?"

"Uh… yeah, we are." Bukinero felt both embarrassed and thrilled. "I'll see you when I get there."

Chitolla spread her wings. "See you later."

Bukinero bobbed his head in farewell, his tongue refusing to work as he watched her glide into the sky.

Hearing snickers echoing off the cliff wall, Bukinero lowered his head to search for their source. Chiol's smiling face and big eyes peeked out of the nest at him. "I knew you lick-ed her!"

* * *

When Bukinero arrived at the Stone Place, his primary concern was finding Chitolla. He perched on a tree limb, glad to finally rest his wings after the long journey, and contemplated his options. He could see a bevy of fellow swallows before him, circling the Stone Place and chattering loudly about where to build and who owned what spot.

The Stone Place was a large ruin atop a jungle-covered mountain. Each of the structure's grey rocks had been chiselled to fit perfectly with its neighbouring stones. The Stone Place had stood on the mountain for more years than the swallows could count.

The little birds ignored the structure's interior. They had taken to living in the tiny crevices and holes that had formed over time along the outside wall, created by vines and small trees and the wind and rain.

As the cliffs where Bukinero grew up became too crowded, rumours spread that the Stone Place was prime property, nearly empty of inhabitants. Bukinero saw now that this was far from the truth: already he could hear many swallows suggesting that it might be better to move on in search of more secluded spots.

Over the next hour, as the crowd thinned, Bukinero kept his eyes and ears roving the jungle for signs of Chitolla. Fearful that she may have decided to join the swallows who had moved on, he debated doing the same.

"I don't like this place," Bukinero overheard one young swallow whine to her husband. "It's in the middle of nowhere, and isn't as pretty as the cliffs. Why couldn't we go back and build a nest there?"

Another bird's words carried over to his ears. "Most of the other swallows think we should move on. There's not much space here, and there are nicer places to live."

"I don't understand why everyone keeps saying that. I like it here. It's beautiful."

Bukinero's heart skipped a beat at the sound of the second swallow's voice. *Could it be?* His eyes darted around until they found the source of the conversation. *It's her!*

Spreading his wings, he thrust himself into the air without even thinking about what he would say when he reached her.

Soon, he found himself gently landing on a corner of the stone building's roof, inserting himself into a small group of clay-coloured swallows. Three sets of eyes turned to the newcomer with slight bewilderment, but Bukinero's attentions were focused only on one.

"Hi, Chitolla." Realizing from her puzzled look that she may not remember him, Bukinero continued, trying not to allow any hint of embarrassment to creep into his voice. "I'm Bukinero. We talked on the Southern Cliffs."

Chitolla nodded in recognition. "Yes, I remember. Hi."

The other two exchanged odd looks. One spoke up. "Hi, I'm Vita."

Bukinero glanced in her direction. "Hello."

"Are you moving on with the other swallows?"

"Haven't decided yet." Bukinero returned his attention to Chitolla. "What are your plans?"

Chitolla hesitated. "Well, I don't know… I really like it here, but most of the swallows are older, and I don't honestly know if I'll be able to find a mate."

"I'm considering staying," Bukinero said. Vita rolled her eyes, but he didn't notice. "Are you hungry? We could go foraging together—I could help you find something to eat."

"Can we join you?" the other swallow inserted.

Bukinero looked at her, bewildered. "Hmm? Sure."

"Nah, Maria, why don't we go hunting together and let the ol' pals catch up?" Vita nodded in Chitolla's direction, attempting half-heartedly to contain her teasing smile. "See you when we get back."

Vita encouraged Maria with a gentle shove, and the two took off.

"Well," Chitolla said once they were alone, "I wouldn't mind getting something to eat."

"Great."

As Chitolla took off, Bukinero followed after her. Soon, they were flying side-by-side, Bukinero making small motions with his beak as he directed Chitolla to what he believed would be the best feeding areas.

"So," he said, not too concerned about catching any insects himself, "what's your favourite pastime?"

"Pastime?" Chitolla had to consider that for a moment. "Well, I really like stories, listening to storytellers or travelers telling of their adventures... I suppose that's not exactly a pastime, just something I really enjoy."

"I think it counts. What's your favourite story?"

This also appeared to be a tough question. "Honestly, I don't know. I like stories about unexpected heroes and journeys to exotic places. What types of stories do you like?"

"To tell the truth, I've never really been into stories. I like practical things. But I wouldn't mind hearing a story from you."

Chitolla giggled softly. "Really?"

"Yeah. Go ahead, tell me a story."

"Like... what story?"

"What's the last story you heard that you really enjoyed?"

Chitolla thought for a moment. "Well, this sparrow came to the cliffs not long ago and told us about some of the wonderful things he saw during his time in the north."

Bukinero listened intently as Chitolla told him about all the different things the sparrow had mentioned seeing, like treeless mountains, fluffy white rain, and strange honking birds. Chitolla's confidence and joy rose greatly as she carried on, and neither noticed as the sun faded from the horizon and the stars showed their light.

* * *

Months later, Chitolla found herself busily pasting together her first nest. She carried one beakful of mud at a time to a crevice on the wall of the Stone Place, caking the fresh mud onto what was already there. She would then fly off, returning shortly with another bit of mud to add to the developing nest.

After delivering yet another clump to its proper place, she paused to examine her work. The task was almost complete.

Bukinero should be pleased, she thought. *I've gotten a lot done since he left to find food.*

Chitolla stopped for a moment to take in the world around her. She listened to the insects, chirping and buzzing in the trees, and slowly breathed in the warm, moist air. The trees stretched their arms out over the deep green world above her, their leaves reaching out to touch the rays of sunlight that fell from the clear midday sky. Covering the ground some distance below was red earth, a perfect nursery to small ferns, young trees, and colourful flowers with thin, stringy roots. Everything was peaceful. Chitolla could hear the familiar and comforting calls of other swallows, many originating from cracks and nests similar to the one in which she herself now perched.

She suddenly noticed another creature below her, plodding over the red earth with slow, deliberate steps. The animal looked almost like it had been chiselled out of brown rock; a heavy shell covered its back and it walked along on short, stubby legs.

Curious, she called out in greeting. "Good morning, sir tortoise!"

The creature turned its head to leisurely look up in her direction. A smile creased its already wrinkled face. "Good morning, young sparrow!"

"Actually, I'm a swallow, sir tortoise."

The tortoise took a couple steps towards the wall on which she perched. "Sorry, I've never been able to remember how to tell you guys apart. My name is Hermain. Who would you be?"

"Chitolla. Do you come here often? I don't believe I've seen you before. We don't get very many of your kind around here."

"Oh, no," Hermain said with what Chitolla thought was an odd tone. "I haven't been in this place for many years. The last time I was here would have been—1635, I think. Long before you were born."

"1635? My, that was a long time ago!" Chitolla mentally did the math. "About… 160 years ago…" At first she was incredulous, but she soon recalled having heard that tortoises could live as long as two hundred years. "What brought you back?"

Hermain surveyed the wall, examining the stone building. A distant and somewhat amazed appearance overcame his wrinkled face.

"Are you looking for something, sir?" Chitolla yelled down. "Perhaps I can help."

"I came to see if the rumours were true… and it appears that they are."

Chitolla shuffled a bit, concern in her voice. "The rumours?"

"Good rumours," Hermain replied, relieving her of her worries. "Very good rumours. Tell me, Chitolla, how long have you lived on this mountain?"

"All my life, sir. I grew up along the Southern Cliffs. My family and I moved up here after my youngest siblings learned to fly."

"What do you think of it here?"

Chitolla looked up at the dazzling blue sky. "Oh, it's beautiful!"

Tired of yelling, she darted down to a nearby tree stump so she wouldn't have to call so far.

"The cliffs were nice too," she said. "They had a good view, but here, the air is crisp, insect and bird songs are sung continuously, the soil is soft, the rocks colourful, the flowers so varied, and no matter where you look there is every shade of green imaginable. It's so… alive!"

Chitolla stopped, feeling a bit embarrassed at how overcome with emotion her words must have seemed to this near stranger.

But Hermain didn't chuckle or even smile. Instead, he spoke with gravity. "This used to be a place of death."

THE MYSTERY

CHITOLLA REPLIED WITH STUNNED SILENCE. *DEATH?*

Hermain hung his head, as if saddened by the memory that washed over him. "Chitolla, would you like to come down here and learn the story of this Stone Place? If not, I understand. It isn't a very pleasant story."

Chitolla loved her new homeland very much, so she wanted to know why this strange tortoise would speak of it with such sadness. She flew down to the ground and stood respectfully beside him.

"You can tell me," she spoke quietly.

"Do you know who built this place?"

It was a question she had never considered. "Other creatures, I suppose. The older swallows say it's been here for many generations, longer than anyone remembers."

"Do you know why it was built?"

She looked a bit ashamed. "I never thought to ask."

"Years ago, the Stone Place was put together as a temple to honour the god of a kingdom that was once here. A kingdom of bats."

"Bats?" Chitolla responded. "There aren't many bats on this mountain."

"Well, during the time of this kingdom, there were many bats, all ruled by a giant, flesh-eating bat whom they considered to be a god. This bat would order the other bats to serve him. They lived under his authority, at times even bringing themselves to him as an offering. There would be a ceremony of sorts, where they asked for his blessing, and in return they allowed themselves to be fed to him."

Chitolla's eyes filled with horror. "Not here!"

"Yes, here," Hermain replied gravely. "These bats knew what was to happen to them, and they agreed to it, for the sake of pleasing their god. They believed that, as they gave themselves to their god, he would bless them and their families with honour and power—even immortality."

"That seems foolish, if I may put it bluntly."

"Over time, the kingdom grew larger and stronger, and it conquered nearby lands. The bats began to enslave fellow bats and other creatures, forcing them to expand the temple, then taking them to their 'god' to be tortured, killed, and devoured."

"That's dreadful!" Chitolla cried. "Why would they do such a thing?"

"To prove their power. Long ago, the screams of their captives rang through the forest as they were forced into the temple. It was a rare day that the place wasn't covered with blood. Their god said he loved the sight of blood, so the bats painted the walls with the blood of their captives, to keep his blessing on them."

Chitolla shivered at the image that passed through her mind. "That's terrible. Horrible. How was this disgusting practice ended? Clearly no one has been forcibly fed to a flesh-eating bat in this Stone Place, this—temple—for a long while. In fact, no one even enters the temple now, and certainly no one lives in it. Where did the so-called god go?"

"Well," Hermain said, "that is the question of the day."

Chitolla was shocked. She wanted answers. "How were these horrible practices ended?" she asked again.

"I have no idea."

"Why not? No one will tell you what happened?"

"No one seems to know. Several seasons ago, one of my friends came by here on his way to another spot, and he found it as you see it now. You swallows do not have stories of how the bats left?"

"No," Chitolla replied. "All I know is that friends of my family moved here some time ago, and recently, my family has joined them."

"Amazing," Hermain said with a smile. "Vanished. Well, perhaps they weren't powerful for very long. Perhaps." Hermain pondered his own words, seemingly lost in thought. Finally, the tortoise returned to the world of the living. "Well, I must be going."

Disappointed, Chitolla asked, "Are you not staying a while longer?"

"No, just passing through. My time here is up. It was certainly nice to speak with you, young swallow."

"It was a pleasure meeting you, sir tortoise."

Hermain gave her a wide and wrinkly grin as a goodbye, turning his head as he resumed plodding towards destinations unknown.

Then, unexpectedly, he paused. "If you're really interested in delving into this mystery, there's a place you should check out. A friend of mine, Flammeus, has established a library in her tree hollow. Ask around—I'm sure the other swallows know where it is. I plan on going there to see what dear Flammeus knows about the disappearance of the temple's former resident."

"I'll be sure to look into it. Thank you, Hermain."

Chitolla watched the slow-moving figure a moment longer before spreading her wings and taking off. She flew back to her small home, gently landing in the crack along the grey stone wall. She briefly contemplated the nearly-finished mound of mud that had previously occupied her.

Not in the mood to continue working, she gazed at the well-arranged grey stones below, examining the wall in which her shelter was located.

Something seemed to have changed. The stones appeared sharper than she recalled, and the woods darker. She could imagine the sounds of screaming captives, peace-loving creatures, being forced towards their doom. The red soil now resembled blood.

She turned quickly at an unexpected sound, half-expecting the horrible form of a giant, ashen-coloured bat with blood-red eyes and long fangs… but it was just a cricket, nestled in a crack below her perch, chirping happily.

A glint of sunlight caught the young swallow's eye and she hopped forward to reach it. The horrible screams faded as the familiar sounds of cicadas and bird calls reached her ears again. The blood washed away in the sunlight, the evil slowly buried, silenced by the peace and beauty that now filled Chitolla's heart.

This is a beautiful place.

At that moment, a thought came back to her: *I must finish my nest!* She swooped to the ground once again to search for those few remaining bits of mud.

* * *

"You're sure about this, Chitolla?" Bukinero soared alongside his mate. "You really want to fly all that way to look at a… what was it again?"

"A library," Chitolla patiently explained, as she had already done a few times before. "I asked some of the other swallows about it. It's in a large tree hollow on the other side of the mountain."

"So, you actually *want* to fly that far to look at a couple of books?" Bukinero looked bewildered. "Chitolla, you've never been excited about travelling before, except to visit the Southern Cliffs. Why the sudden interest in a library?"

Chitolla shrugged as best she could in mid-air. "I'm—curious, that's all. Remember what I told you about the tortoise, Hermain?"

"Of course," Bukinero said with a small sigh. "He's to blame."

A few days earlier, Bukinero had come home from his hunt with a mouthful of damselflies as a special treat, and she had told him about her encounter with the traveling tortoise.

Shouldn't we be more focused on our nest? Bukinero thought to himself. *Our nest, our coming chicks, our family—our future. Not the history of this building, what it was originally used for… None of that matters anymore!*

But somehow, after speaking with that tortoise, it had begun to matter to Chitolla.

"You're sure about this?" Bukinero again asked. "Wouldn't you rather be at the nest right now?"

This time, Chitolla didn't try to explain. "If you really don't want to go, Bukinero, we can turn back." Though she said the words kindly, her voice betrayed disappointment.

"No, that's fine," Bukinero insisted. "Really. If you're this thrilled about going, we should go. It's just… unexpected, that's all." He smiled at her. "It is nice to have some time alone together."

She giggled, pulling herself closer to him. "By the time we get to the library, we won't be alone."

"Really? Why not?"

"The librarian will be there, of course."

"Of course," Bukinero said with another sigh. "Well, at least we can enjoy our trip together. What is the librarian, anyway?"

"Hmm—that's a good question. I *think* she's the keeper of all the books."

"Funny. I meant, *what* is she?"

* * *

While Chitolla engrossed herself in the books lining the walls of this rather large tree hollow, Bukinero stared nervously at the "keeper of all the books."

This librarian was covered in an array of fiery-coloured feathers and armed with a small, hooked beak and sharp talons. She was an owl, five times his height, which was perhaps small for this race of owl, but she was nevertheless frightening.

Chitolla had asserted that the swallows who had told her about the library agreed this owl was trustworthy, and only ate lesser, non-talking animals. Still, Bukinero felt neither confident nor safe around the other bird—though he had decided it was best to keep that fact hidden.

Looking up at the owl's face, Bukinero let out an abrupt chirp to clear his voice. "So… you collect books?"

The owl swivelled to make eye contact with him, blinking quickly. Bukinero hopped backwards, not expecting those golden eyes to be so intimidating.

"Collect?" the owl responded in whispery tones. "Gather, more like. But collect… yes, I suppose so."

Her voice seemed sinister to Bukinero. "What subjects do they cover?"

"Subject, subjects," the owl repeated, moving along the shelves to pull out books. "Well, I have books on many things: trees and herbs, medicine and tools... there are stories, histories... kingdoms, lands, maps... and animals—many, many books on the animals that inhabit our world." At this, the owl hopped to the shelf across from Bukinero. "This section is all about animals."

Chitolla, mesmerized by the many titles, barely noticed the conversation her mate was having with the librarian. Her eyes darted excitedly in all directions. Already, she had flipped through several volumes, but she remained hungry for more.

Suddenly, her eyes locked onto a book far above, a thin, faded piece. She felt unexpectedly drawn to it as she read the words along its binding: *The Story of Worlds*.

"Librarian," she called out, using her beak to point out the book, "what is that one about?"

Bukinero was soon at her side. He didn't see any reason why this particular book should draw his mate's attention. It looked like all the others: dark brown and a little old.

But the owl, also quick to reach Chitolla's side, made an excited chirring sound.

"This book is very special," the owl said, using a few wing beats to level herself with the top shelf. She pulled it out and floated back to the ground, laying the book out so the two swallows could see it. "This is one of the few books I have managed to collect that speaks of both worlds, the Veil and the Echo."

"The Veil?" Chitolla asked curiously.

"Why, *our* world!" the owl replied, chirring once again. Bukinero took it for laughter. "The world of talking animals."

"There's another world?" Chitolla's voice was filled with something between doubt and curiosity.

"Oh, there *is* another world! Our world is connected by the Bridge with the Echo: the world of bats, where no other animals speak."

"Where is the Echo?"

"Right across the Bridge from our world, of course! My, this all seems to be very new to you!"

Chitolla gazed in wonder at the volume in front of her. She hesitantly ran her claws along the edge of the special book, as if considering whether or not it would be proper to open it. Slowly, she flipped to the first page.

The owl's eyes began to gleam. Bukinero looked on with faint curiosity.

Chitolla examined the book's off-white and wrinkled pages, noting its cracked binding. "It looks like it's been read a lot."

The owl's head bobbed up and down. "Yes, it is one of my favourite books! I've read its tales many times. It is a beautiful work of art, and its stories so touching and exciting and thought-provoking."

"What are your other favourite books?"

"My other favourite book also talks about both worlds." The owl whirled her head around, then took off. "This book is treasured by many—and it is very special. I have many copies, and many books written by those who have studied it and pondered it."

Huh? Bukinero's head spun at the thought. *Are you saying there are books about other books? Who makes those?*

The owl returned from another section of the library, bringing to Bukinero and Chitolla a smaller but nonetheless thick book. "This," she said excitedly, "is the most important book in my library—the most important book *ever*."

"What is it?" Chitolla responded eagerly, looking over the volume. Bukinero, meanwhile, stared at the dark talons holding it.

"This is *Creator's Book*, a book with stories given to us by the Uncreated Maker. Through them, we learn about him, and we learn about ourselves."

Bukinero knew who Creator was: the God who ruled over the world, who, as his title implied, was credited for the existence of this world. But he nodded absently, not particularly interested.

"Yeah, I've heard of this book," he said. "You have too, Chitolla. Your mother showed us a copy her friend had. The swallows I used to live with memorized the stories in it and told them to each other. *Everyone* knows about this book."

Chitolla turned away from him to stare again at the thick, darkly-coloured volume. Bukinero was surprised she was so enchanted by it.

Wasn't it just an ordinary book that happened to be very well-known? Why did she care so much?

He sighed with realization. *It's the owl. The owl making a big deal about a commonplace book. Just like a random travelling tortoise getting her so interested in the history of some ordinary stone building.*

Bukinero watched as Chitolla flipped open the book and scanned a section of it. Bukinero hopped closer, reading over her shoulder. The tale was about sky-beings coming to the rescue of a weasel and his family from a soon-to-be-destroyed kingdom, because Creator had made a promise to this weasel's brother.

Baffled by the strange ideas contained in the story, he soon stopped reading. But to his shock, Chitolla appeared spellbound, soaking in each word.

Bukinero glanced sideways at *The Story of Worlds*, which remained on the floor, opened and waiting to be read. Wondering how many other books Chitolla could become engrossed in, Bukinero surveyed the many shelves in the spacious tree hollow, attempting to count the books. He decided they had better leave before the owl had a chance to capture his mate's imagination with yet another volume.

"Well, it has been very interesting seeing your... collection," he told the larger bird. "Perhaps we shall come back another time. It was nice meeting you, uh…"

"Flammeus is my name," the owl responded, her voice friendly, "Flammeus. And it has been a pleasure having you here. I do hope to see you both again."

Glad for the opportunity to leave, Bukinero darted out of the hollow in a hurry. Chitolla reluctantly hopped away from her reading, said a polite farewell to Flammeus, and set out to catch up.

* * *

It was weeks before Chitolla and Bukinero returned to the library.

Flammeus was rearranging books in the tree hollow, chirring at memories from days long past, when she heard the two swallows arrive. She hopped over to the hollow's entrance to greet them, a joyful tone in her owly voice. "Good morning! Good morning! Sir Bukinero and sweet Chitolla, I see. You've returned for another look?"

Bukinero nodded, but the frown that crossed his face suggested he was a little put off by the owl's good mood.

Flammeus regarded the two swallows, noting that their countenance was more solemn than on their previous visit. She cleared her throat, hoping to cheer them with some pleasant conversation. "Oh, Chitolla, I had some friends of yours here a week or two ago! Vita and Maria. They mentioned you two had just had your first batch of eggs! Congratulations! How does it feel being a parent? I would love to meet the little chicks when they hatch!"

A short moment of silence followed.

"Actually, our eggs died," Chitolla spoke softly. "We'll have to start a family next season."

Flammeus' ear-tufts fell back. "Oh, dear," she said, troubled. "I am so sorry to hear that. Is there any way I can help you? I know that reading some of the stories in *Creator's Book* comfort me when I'm in distress."

"Me as well," Chitolla replied. "Actually, I've been reading it a lot. One of the other swallow families in our area has a copy. They've been very kind to share, and we've become friends through this difficult time."

Chitolla sounded grateful and comforted by this fact, but Bukinero didn't feel the same way.

Perhaps someday, he realized, *I'll be glad for these new friendships.* At this point, all he felt was loss.

"Actually," Chitolla continued, "I've been very curious about *The Story of Worlds*. No one seems to have a copy of it. In fact, no one seems to have heard of it."

Mention it, and you get blank stares, Bukinero thought. *Mention other worlds, and you generally get very strange looks.*

Flammeus flew up to that higher shelf and brought down the special book. She opened it. "Alright. What would you like to know?"

Chitolla considered for a moment. "Nothing specific… except, why is our world called the Veil?"

"Well, sweet swallow," Flammeus replied, "when the worlds were first created, Creator asked the creatures living at that time to give their world a name. We, the talking animals, called our world the Veil. Something about the early clouds covering our world was reminiscent of a thin veil stretching across the sky. Of course, with time, this 'veil' has mostly faded, but in some places—"

"Who would know that?" Bukinero interrupted suddenly, his tone incredulous.

Ignoring Chitolla's surprised stare, he hopped over to the worn volume and furiously flipped through its pages.

"Why would *anyone* believe in other worlds?" he pressed. "If there is another world, why do so few books talk about it? Why should we just accept—"

Hearing a ripping sound, Bukinero stopped flipping the pages and stared down with an abashed look at the page he had accidently torn out.

Flammeus pushed Bukinero out of the way and grabbed the page from his grasp. She gently placed the page back in the book and closed it. Slowly, she turned to Bukinero, her golden eyes blazing with fiery intensity.

"This," she said, taking a deep breath, "is a *very* old book and *very* difficult to find. *Be gentle with it*—it is *very* rare and *very* precious."

Bukinero shrank back under her stare, imagining that her sharp beak was poised to snap out at him. Flammeus, not having intended to startle him, relaxed her gaze and backed away. She flattened her feathers, hoping to appear smaller and therefore less threatening.

"It's fine," she said gently. "It's just a book. It can be healed. No harm done."

Quaking in fear, Bukinero turned to Chitolla, who was watching him with a puzzled look.

"Is something wrong?" She took a few steps towards him.

How could she ask that?

"Everything's wrong! Every... no." He sighed, closing his eyes as he let his anger subside. "No. I'm sorry, Flammeus, I didn't mean to wreck your book."

"It's alright," Flammeus said patiently. "You've both had a very rough few days."

Chitolla hopped over to her mate's side. "Do you want to go home?"

Bukinero shook his head, reaching over to run his beak through her feathers. He dwelt on the feel of her, so close to him, her warm breath touching him. "No. I just need to get my mind on something else." He stared into her dark eyes. "So… don't you want to read that book?"

Chitolla's gaze returned to *The Story of Worlds*, its keeper gently arranging the torn page. Flammeus took a step back from the book so that the two swallows could squeeze in front of her. Gently, she flipped back to the first page, and Chitolla began to read.

Long ago, the worlds of the Veil and the Echo were in easy access of each other. There was a Bridge between them, clearly visible, and the Bridge was crossed often, as the two exchanged goods and tools and ideas and stories.

On both sides, the entrance to the Bridge was marked by a sparkling blue spiderweb, spun by Elabra, the sapphire orb-weaver whom Creator assigned to the task.

But a terrible tragedy occurred, one that will be explained in further detail later in this book. Suffice to say, the Bridge has now become a terrible place, and the webs of Elabra are not as clearly visible as they once were…

MISTAKES

3

A FEW WEEKS LATER
Tell me that you love me;
Tell me that it's true.
Tell me, 'cause my love,
I wanna live my life with you.

PATAS CHUCKLED TO HIMSELF. *I'M GOING TO MAKE THAT MY AFFECTION song: a song for that special moment when I finally meet the special girl who actually* wants *to put up with me for the rest of her life.*

As he crawled through the underbrush, his thoughts returned to when he was a pup, back to the night his mother had taught him his first song.

"Songs are important to us, Patas," she told him as he rested comfortably under her delicate wing. "They change how we see the world around us. We never really live in the dark, because with these songs, we can make the world appear bright. We can even sense how an object feels without touching it."

Right now, through the song he hummed to himself, Patas could see the towering forms of widely-branching trees all around him. He detected the smooth texture of their papery bark, and he could navigate around the spreading ferns and thin, stringy grasses dotting the ground.

He located the trunk of a nearby tree and made his way up, gripping the bark with two sharp thumb-claws, humming softly as he carried himself further into its branches. Spying a nice, thick bough, he thrust himself off his current perch, leaping through the air and landing on the branch. He scurried along the length of the tree limb, propelling himself with his arm-like wings and powerful feet.

He made his way up the tree and into the canopy. His ears and eyes busily scanned the branches for signs of his target. Finally, he spotted it: a dark figure hanging from a nearby bough. Crouching low, he approached slowly.

"You know, Patas, sometimes I wonder how you manage not to starve. Your stealth mode lacks... stealth."

Patas smiled. "Hey, c'mon, Mano. I manage to sneak up on wild boar and sleeping deer without *them* noticing anything. I get my share of blood each night—the few ounces I need to fill my stomach."

"You should learn to crawl without making so much noise."

"Hey, it's not like I *need* to be able to sneak up on fellow bats." Patas fluttered over to his friend. Sighing contentedly, he gestured to the sky. "Beautiful night, eh? Cloudy, overcast, heavy air, we'll probably get rained on before too long. We'll get back to our caves with water pouring out of our fur. Hey! Maybe we could bring back enough water to make a swimming pool on the floor! Then we could learn to become water Vampires and drink fish blood!" He contemplated his own words, then continued with slight disgust, "Actually, I'm not sure I want to know what that tastes like."

Mano rolled his eyes. "Are you going to stop blabbering long enough to go find your little brother, Ézo?"

"Ah, that's right—the three of us were going to hang out tonight, weren't we? Though I suppose just *hanging* may not be the funnest of activities—"

"If you can tear him away from your mother long enough, we could visit the Whispering Caverns."

"That shouldn't be too hard. Mom needs the break. Ever since he learned to fly, Ézo has found himself a never-ending supply of energy and entertainment—constantly going in circles, chattering nonstop."

Mano snorted. "Sounds like someone else I know."

"Ha ha. Hey! Ézo could be our experimental fish-chaser! He chases everything else—bugs, leaves... girls. Unsuccessfully, but it's a start."

"Are you getting him or not?"

"I'm going!" Patas spread his wings wide, preparing for takeoff.

"Just out of curiosity," Mano continued, "what was that song you were humming to yourself?"

"The song?"

"Yeah. Reminded me of that silly little ditty we sang when we were pups. You know, about the different races of bats."

"Hmm. Haven't heard that song in a while." Patas contemplated for a moment. "It was pretty silly. Although, if you think about it, it probably formed the basis for how we think of the other races. Almost manipulative of Cattae to teach it to us..."

Mano sighed deeply. "Patas, there are moments when I want to tell you to talk less and think more. And then there are moments when I want to tell you to stop thinking so hard." He shook his head. "Pains me to be your friend sometimes."

"Well, enjoy the pain, 'cause your about to get a whole night of it—times two."

"Bring it on."

* * *

As Patas flew through the dense jungle towards the tree where he hoped to find his mother, he found it hard not to think about the song Mano had mentioned. He hadn't thought of the song in years, but now he could hear the words playing in his mind, just as clearly as he had when he was younger.

> Four bats in our kingdom,
> Four races there are.
> Four bats in Thériava,
> The home of our god.

Nectar-Drinkers came first,
Sipping daintily from flowers,
Looking at us with disgust,
And saying, "We're much better!"

Stripe-Faces come from islands
In the Sea of Deception;
With mouths stuffed with fruit,
Da bein' talka lika disen!

Our god and our priest
Flesh-Eaters, are called;
Their food is our meat,
So treat them with awe.

The fourth race are we,
Spectral's servants we are.
He taught us to drink blood:
Vampires, we are called.

It was a silly little song. But now that he was older, Patas could see clearly that it had influenced how he thought of the other races: Nectar-Drinkers were vain, Stripe-Faces talked funny, and the Flesh-Eaters were to be worshiped. The more he thought about it, though, the more convinced he was that the four races weren't all that different from each other. The ancestors of the Vampires, in fact, had been Nectar-Drinkers. Drinking blood had changed them physically, as had crawling and hopping along the ground—a habit the other bats considered dirty and unnatural—but that didn't change where they came from.

Cattae himself insisted, "Vampirism is just the step between Nectar-Drinking and Flesh-Eating. Spectral and your ancestors were Nectar-Drinkers, and I was once a Vampire like you. If Spectral chooses you, as he has chosen me, you will become a Flesh-Eater as well."

Patas shivered. He didn't like the thought of eating other bats, but Cattae said it was the only way to become immortal. *Maybe I'd rather die instead.*

He knew he could get in trouble for saying something like that aloud, so he made a point of pushing the thought from his mind.

Catching sight of a familiar figure hanging not far away, Patas smiled. He rushed towards his mother, wrapping his wing around her shoulders.

"Hey!" Patas greeted, holding her tight. "I haven't seen you all night! How have you been?"

Péla placed a claw on his shoulder. "Ah, Patas, It's... it's good to see you."

Her quivering tone made him uneasy.

"Mom, what's wrong?" He scanned the trees for signs of his brother. "Where's Ézo? Mano and I wanted to hang out with him."

Péla didn't respond.

Patas used his wing to gently turn his mother's face towards him. When he did, he saw that her normally bright eyes had turned to strange, black voids. She stared back at him with an empty expression.

"Mom...?"

She remained still, eyes unblinking. Then her lips trembled, and she spoke in a strange, automated voice. "Cattae took him."

A cold feeling overcame Patas, and for a moment he stopped breathing. "Took... Ézo? For... for his initiation, right?" Patas tried to calm his nerves by holding his mother close. "Like the one everyone goes through. He'll come back, don't worry."

Tears streamed down her face. "He's not coming back, Patas. Spectral... wanted him..."

Patas shook his head in confusion. "What do you mean? Spectral wanted him for the initiation, right?"

"No," Péla whispered faintly. "Cattae..."

Patas pushed himself away and took off into the night sky. Mind becoming numb with panic, he tried to convince himself that his mother had misunderstood. *Cattae just took him for the initiation, that's all. If I can find Cattae, I can clear this whole thing up.*

There was only one place he knew to look for Cattae. Beating against the humid air, he glided above the canopy. Below, the murky rainforest covered the land, reaching farther than Patas' eyes could see or his songs could reveal to him.

It wasn't long before he found what he was looking for: a huge stone construction, pale grey and gleaming in the moonlight. He powered towards Spectral's Temple, scanning the clearing for any sign of a giant grey bat.

* * *

Cattae was casually cleaning his fur when Patas approached him, breathless and gasping. "Where's Ézo?"

Cattae paused to gaze at the smaller bat. "Who?"

"M–my brother. Small guy, still a pup. Mom said you took him because Spectral—"

"Ah, him." The Flesh-Eater's expression betrayed disapproval. "Don't you have better things to do than chase down your priest?" Patas stared up at the larger bat expectantly. Turning his face from the Vampire, Cattae continued in a calm, controlled voice. "Spectral was hungry. He wanted a younger sacrifice this time, someone with more 'youthful vitality,' as he put it."

Patas' stunned silence spoke volumes.

"Don't worry about him," Cattae went on. "You know that Spectral has to feed on flesh. Your sacrifice is a worthy price to pay for his guidance, his protection, the shelter he offers by allowing you to live freely in his kingdom. As long as we stick with him, we have nothing to fear except his hunger and wrath. As a matter of fact, you should be glad to know your brother did his part to keep Spectral appeased."

"Appeased." The word exited Patas' mouth in a whisper.

Cattae gave him a questioning look. "Yes. We must keep him happy. He is a god, after all."

"A god."

Clearly bored of the conversation, Cattae spread his massive wings and took off into the forest, leaving Patas alone.

"A god," he whispered. "Spectral is a god."

Ézo had to die. Spectral must be kept happy. He's a god. He is a god.

Tears flooded Patas' eyes as he thought of his little brother—gone. What had his last moments been like? Had he been afraid? Had he died quickly, or… No! Patas' heart filled with anger at the very thought of his little brother being killed brutally.

"He's not *my* god!"

Patas was shocked to hear himself yell out the words. He quivered in fear, expecting Cattae to leap out at him. But the forest was dead silent.

"He's not my god," Patas repeated, this time more quietly. Tears rushed out of his eyes as he continued murmuring. "He's not my god."

Patas suddenly found himself staring up at a bell-shaped blossom hanging just above him. As he eyed the yellow flower, a new thought came to him: *Spectral isn't the god of the Nectar-Drinkers.*

True, the other bats were afraid of the Flesh-Eaters. Who wouldn't be? But they didn't worship them. The Nectar-Drinkers had fled when Spectral and Cattae forced them out of their homes, but they hadn't allowed Spectral to make them his servants.

Spectral isn't the god of the Nectar-Drinkers…

Patas' next action came without thinking; it came through a sudden impulse to rebel—to prove his own words.

He thrust his face into the yellow blossom and reached out with his tongue until he felt it touch the cool liquid inside. He blinked back his shock, new tears forming in his eyes as the overwhelmingly sweet flavor hit his tastebuds. For a creature that had never before drank anything but blood and water, the sugary taste was almost unbearable. Patas had to force himself to continue drinking, until finally he lapped up the last drops. Pulling his head back, he sneezed at the pollen that had gotten all over his face.

Turning, he caught sight of a nearby pink bloom. He darted to it, his tongue reaching out, his eyes blinking in anticipation of the overpowering sweetness. But with a gasp, he pulled himself away from the flower. His wings beat furiously as he attempted to fly away, but he was too late.

Striking with snake-like speed, Cattae's jaws clamped around Patas' flailing body, nearly crushing his bones in their vice-like grasp.

"Traitor! Spectral has decreed that you drink blood. You have rejected his gift! Don't expect to live much longer, fleshling. Spectral never leaves a betrayer unpunished."

With that, the Flesh-Eater spread his wings and carried Patas off into the night.

* * *

Adila got up from the ground, her eyes stinging with tears. A trickle of blood oozed out of her arm, a wound inflicted by the short sword Dumisai held. She looked up into the eyes of her foe. "Dumisai, don't be like this," she pleaded. "We were in love. I don't want to be enemies."

"We can't be lovers as long as you don't understand!" Dumisai shot back, his dark form blending into the shadows that filled the tunnel in which they now stood. He lifted his blood-stained sword and pointed it at her. "I had to kill the rest of the mob—those who wouldn't accept me. Don't you see? I grew up under their hate, wondering what I had done to deserve it."

"They didn't understand you, Dumisai! But you never had to become like this! You never had to kill them!"

Adila's desperation did nothing to calm her companion's rage.

"Your father wouldn't let me marry you, and all the other meerkats treated me like an outcast, ever since I was born." Dumisai stepped closer to Adila, stretching out his sword arm. "I tried to prove myself to them. With intelligence. With ideas. Nothing worked. Your father loved you, and even he didn't care how we felt about each other!"

Dumisai's voice rose in excitement. "Then, I got it. Kondo helped me see it. The reason they hated me was that they feared me. They knew I had been destined from birth to fulfill the prophecies of the Dark One, the one chosen to father a new race of stronger, better meerkats, killers that even the great Lion and Cobra cannot stand up to!"

"Kondo is a murderer!" Adila screamed. "He made up these stories to trick you! Can't you see that?"

"Exciting book?"

Chitolla jumped at the unexpected voice. "Oh, Flammeus, hello. I thought you wanted to spend the day sleeping so you could return to being nocturnal."

The owl chirred in a friendly manner. "Yes, yes I did. I just got up to get a drink of water. I see you're enjoying a tale from *The Story of Worlds*. Hadn't you finished reading that already?"

"Oh, yes, but I really like the story of Adila, and wanted to read it again. Since you're up, I was wondering: what is a meerkat exactly?"

"What is a meerkat... hmm... well, I don't know what to compare them to that you would be familiar with. Try page 202 in *The Book of Mammals*."

Chitolla nodded, her eyes turning towards the shelf where she knew the volume was located. "Thank you. Have a good rest."

"Enjoy your day, sweet Chitolla." Flammeus waddled off.

Chitolla turned her attention back to the books before her. Besides *The Story of Worlds*, *Creator's Book* lay at her feet, along with an assortment of texts about everything from faraway kingdoms to birds that lived further north to how the cure for a long-eradicated disease was found... anything that caught her interest that day.

Coming to the library had become a regular habit. Usually, Bukinero joined her, even though he had little interest in reading. He simply listened as Chitolla explained the interesting things she learned.

This morning, however, Bukinero had been invited by some of the neighbouring swallows to go dragonfly-hunting. He and Chitolla had agreed to return home by noon.

Uh-oh... Chitolla darted around the shelves and over to the hollow's large entrance. Outside, the sun had passed its peak spot in the sky. *Its afternoon—I'm late.* She turned back to *The Story of Worlds* longingly. *Well, I suppose I already know how it ends.*

One by one, she returned the books to their places, making a mental note as she passed by the shelves dedicated to animals: *The Book of Mammals, page 202.*

She changed her mind about waiting and quickly flew back to the shelf. She flipped to page 202, studied the illustrations, then slid the book back in place.

So, that's what a meerkat looks like. She mentally compared the pictures to the descriptions in *The Story of Worlds*, combining the two to create her own image of Adila and Dumisai together.

Her imagination satisfied, she dashed out the door and into the jungle.

* * *

"Bukinero?" Chitolla called as she approached the Stone Place, her eyes scanning the structure's cracked grey wall. "Bukinero!"

When she looked inside the crevice that held their nest, she was surprised to find it empty.

Is Bukinero late, too? Or has he gone looking for me?

Just in case it was the latter, she decided to loop around the building. Perhaps he had gone to visit some of their neighbours. But as Chitolla prepared to dart off, something caught her eye. Further back in the crevice, behind their nest, a dark, vertical crack had appeared in the wall. A musty smell wafted through it.

Hmm... that wasn't there before, she realized. Of course, it wasn't unusual for new cracks to appear in the deteriorating stonework, and the frequent earthquakes and tremors that rattled this mountain often shook loose shards of rock. It was the smell that surprised her.

Chitolla hopped over to the crack, examining it carefully. The hole was just wide enough for a little bird to pass through. But the darkness inside swallowed up any rays of light.

Curiosity winning over caution, Chitolla pushed herself through the new crack. It was deeper than expected, and the smell increased in intensity as she ventured inside. She was shocked when she felt the crack give way to open space. She looked around in the darkness, her eyes finally adjusting.

I'm inside the Stone Place!

The building was dark, lit only by the small beams of light that managed to squeeze through cracks in the walls. The air was stale, and the only breathing she could hear was her own. The grey stone floor was barren, with no signs of vegetation, living or dead. There wasn't even the usual array of scurrying cockroaches, no buzzing flies, nothing. The place felt completely desolate.

Chitolla could only remember having been inside the Stone Place once before. The swallows avoided entering the building—not because they had any rules about it, but because they hated the feeling of emptiness.

Her thoughts drifted back to the day Hermain had passed through, and what he had said about the building's history. Was this evil bat god's influence so great that even now, generations later, his aura couldn't escape from the temple in which he had resided? Did the building somehow recall its blood-soaked history, refusing to let the memory go?

Chitolla shook these thoughts out of her mind. *Perhaps the inside just isn't… habitable.* Even this logical thought did little to calm her nerves. Overcome by discomfort, she prepared to exit through the crack she had come through and return to the daylight.

But a strange sliver of light caught the corner of her eye. Blinking in surprise, the swallow directed her gaze to the building's floor.

For the first time, she noticed a circular hole carved into the stone. As unusual as the hole seemed, she thought little about its oddly perfect shape. It was what was inside the hole that drew her attention: a layer of shimmering blue lights, each rippling in recurring patterns. As she watched, the recurring patterns blended together in her mind's eye, and she saw they formed a spider's web.

Yet it's not a spider web… is it? Spiders don't have glowing blue silk…

Chitolla's heart skipped a beat as she recalled the words in *The Story of Worlds* pertaining to Elabra's web:

On both sides, the entrance to the Bridge was marked by a sparkling blue spiderweb, spun by Elabra, the sapphire orb-weaver to whom Creator assigned the task.

Chitolla leapt off her current perch and headed down to the beautiful lights, heart racing with excitement.

In that moment, Bukinero appeared through the crack and peered inside. "Chitolla!" he called out with relief. "There you are! What are you doing in here?"

"Bukinero, look at this! Remember what we read in the book? Isn't this amazing?"

Chitolla hovered in midair, just above the strange beams. She stretched out a clawed toe, reaching towards a ray of blue light.

BATS

THE INSTANT HER CLAW MADE CONTACT, A STRANGE SENSATION overcame Chitolla's body. Her vision blurred. The air seemed impossibly thick, almost liquid. Her wing beats slowed.

Faintly, she heard Bukinero. "Chitolla! Where are you? What just happened? Chitolla!"

She wanted to turn and face him, to answer his calls, but the world seemed to shift. Bukinero's voice abruptly faded and she felt the Stone Place move away from her.

For a moment, all she could see was darkness, and all she could sense was her heart inside her chest, pulsing with fear.

The darkness vanished, replaced by burning light—and with it a powerful, suffocating heat. Her eyes watered, stinging from the smoke that rose up all around her.

As her vision snapped into focus, her eyes adjusting to the brightness, she realized the enveloping light was really flames, monstrous flames, towering from the unseen ground below to many meters above. The air grew hotter and hotter, and she was convinced she was burning alive.

Desperate to escape, Chitolla unconsciously chose a direction and threw herself forward. The thick air rebuffed her little wings, but she fought nonetheless, curving her feathers around the resisting air in wide, powerful strokes. She closed her eyes to the flames and forced herself to take deep breaths of the stinging, toxic smoke.

I'm going to die.

The thought, though repeating in her mind, didn't stop her wings from beating against the air or her lungs from taking in large, painful gulps of it. She would press on until the flames gave her one final embrace.

Chitolla felt a sudden breeze tickle the feathers of her face. It rushed against them as if something were whizzing past her. She opened her eyes for a moment, wondering at the strange spot of bright blue light in front of her. She felt it pulling, reaching towards her with a gravity that overpowered even the liquid-like air. Chitolla couldn't fight it; she could only watch as it drew her in, covering more and more of her vision until all she could see was radiant blue.

She then felt the bizarre shift that had first signalled Bukinero's disappearance, and the world was dark again. The air returned to normal, no longer burning her eyes or smelling of smoke. She folded her wings and felt her feet hit solid ground. The stale taste of air and the feel of weak light against her body convinced her she was inside an enclosed space. For a moment, she wondered if she had returned to the Stone Place.

As her eyes adjusted, the darkness became dotted with black circles. At first, dozens. Then, hundreds. Eventually, there were thousands, all lined along what she guessed to be the walls of this building.

Then it dawned on her: *Those aren't black dots... those are eyes!* Thousands of black eyes belonging to thousands of bats. The faces Chitolla could see clearly wore solemn masks.

She wasn't sure why, but she felt the need to hide. The frightened eyes weren't looking at her—their attention appeared to be drawn elsewhere. She felt exposed and in danger. Crouching, she glanced in all directions.

The spot where she stood was surrounded by large, jagged rocks and scattered pebbles. Her eyes locked onto a long shadow, created by the irregularly-shaped stones piled around it. She dashed along the ground towards it, not wanting to spread her wings and draw attention to herself. Her legs pumped up and down as she threw herself into the shadow's cool embrace.

Huddling down, Chitolla began to pant, a wave of dizziness overcoming her. The thought came that it must have been from breathing the strange, smoke-filled air, or perhaps from fighting against it. Maybe she could blame her panic, or having to run across the floor—a greater distance than she had ever before travelled on foot.

She wondered whether she was about to pass out. An image of Bukinero flying around the Stone Place flashed through her mind. The next moment, the giant flames returned, burning themselves into her memory.

As she drew deep, calming breaths, soaking in the stale air, Chitolla felt her mind clear again. The faded, confused images left her. She blinked a few times, suddenly quite grateful to have her vision fully restored.

She began to focus on what was going on around her. Listening intently, she could pick up hushed whispers reaching her ears from all sides. The voices belonged to the many bats covering the walls of this stone building, but she couldn't make out anything they said.

Deciding that a peek out from behind her hiding place might yield more information, Chitolla hopped to the edge of the shadow and peered out from between the towering rocks.

Gasping, she drew back, huddling under the protection of the stone.

Just outside her hiding place, no more than a few short hops away, was a dark and winged monster.

* * *

Bukinero flew in circles, trying to figure out what had happened. The shimmering lights had vanished before he could reach them, and there was no sign that they had ever been there, no sign of Chitolla, and no sign of a way to bring her back.

What do I do? How could she have just vanished like that? What was she thinking, touching those strange lights?

Suddenly, Bukinero's mind picked up on a solution. His eyes searched for a crack by which to exit the building.

There was a certain owl he had to visit.

Patas stood in the center of Spectral's Temple, heart beating crazily as he awaited his fate. His glance travelled to the building's entrance; much to his dismay, Cattae covered the opening. The giant Flesh-Eater's eyes rested on Patas, as if daring him to attempt an escape.

He shuffled nervously under Cattae's stare, knowing that the next few moments could very well be his last. Nevertheless, Patas did manage to find amusement in his current situation as he looked around at the thousands of Vampire eyes crowding the walls and cleared portion of the floor. Everyone he had known since puphood—his friends, family, acquaintances, and not-so-charming rivals—were gathered to watch lil' ol' him, standing on the stone platform. Patas smirked mischievously as he contemplated breaking out into random dance moves, or perhaps coming up with a few jokes to break their solemn faces into cheerful smiles.

The situation grew much less entertaining the moment a dark figure, previously hidden by large stones scattered across the floor, arose from the shadows. The room went silent, all hushed whispers stopping abruptly, all eyes turning their gaze to the creature.

Patas gulped as the dark figure crawled towards him on long, muscular forearms and talon-bearing feet. The giant bat eased across the floor with confident steps, his eyes locked on Patas.

The monster stopped just one step away from Patas, who became quite aware of his own size next to this King of the Underworld. All thoughts of laughter fled from his mind as Spectral gazed down at him, the Flesh-Eater's thin slice of a smile revealing large fangs.

Patas closed his eyes tightly, trying to lock them away from Spectral's overarching form. He could feel the monster's breath against his face, glowing white eyes boring into him.

"Patas Pélonas Desmodus."

A tremor went through Patas at the sound of his own name. He forced open his eyes to look into Spectral's terrifying face.

"You know why you have been brought here, Patas. The crimes you have committed. You have rejected my gift to you, my gift to your ancestors: the gift of lifeblood as your sustenance. That, as you have known since puphood, is an act of treason, and an offence to me, your god, the Lord of the Underworld."

Patas desperately desired to argue, to repeat the words he had said earlier in the forest: *Spectral is not my god.* However, hearing the calm, assured declarations of Spectral himself, seeing his powerful body, hearing his strong voice, and feeling overshadowed by his intimidating presence...

"However, to show my great kindness..." The final word left Spectral's mouth as a vicious hiss. He stretched out a large, leathery wing and pointed a bony wing-finger behind and to the left. "...I will allow you to choose between two forms of punishment."

Patas' eyes drew to where the monstrous bat pointed. His heart pounded in his ears as he recognized the circular hole in the temple floor. Memories came back to him against his will: of going down that hole, of touching the strange blue lights, of the hour he had been forced to remain in that horrible world.

Patas' lips refused to move, but he could hear his own voice screaming in his head: *Eat me. Please, eat me. I won't fight. You can tear out my wings. Rip off my head. Anything. Please. I can't go there again...*

Seeing the look on Patas' face, Spectral laughed dryly. "If that is not your desired punishment," he continued, drawing his wing back, "I have another option for you."

Patas' eyes glowed with desperation. *Okay. I'll let you eat me. Any way you like. I'll drink blood again, really. I'll never again say or do anything you don't like. I'll even call you my god.*

This thought sent a painful pang through his chest, and he was suddenly unconvinced that he would. But the rest, he knew, he would do quite readily, as long as it meant he would never, ever have to return to the agonizing confusion of the Underworld.

Better to be eaten here than to wait forever in constant fear of such an ending there.

Spectral shifted his eyes from the cowering Vampire, turning his head to gaze at another bat who watched the trial from the front row. "Patas, bring me your mother."

Patas cocked his ears in confusion, positive he had heard wrong. "W–what?"

"It would be a proper punishment for you to see how your actions affect others, and a good way to show love for your god." His burning stare returned to Patas, and he repeated: "Patas, bring me your mother."

Patas' eyes blurred with tears as he watched his mother approach with hesitant, shaky steps.

"Mom…" he said in a weak, quivering voice.

As she came closer, Patas rushed towards her and wrapped his wings around her trembling body, tears running down his face. "Mother, I'm so sorry. I shouldn't have—"

"No, Patas, I understand… it's okay… please don't… I…" She shook so badly that she could barely speak.

He pulled her closer, holding her tight. Closing his eyes, he focused all his attention on Péla's comforting smell and the softness of her fur. "Mom," he said, "I'm sorry I can't see you ever again. I love you." He pressed his lips to her forehead. "Mom, do you remember when I was a pup, and had just learned to fly?"

Péla's nod was hard to differentiate from the shaking that overtook the rest of her body, but Patas could tell she had heard him.

"I was so excited about flying that you said it was like I never wanted to stop." He smiled at the warm memory. "Do you remember that? How happy I was?"

Péla laughed in spite of her fear, and Patas' tears changed from signs of pain to echoes of joy. "That's how I want you to remember me, Mom. Please don't think of how I'm doing. Just remember how I was that night. And I'll never forget the song you sang to me. Okay?"

Péla's trembling subsided as his words sunk in. She looked up into his face, confused. "Patas? You mean, you choose—"

Patas gently pushed her away and turned his attention back to Spectral, announcing loudly, "I choose banishment."

If Spectral was surprised, he hid it quite well. He eyed Patas, as if searching for any sign of indecision. Patas, though dizzy with fright and grief, stood as tall and straight as possible in order to convince the Flesh-Eater of his resolution.

After a moment of silent observation, Spectral finally continued. "Very well. Patas Pélonas Desmodus, I sentence you to banishment in the fiery Under—"

"Hey! Get back here, you disrespectful creature!" Cattae's booming voice filled the temple, startling everyone within, just as a flash of white looped around in the air above them.

With all eyes glued to the unexpected distraction, the bats recognized that the creature was a tiny white bat. She glanced around the temple fearfully, apparently confused as to where she was. Doubling back, she dashed towards the entrance, whizzing past Cattae, who was shocked and dumbfounded.

"Cattae!" Spectral was unable to hide his own surprise. "How could you—?!"

"M—my master! Some oblivious little imp just flew into your temple, and she did so without any consideration to your majesty and without any acts of respect!"

Spectral grunted angrily. "I saw that! Find her and kill her!"

"Yes, master!" Cattae flew off, giving chase to the little flash of white.

Spectral sighed in disgust, then looked down to the traitorous Vampire he was in the process of banishing. Only, the spot where Patas had once stood was now empty.

Spectral roared in frustration.

* * *

Outside her hideaway, Chitolla heard the flurry of confusion and the leathery sound of bat wings. She tried to make sense of the yelling that echoed throughout the building, originating from the many bats she had earlier seen lining the stone walls.

"Where did the white bat go?"

"Where's the criminal?"

And then from a horrible, coarse voice, "I want the place thoroughly searched!"

As she huddled down, not understanding what was going on around her, she felt something warm and bony wrap itself around her. Before she even thought to resist, it had dragged her deeper into the shadows of her hiding place, then down into a small tunnel.

"Come, little birdy," said a strange, high-pitched voice. "I don't know how you got in here, but this place isn't safe for either of us."

* * *

Secha's snow-white form raced across the moonlit sky, her flight pattern wild and erratic as she worked to shake the huge grey bat chasing her. She focused on the path ahead, though her ears at times turned back to listen to the giant's powerful wings flapping against the steamy air. He was close enough that she could hear him mumbling to himself under his breath.

"Obnoxious little bat. Never seen a bat so stupid. Cattae here is going to devour you, pretty little white furball..."

Secha hoped he wasn't serious, and considered how she could talk him out of his frustration. *I didn't mean to startle you. I didn't realize I wasn't supposed to go into that stone place. When I flew up to it, saw you, and said hello, I was being friendly. You didn't have to look at me so oddly, and you could have stopped me from going inside... and you don't really eat fellow bats... do you...?*

Moonlight reflected off Secha's white fur, making it easy for Cattae to track her. She remained above the canopy, trying to think of a song to help her current situation.

"*Light a path beneath...* no... *sing out a song of stars and...* it doesn't go like that, Secha... *help me find...*"

A large, dark wing suddenly rose above her, blocking the light of the moon. The powerful wing closed in around her, pulling her down into the trees. Secha closed her eyes, convinced that the horrible cannibal had finally won.

Oddly, however, the dark wing unfurled. Secha, clinging to the fur of another bat, saw again the murky shapes of tree limbs, tangled vines, and wide leaves. The powerful wing came down again, but, as before, it soon unfolded, reaching out in an upwards stroke.

"You should na fly in straight moonlight," a thickly accented voice spoke out. "You will die that way. Come down into da forest."

The bat sang out as he lit the way for both of their eyes:

> Fly, it na matter what lie behind, bohah
> It na matter what you leave long agohah

Secha stole a glance to the side, hopeful for a glimpse of her rescuer's face. His oval-shaped eyes stared ahead. His fur was mostly dark brown, though he had a few streaks of white crossing the side of his face. He was twice her size, not quite as large as the bat chasing her.

"Higuero!" Cattae shouted from somewhere behind them. "Decided to interfere with my business, eh? Why don't you take your own advice and leave like all the others? You know, to the place you left *long ago-ah*…"

"You lookin' into my personal life, Cattae?" Higuero replied in an unexpectedly casual tone.

"Na," Cattae's voice was rough and harsh, "your strange talk gives it away—or rather, the fact that you *can't* talk."

"Perhaps my talk es good and your talk es strange."

Higuero managed to weave in and out of the branches of the trees, deftly evading Cattae's grasp. Cattae's attention had been successfully drawn away from Secha and onto her rescuer. The Flesh-Eater frequently reached out to grab Higuero, either with his jaws or large back claws, but Higuero would duck under the cover of a thick branch or twisting vine. Cattae, forced to slow down in order to avoid crashing, fell further behind. Cursing under his breath, the Flesh-Eater refused to stop, pumping his wings furiously as he followed Higuero through the trees.

All it takes is one mistake, fleshling, Cattae reassured himself as he narrowed his eyes in eager anticipation. *One mistake, and I win.*

Secha's heart raced as she tried to keep her breathing steady. She wondered if the giant cannibal would ever give up his chase.

> Fly, it na matter what lie behind, bohah
> It na matter what you leave long agohah

Suddenly, an unexpected shape appeared in front of Secha.

"Fly away! Fly away!" Secha warned the newcomer. "We're being chased by a cannibal!"

This new bat, hanging from a thin branch, caught Secha's gaze and turned her head, but didn't leave her roost. She was nearly twice the size of the small white bat, with silver fur. Her face lifted into a small smile, her wing stretching out to wave at Secha.

"Didn't you hear me?" Secha tried again, panicked at the bat's serene reaction. "There's a cannibal chasing us!"

Higuero veered away from the silvery bat. Then, grasping a thick tree limb, he fell into a hanging position, panting heavily, with Secha hidden under his wings. When he spread them again, he found her clinging tightly to him, each tiny thumb-claw hooked to one of his shoulders.

"Why are we stopping?!" Secha cried out fearfully. "Cattae will kill us!"

"Take it easy," Higuero whispered reassuringly. "It's all good."

Cattae was the next to appear out of the foliage. He spread his wings wide to slow himself, apparently confused about where his prey had gone. His eyes locked onto the silvery bat hanging not far in front of him. A huge grin engulfed his face.

"Well, well, little Chinaca!" A coarse laugh echoed out of his throat. "What a surprise! Looks like tonight is my night to visit all our pesky neighbours!"

"Why hello, dear Cattae." The silvery bat's voice remained shockingly calm. "Have you missed me?"

Cattae reached his knife-like claws towards Chinaca, who didn't even try to evade his talons. Instead, she watched them rush towards her, observing intently as if calculating the speed of their approach.

Secha watched with unblinking eyes as Cattae's claws closed in around Chinaca.

Suddenly, Chinaca dropped from her perch. In the next moment, she darted back up, a small vine now clasped tightly in her teeth. As she flew upwards, pulling the vine along with her, the network of branches surrounding Cattae folded in around him, snapping together like a sprung trap.

Secha gasped. The whole event had happened in the course of one or two seconds, but she saw it play out in slow motion. She regarded the trap with awe, wondering why she hadn't noticed the strange positioning of the sturdy branches and thick vines earlier.

Cattae, startled and struggling to claw his way out, clearly hadn't noticed either.

"Chinaca!" The Flesh-Eater's tone was dark and angry. He squeezed his wing through the "bars" of his cage to grab at the silvery bat. "You're as good as dead, fleshling! This is the last trick you'll ever pull on me!"

"You said that last time," Chinaca said defiantly, settling down on a roost just outside Cattae's grasp. "In those exact words, in fact. Besides, I'm not done yet. This trap may be temporary, and I know you'll break through in… oh, maybe half an hour or so. But consider it a warning: when the time comes, I'm going to make sure both you *and* Spectral are gone." Chinaca lowered her voice threateningly. "You can't get away with murder forever, cannibal. I'm going to make sure you're stopped, one way or another, along with all the dirty Vampires who serve you."

Cattae burst out into harsh, wicked laughter, breaking eye contact with her for just a moment before returning with a mocking, teasing stare. A sly grin crept across his face. "Why don't you ever ask me what they tasted like, dear fleshling? Your colony. Come on, ask me how much fun it was to rip apart your brothers and mother, your father, your friends…" He watched her reaction. "Are you frightened of me, dear Chinaca? My, your face has gone pale with—"

"Chinaca!" Higuero's voice boomed in warning as Chinaca flung herself at the caged monster, teeth bared, forgetting for a moment that she was putting herself within his reach.

Before Cattae could grab her, Chinaca pulled herself back, breathing heavily.

Cattae chuckled. "Poor little fleshling, did I scare you?"

"Chinaca," Higuero said again, "now es da time to leave, before Cattae does."

Secha returned her attention to him. She noted with slight

bewilderment that he seemed neither impressed nor surprised by Chinaca's amazing stunt.

Does this happen often?

Hearing a harsh sigh, Secha turned to look at Chinaca. "Fine," the silvery bat spat. "I guess that means you expect me to debrief with you again, lesser bat?"

Secha was shocked by Chinaca's demeaning tone. *Who was the "lesser bat"?*

"Higuero saved my life," Secha spoke up defiantly.

"Sorry," Chinaca said, startled. "Didn't see you there... uh..."

"Secha."

"Got it. Secha." Chinaca studied her for a moment. "What race are you?"

"I don't..."

"Are you a Nectar-Drinker or a Stripe-Face, youngster?"

"Youngster? I'm full-grown. And I'm a Tent-Maker, from the Iridescent Forests."

"Iridescent Forests, huh? From over the High Mountains?" Chinaca mulled over the information before continuing. "Well, a foreigner can't be too bad. Welcome!" Chinaca's glance returned to Higuero. "Well, since the *harem leader* is clearly impatient, we should get going." She spread her wings and dropped from her perch, dashing out into the jungle.

Assuming Higuero wanted her to follow, Secha released her grasp. She and Higuero flew after Chinaca, leaving Cattae alone to work his way out of the trap.

* * *

The tunnel was dark and barely big enough for Chitolla and the one dragging her to fit through. The swallow could see nothing in the darkness, but she sensed her feathers brushing up against the rough stone walls, quickly becoming plastered with cobwebs and dust.

It was a long, twisting tunnel, and more than a few times she wondered if it would ever end. Nevertheless, she didn't struggle against the one pulling her, or try to argue with him. She held on to the hope that he was guiding her to someplace more hospitable.

Finally, as she stumbled forwards, her leader's bony arm wrapped over her shoulders, Chitolla caught the sweet and familiar scent of rainforest air. Her eyes focused on a thin beam of light up ahead. The creature pulled her closer and closer to the faint light, until Chitolla was near enough to see that the beam poured through a wide opening in the roof of the tunnel. The swallow looked up gratefully, staring out at the bright moon and open night sky.

"This is where you exit, little birdy."

Chitolla turned to see her rescuer for the first time. *A bat!*

The male bat was almost the same size as Bukinero. His fur was dark brownish-grey, but as he hunched over she could see a patch of silver hairs between his shoulder blades. His relatively flat face held wide black eyes and a strange-looking nose. Two sharp incisors peeked out under his top lip.

He smiled at her oddly, as if waiting for her to do something.

Chitolla looked up to the hole in the roof. The first thought to enter her mind was, *I should fly back to Bukinero.* Of course, she quickly realized she couldn't. *I don't know where I am, or where Bukinero is, or how to get home.*

Chitolla returned her gaze to where she had last seen the bat. To her shock, the spot was empty. The bat had vanished.

However, as she listened carefully, she could hear his high voice coming from somewhere in the darkness ahead. The bat had left her behind, expecting her to exit through the hole while he made his way further down the passage.

Panicked at the thought of losing her only help, she took off down the tunnel, spreading her wings. Hitting a wall, she tried flying to the left, only to find another wall. Taking off to the right produced another painful crash. Finally, she figured out that the path curved upwards.

Chitolla learned from many similar experiences that the tunnel's unseen curves made flying too difficult, at least for someone who couldn't see in the dark. She instead chose to hop as fast as she could, but the twists and turns produced the same results. Eventually, she adopted a sort of flying-hop method of travel.

She stopped for a moment, trying to hear over the beating of her own heart. Hearing nothing, she called out, "Help! Are you still in the tunnel? Where are you?"

"Who's that?" There was clear puzzlement in the bat's strange voice.

"It's me! I don't know how to find my way!"

There was no response from up ahead. Chitolla waited in silent expectation.

Finally, she heard his distant voice echo through the passageway. "It's the pointy rock."

"What?"

No answer.

Confused, but desperate to reach the bat, she continued forward, hitting a wall and then going down, up, left, and right until she found the way the path turned.

Eventually, she came to a wall that defied all her attempts to find a way around it. She sighed, stopping to perch on the ground. *Dead end.*

She listened intently, panting heavily, but heard nothing. Blinking a few times, she noted that her vision was exactly the same when her eyes were open as when they were closed.

The bat isn't here, so he must have gotten past this. But how do I find the way if I'm completely blind?

Chitolla used her wing to feel along the stone wall, sensing every crack and bump along its uneven surface. She felt her wing brush against something sharp, then carefully used the rest of her body to gently run along the edge of it, discovering its shape. She tried to imagine what the rock would look like if she were able to see it.

It's triangular, about two or three times my size, I think. She reached along for a smoother part of the stone and pressed against it with her body. *Hmm. It's not tightly held to the wall, but the two are somehow connected.*

Flying up to the sharp, narrow point, she pushed it hard against the stone wall. The rock jiggled a little, then refused to move. She gently grabbed its edge and tried pulling it away from the wall.

The rock moved with ease, and as it did so, Chitolla heard a grating sound reverberate around the tunnel. She blinked a little as a small burst of soft light flooded the passageway.

Turning, Chitolla caught sight of an entryway to her right. Pleased, she congratulated herself on finding her first secret door.

QUESTS

5

SECHA GLIDED THROUGH THE DARK JUNGLE, LED BY HIGUERO AND Chinaca. They hadn't spoken a word since their escape from Cattae. Their wing beats were focused and noiseless, and they stayed under the cover of the understory, trying to remain unseen. Secha wasn't sure why they felt the need for secrecy, but she decided it was best to follow their example.

The group had long been approaching a tall, sheer cliff of red and grey stones. Secha assumed they were going to find a safe nook in the rocks. However, when the trio was just a short distance from the rockface, Higuero pulled ahead and flew up to a grey stone jutting out from the cliff. He landed atop it, pushing down on it with his weight.

Secha watched curiously. *What's he doing?*

Suddenly, the rocks within the cliff grated against each other, and a group of them shifted from their places, making way for a large, circular opening, easily big enough for all three bats to enter at once.

Secha, filled with awe and childlike delight at this strange bit of technology, flew ahead of the group, darting through the hole.

Beyond the entrance was a short, square tunnel which gave way to a huge cave, lit brilliantly and filled with cool, damp air. A deep pool of water covered the bottom of the cavern. The pool teemed with an array of small, sleek fish, which, to Secha's amazement, appeared to glow from the inside. There were so many of them, darting back and forth in large schools, that their presence filled the cave with dancing rays of light.

The four walls were flat, aside from a pattern of small grooves. These grooves allowed woody vines, fed by the waters below, to reach the roof. The roof appeared to be designed to allow for the plants to grow across its length and width. Tangles of branches and bunches of pale green leaves hid much of the stonework from view.

The branches—small, round, and strong—made perfect roosts. As the others followed Secha into the cavern, they each picked out a spot. Secha grasped one such vine, landing upside-down, facing the pool of tiny fishes. Pulling in her forearms, she snuggled up contentedly, taking in a deep breath of cool air.

"You doin' well?" Higuero asked. He hung nearby, his eyes on her.

She smiled gleefully. "Yes—this is amazing! I've never seen anything like it!"

Higuero returned the smile. "This place es a safe shelter. We come here often to escape Spectral's servants. Now, what are you doin' in this jungle? Thériava es na a safe place to live, and Spectral's Vampires are common in this part of their kingdom."

Secha allowed his accent to grow on her. "I came here a few nights ago, looking for a new home. I didn't realize it wasn't safe." Then, her face became puzzled. "Who is Spectral? And what's a Vampire? Is that what Cattae's race is called?"

"What's a Vampire?" Chinaca gave Secha a quizzical look. "Wow, you've lived a sheltered life."

Taken aback, Secha turned to Higuero for a more considerate reply.

Before he could respond, Chinaca continued. "The Vampires were once Nectar-Drinkers, like me. But Spectral taught their ancestors to live off blood. Cattae is a Flesh-Eater, like Spectral."

A look of disgust came over Secha's face. "They drink *blood?*"

The silver bat nodded. "You see, over a hundred years ago, Spectral came to our rainforest, demanding allegiance and destroying the first few colonies that didn't give it to him. Those who agreed to serve him built a temple—that's the stone building at the top of the mountain—and he taught them to drink blood and worship him as their provider."

"Wait… over a hundred years ago?" A chill crept through Secha's spine. "So, this Spectral is older than that? Isn't that… kind of impossible?"

"He claims to be immortal. Whatever the case, most of the Nectar-Drinker and Stripe-Faced colonies that once lived here have either fled or been destroyed by Cattae and his Vampire army."

"Many of da bats have moved northward," Higuero added, "into da Desert Mountains."

"Okay," Secha said, feeling she had gained some understanding. "So, you stayed here together because—"

"Whoa, no no no no!" Chinaca contended zealously, raising her wings in defence. "*No.* We are *not* together."

"But you both came *here*," Secha responded hesitantly, "to this cavern… *together*…"

"Well, yeah," Chinaca relented. "However, we aren't *working* together. We stayed in Thériava for different reasons."

Higuero explained, "I am here to help other bats on their way to da Desert Mountains. I know da place, I came from near there, so I can help them as a guide."

Secha's eyes again rested on Chinaca. "But you're not here helping other bats get out?"

"Actually, I'm here trying to convince them to stay," Chinaca said bluntly. At Secha's perplexed look, she went on. "Leaving isn't going to help anything. Cattae will continue to extend the boundaries of Thériava, and Spectral will continue demanding that more colonies serve him. What we need are bats who are willing to stand up to Spectral and find a way to stop him. I'm here searching for warriors."

* * *

Upon exiting the secret passage, Chitolla was positive she was done crashing into things. However, the first thing she felt outside the tunnel was her body hitting a thick wall of twisted, tangled vines. Their woody branches refused to let her pass, their velvety leaves tickling her face. She backed out of them quickly.

Scanning the area with her eyes, she realized the secret passage opened into a wide corridor. The corridor, bordered by smooth stone walls to the left and right, led to a mass of jumbled vines.

Along the rock floor, Chitolla caught sight of the bat who had led her through the tunnel. He stood upright on his back feet, peering through a break in the vine barrier. His ears were perked.

Chitolla cocked her head slightly. *Are most bats able to stand upright? I've never seen them do that before.*

The swallow flew towards the bat, landing at his side.

Glancing at her briefly, the bat motioned for her to be quiet before returning to his careful listening. Then, as if realizing something, he did a doubletake and turned back to her with a puzzled expression.

"Where did you come from?" he asked. Before Chitolla could respond, he shrugged it off. "Oh well, I guess you're just a strange little birdy. Look over there! The bats! See them?" Chitolla made a move to do as he suggested, but was soon distracted by his squeaky voice. "Of course, you're a bird, so you don't know what I'm saying."

Pardon? Why would you think—

But the bat was clearly oblivious. "Chinaca is incredible! Listen to her: a Nectar-Drinker who wants to stand up to Spectral!"

Chitolla manoeuvered around the thick vines to get a better view. There was a silver-grey bat, about Chitolla's size, a larger brown bat with white lines running above and below his eyes, and a tiny white bat. Chitolla, straining to listen, picked up on the tail end of their conversation.

"War is na goin' to work," the brown one said in an unfamiliar accent. "It's best that everybody leave."

"There are ways to defeat him!" the silver bat argued. "Perhaps there are no other bats his size or with his longevity—"

"Na with his armies."

The silver bat sighed in frustration and directed her attention to the little white bat. "Secha, what this harem leader here doesn't seem to get is that Spectral has displaced millions and millions of bats from their homes! If everyone joined together, rather than fleeing, we could easily defeat him!"

"She's right!" a new voice declared.

Chitolla quickly realized her rescuer was no longer beside her. He had left the shelter of the vines to present himself before the others.

"Your idea could work," he continued excitedly, "and I—my name's Patas, by the way, it is awesome meeting all of you—I can help!"

Higuero and Secha responded to this with odd stares, surprised at Patas' sudden appearance.

Chinaca's shock gave way to a repulsed frown. "That, little Tent-Maker, is a Vampire bat," she said to Secha. "The least honourable of all bats, the ones who accepted a diet of blood."

"Actually," Patas put in, "tonight I drank nectar—"

Chinaca went on as if she hadn't heard him. "We do not talk to them, we do not learn their names, and we certainly do *not* ask them for help."

"You never had to ask! I offered!" Picking a roost next to her, Patas fluttered over. "I'd love to help. I could give you inside info. I've never liked Spectral and he was actually just banishing me for betraying him and why are you not looking at me?"

Chinaca had turned her attention towards the playful fish in the pool below, her ears focused on the little critters. Her face was a mask of complete oblivion.

"But... but I *want* to help!" Patas insisted, his voice rising in desperation. "All of us Vampire bats live in fear of Spectral. With your plans, we could defeat him!"

His attention focused entirely on Chinaca, Patas didn't notice Secha looking him over with curiosity.

"Maybe you should listen to him," Secha said to Chinaca. "Don't you need to know things like numbers and strategy and other insider information to win a war?"

"And if it's a trick?" Chinaca argued.

"Spectral and Cattae call us nuisances, na threats," Higuero said. "Why would they bother to trick us?"

"Besides," Secha continued, "didn't you say something about being banished, Patas?"

Patas nodded enthusiastically. "Yep! In fact—what's your name again?"

"Secha."

"Secha, that's pretty. I've never seen a white bat before. I bet you get hit on a lot."

Secha's face turned puzzled. "You think I get hit a lot?"

"It's an expression. Ask Higuero, I'm sure he gets me. Anyway, I was on trial for—ahem—drinking nectar…"

Patas waited for a comment from Chinaca, but she just stared at him through drooping eyes, her face wearing an expression of borderline boredom.

"…and I was just about to be banished to the Underworld, when all of a sudden, a tiny white—" Patas froze unexpectedly. Amazement filled his eyes as he looked at Secha. A big smile consumed his face and he rushed towards her, his wings engulfing her small, furry body. "It was *you!* Secha, you are a lifesaver! Thank you! Thank you! Thank you!"

Patas spread one wing while holding her tight with the other.

"You flew into the temple, distracting Spectral and Cattae," he continued. "I snuck into one of the hidden tunnels, grabbed a birdy, went down, and came up here!" Patas concluded with a wide sweep of both wings.

"Really? Well, you're welcome." Secha released a short laugh, wondering why she felt the sudden desire to ask him to put his wing around her shoulder again. "But what does the bird have to do with any of it?"

"Oh, she's been following me around. Hey little birdy, come here!"

Chitolla, imagining this must be her cue, pushed herself through the little crack in the wall of vines and soared over to the group of bats.

She quickly realized, however, that there was nowhere for her to perch. The bats appeared to hang effortlessly from the many creeping vines, but this bat-made cavern had no comfortable place for a bird to sit.

Clearly, when they built this place, they weren't expecting birds to visit.

Chitolla circled the cavern. She dashed to a vine that hung down across a portion of the roof, apparently having lost its grip, and landed, hoping it would hold her weight. Balancing precariously, she looked up to see the four bats staring at her with strange expressions on their faces.

Did I do something wrong?

"See?" Patas said, pride filling his voice, as if he had accomplished an amazing feat. "She seems to like me a lot, she follows me everywhere, even made it through the tunnel and secret door." His face turned puzzled for a moment. "Hmm… come to think of it, I'm not sure how she did that… but she got here, so she must be one smart birdy!"

Higuero peered at Chitolla through narrowed eyes. As if noticing something peculiar, he spread his wings and left his roost to move closer to the swallow.

"Patas," he spoke slowly, hovering a short distance from her, "never have I seen a bird like this."

"What do you mean?" Secha asked, searching the swallow for whatever feature Higuero found unusual.

"Her eyes!" Chinaca exclaimed. "And her face…"

Chitolla, creeped out by the bats' stares, spoke up. "What about my face?"

The black eyes of each bat widened immensely. Higuero backed away, grasping a roost and spreading his wings as if expecting an attack.

Chitolla responded with a shocked look of her own, confused. *These bats think I'm weird…* Her thoughts returned to the odd things Patas had said to her, the way he had addressed her since their first encounter.

In all the excitement, she had forgotten about her experience in the raging inferno, touching the strange blue lights back in the Stone Place. *I touched them because they reminded me of what was written in* The Story of Worlds, *how sapphire webbing marks the door to the Bridge between the worlds…*

"That's it!" she cheeped.

Everything clicked into place: she had crossed the Bridge between worlds, and in doing so had left behind the Veil, the world of talking animals, and was now in the world where only bats spoke.

"I'm in the Echo!" Chitolla bounced up excitedly, forgetting the weak state of her current perch. "I made it to the other world! The Bridge can still be crossed! The Traitor's flames haven't stopped passage between the Echo and the Veil! We can still get across!"

Her thrilling realization, for the most part, did nothing to change the bats' shocked expressions. However, as Chitolla continued to leap with joy, the puzzlement faded from Secha's face.

"Wow," Secha said, her voice filled with awe. "There are secret caverns, Vampires, and now other worlds, too. I never thought the lands beyond the High Mountains could get any stranger, but they just did!" She smiled at Chitolla warmly, no longer fazed by her speaking ability. "What's your name?"

"Chitolla," was the sweet response. She nodded to each of the bats as she addressed them. "And you are Secha, Higuero, Chinaca, and Patas. Thank you for rescuing me, by the way."

"Err, ah, yeah," Patas sputtered abashedly. "Sorry for talking to you like an animal—I mean, a lesser animal, that is. And you're welcome. I couldn't exactly leave you there for Spectral. He eats swallows, too, you know. Even talking—well, I don't think he's ever met a talking bird, but if he did, he'd probably eat it—"

"Patas," Higuero said, "you said somethin' back their about a tunnel and escapin' Spectral?"

"Well, yeah," Patas responded, confused. "I was about to be banished, but I snuck through the secret passageway—"

"Does Spectral know about it?"

"No, of course not."

"Do you think he will na find it? Even after he finds you missin'?"

Patas' initial response was silence, followed by a slow, hesitant, "Uh… yes… he's probably realized by now that I escaped through a tunnel… and, ahem, he may have even found the one I went through…"

"So," Higuero continued, his voice becoming somewhat annoyed, "es there any chance Spectral could be sendin' out Vampires through that tunnel to find you and bring you back? That he could very well be comin' to capture you right this moment?"

Patas quivered, nodding. "Mm-hmm."

"Den why are we still here?"

"'Cause… I, uh, didn't think of that…"

"That's alright," Secha said quickly, her mood not darkened by this unexpected problem. "Higuero's specialty is taking bats out of Thériava and into the safety of the Desert Mountains." She beamed encouragingly at Patas. "He can help you escape north."

"Great," Chinaca put in. "Then let's get going."

Higuero gave Chinaca a bewildered glance. "You are comin' too?"

"You're stealing away my insider, so yes, I'm coming." Chinaca grimaced slightly at the happy smile Patas sent her way.

"I'll come!" Secha inserted exuberantly. "Chitolla, you're coming as well, right?"

At first, Chitolla didn't reply. She thought of Bukinero, back in the Veil. "Will we be returning to the temple? I think that's the only way back to my world."

"We will be back," Chinaca responded confidently, "with warriors and a strategy for defeating Spectral and Cattae. After they're destroyed, you're welcome to go inside the temple. Until then, it's suicide. By all means, come with us."

Chitolla nodded, seeing the sense in Chinaca's words. "I'll join you, then."

"Alright," Chinaca continued confidently, "to the Northern Passage we go."

"Na," Higuero said quickly, "we can na go that way. Spectral never has lost a prisoner, in all his years. He'd be too embarrassed to lose one now. He will probably send somebody after us—maybe even Cattae."

"Uh, yeah." Patas shivered in fear. "Yeah, he definitely will. Boy, am I glad I wound up meeting someone as brilliant as you, Goo-arrow."

"*Higuero.* We can na take da Northern Passage. Too easy."

Chinaca sighed in frustration. "Right. As if there's another way to the Desert Mountains."

"There es. Over da sea."

"The Sea of Deception?" Chinaca appeared to think he was joking. "So, what, we're exchanging one form of suicide for another?"

"I know da sea," Higuero argued. "I know it like my own wings. I spent my life flyin' around there, and I was born in da islands of that sea. Na of Spectral's helpers know da way to cross it, but I do."

Secha nodded, clearly unfazed by Chinaca's doubts. "Alright," she said simply. "I trust you, Higuero. To the sea it is."

Higuero smiled awkwardly, honoured by the white bat's confidence in him. "We have na time to waste. Crossin' da sea will take two nights. We need a hidin' place, then leave early next evenin'."

Chinaca hesitated before agreeing. Patas nodded furiously.

"Alright," Chitolla consented. "Over the sea, to the Mountains to gather warriors, then back to the temple and the door to my world—and back to Bukinero."

* * *

Bukinero dashed through the tall trees as fast as his sleek, aerodynamic form could carry him, beating his wings only enough to keep himself on track. As the jungle rushed by, he searched for one tree—that familiar thick trunk which held the owl's library.

His heart raced the moment he saw it, standing alongside many smaller, less stately trees. This was definitely the place. He flew in and crashlanded on the wooden floor. He didn't care; he straightened himself up and yelled as loud as he could, "Where is my mate?!"

At first, there was no answer. After a moment's pause, Bukinero heard shuffling behind one of the many shelves lining his view. He hopped towards the noise to find that owl, Flammeus, yawning sleepily and hobbling in his direction.

"Ah, Bukinero, is it? I'm so sorry, but this is one of my off days. I like to become nocturnal every once in a while… is something the matter?"

Bukinero stared up at the owl, his previous fear having been replaced with urgency. "Where is Chitolla?"

"Chitolla? Why, she left some hours ago. Has she returned to the library without my knowing?"

"No, no, she's not here."

Flammeus' tired face turned puzzled. "Really, Bukinero, if you know she's not here, why do you expect that I know where she is?"

"Because you were the one who got her to read the book. Because of that, she went chasing the blue lights, and now she's gone! Gone!"

Flammeus cocked her head for a moment, then shook it slowly

from side to side. "Dear swallow, I'm afraid I have no idea what you're speaking of."

"The book!" Bukinero yelled. "The book with all the stories about the blue lights!"

"Sir, I don't mean to be rude, but your mate has come here quite a few times and has read many stories at this library. I do not know which book you are speaking of. Now, slow down. Deep breaths, young one. I would hate for you to pass out on my floor! Dear me, which blue lights do you mean, and what do they have to do with Chitolla being gone? Perhaps you should tell me from the beginning, nice and slow. That's right, deep breaths—"

"No, you don't understand!" Bukinero sighed. He tried to do as the owl told him, but it was hard to calm his frustration. "Chitolla's gone, because she touched the glowing blue lights, that sapphire spiderweb we read about in the book that talked about the other world, the Echo, the world with all the bats. As soon as she touched it, she disappeared! So, where is she?"

Flammeus' large eyes widened. She appeared dumbstruck. "Bukinero… is this a joke, or are you speaking the truth?"

"It's true!" Bukinero cried desperately. "Would I joke about something like this? She's gone, and I want to know where she is!"

Flammeus nodded. "I see, I see…" She allowed her words to trail off. "If that is the case, Bukinero, then you already know where she is. In fact, you just stated it."

Bukinero sighed in frustration but thought carefully. Slowly, what had already dawned on Flammeus sank into his mind. "So, she's in the world of the bats—the Echo?"

Flammeus nodded again.

"But—but how could that be? It doesn't even exist!"

"Well, if you're so convinced of that, where do you think she is?"

Bukinero pondered this. Clearly, he did have something of a dilemma if he believed in the existence of the web but not the world it led to—and how else was he to explain the sudden disappearance of his mate?

"Okay, fine," he consented. "She's in the other world. How do I get her back?"

"Have you tried touching the silk threads, as she did?"

"They disappeared after she touched them!"

"You are sure the threads didn't simply turn invisible?"

"No! I flew to the exact spot where she disappeared and found nothing there!"

Flammeus seemed intrigued. "Odd. I suppose that's why they haven't been found until now. Perhaps the door is only open on occasion. And your wife had the amazing fortune of being there when the door was present. I suppose it's possible Chitolla can return to the Veil from her side. Although it makes sense that, just as the door can vanish from this side, it can vanish from the Echo as well."

Her contemplations didn't appear to Bukinero to be moving towards the answers he desired. "So, you have no idea how to get her back?"

Flammeus' face remained the picture of a problem-solver trying to overcome a most complex puzzle. However, the faded look in her eyes was soon replaced with golden flame. She hurried towards the back of the library, leaving Bukinero stunned at her change of mood.

"Uh, what are you doing?"

"Getting prepared," was Flammeus' curt response. "We'll need to pack some supplies for the journey."

"What journey?"

"A journey to answers, sir Bukinero—a journey to answers." Flammeus hopped to a nearby bookshelf and pulled out a thin volume. She placed it under her wing before continuing further into the far corners of her library.

Bukinero followed the owl closely. "Where are you going to find answers?"

Flammeus had now reached a small wooden stepladder, which she mounted and rushed to the top of, steadying herself with one wing and continuing to hold the small book with the other. "We, Bukinero. Not I. We."

She used her beak to grab a simple brown bag that hung on the top rung of the stepladder, then again headed downwards. She dropped the bag on the floor and stuffed the small book into it. "We are going to someone—two someones, actually—who know more about the Stone

Place and the world of the Echo than quite possibly anyone else on the face of the Veil."

"Who? And where? You're still not making any sense! And why is this a 'we' thing?"

Flammeus turned to him with blazing eyes, a look that had previously left him paralyzed with fear. "If you wish, you may wait here for her reappearance. But it is quite possible I'll need you on this journey. If you think a trip to the kingdom of Sévéritas is a long way to go for a few simple answers, I would understand. Nevertheless, it may be the only way to bring Chitolla back. Do you wish to come with me or not?"

Bukinero stared into her fiery eyes. They no longer seemed to reveal the heart of a ferocious killer. Now, he realized, they revealed desperation: a desire to help, the necessity for a quest…

A quest for my beloved.

"Of course I'll—"

"Think carefully, Bukinero. We do not know what this journey holds. You may have to abandon previous assumptions you have held as truth. You may have to face greater fears than you've ever faced before. Are you sure you wish to come?"

Bukinero looked into her eyes, trembling at their terrible light, yet standing firm in his decision. "*Yes.* I'm coming with you."

Flammeus' eyes lessened in intensity. "Very good. Very good. We shall soon begin our journey north."

Bukinero nodded in consent, but he still had many questions. "Who exactly are we going to see?"

"Why, Hermain for one, the tortoise your mate spoke to when he came to visit the Stone Place."

"You know him?"

That shouldn't surprise me, Bukerino thought. *The tortoise was the one who made Chitolla want to come to the library. And the two do seem like they'd be the type to hang out together, discussing history and asking questions about other worlds.*

"Why, I know him as a passing acquaintance," Flammeus said. "We have similar interests."

And a similar influence on my mate. "Who else are we going to see?"

"Maxéra Réa, the Guardian Princess. She's one of the leaders of Sévéritas. She will be of great help to us."

"What is she?"

Flammeus was quiet for a moment. "She is… someone who knows much about the Echo and the Bridge. Ancient history courses through her blood." Bukinero was about to clarify his question when Flammeus spoke up again. "Have you ever heard of Sévéritas?"

Bukinero shook his head, and Flammeus chirred cheerily.

"Oh, it is a marvellous place! We'll be arriving right around the Festival of Sinocore. Of course, I suppose we shouldn't get sidetracked by such things. But it is a lovely kingdom." Flammeus pulled the small volume out of the bag and flipped it open for Bukinero to see. "Here is a map. We shall travel north, away from the mountain, over the jungles, to pine forests, and then into the desert—and there, we shall find Sévéritas."

"Sévéritas is in the desert?" Bukinero doubted that deserts could be lovely. He had never been to one, but the descriptions he'd heard sounded horrible.

"Oh, Sévéritas is a very special place," Flammeus said with a twinkle in her eye. "I believe you will like it."

Bukinero wasn't so sure he would, but he didn't care. "So, when do we leave?"

"As soon as you are ready to go, sir Bukinero—as soon as you are ready."

SEA OF DECEPTION

CHINACA BEAT HER WINGS FURIOUSLY AGAINST THE ANGRY WINDS, careful to keep her eyes on their guide, Higuero. She didn't enjoy looking at him so much—it demonstrated too much trust towards someone whom she despised. However, she much preferred it to the terrible queasiness she felt every time she looked at their surroundings: the dark blue-green waters below and cloud-covered skies above, both stretching endlessly in all directions.

She sighed, unsure why she had agreed to go this way. Why hadn't she simply suggested that she, and perhaps the swallow and little white bat, travel up the Northern Passage, letting Higuero take Patas across the sea?

We could always have met up later. The Desert Mountains can't be that big. Chinaca chided herself for not coming up with this plan sooner.

From hours of watching Higuero fly in front of her, she could see that the Stripe-Faced bat's wings were perfect for this weather. Their shape and texture went with the howling winds and salty air. Her wings—well, she wasn't sure what made her wings so different from his, but something was throwing her off.

Glancing to her left, Chinaca saw that Patas had once again moved closer to her; their wing-tips nearly touched. Though Chinaca found this even more irritating than having to allow Higuero to guide her, little could be done about it. Sticking together had been one of Higuero's first instructions.

Patas' eyes drew over to her. The Vampire gave her a weak smile. His face had taken on an unusual green hue.

"Hey!" he yelled to her. "How are you doin'?"

Chinaca averted her gaze, mouthing something under her breath, to which Patas responded, "What? I didn't catch that. These winds and waves are so loud."

Ignoring him, she directed her attention to the right. Chitolla, the swallow, didn't appear to like flying over the sea, either. Her feathers were in complete disarray, but she hung on. To Chinaca, it seemed the bird was having an easier time than either she or Patas.

"Hey, how's the little white bat doing?" Chinaca shouted in Higuero's direction. "I'm guessing better than the rest of us, huh? Don't get me wrong, I like her, but it seems unfair that, while the rest of us have to fight these winds, she gets a free ride."

Higuero bristled at the scornful tone in Chinaca's voice. Instead of responding, he looked down to his chest, where Secha clung like a young bat would cling to its mother.

"You doin' alright?" he asked in a caring manner.

"I'm okay," Secha replied in a quaky voice. "Just kinda cold."

Chinaca got tired of waiting for Higuero to answer. "Hey, lesser race, any chance you'll be giving one of *us* a ride? I'm sure Secha could use the exercise. Some extra muscle could be good for her."

From his initial reaction, Secha thought Higuero just might turn and attack the silver bat, but he quickly got himself under control. "Chinaca, Secha es very small. If she flew, she would be taken by da wind. Understand?"

Chinaca was clearly irritated by the sense in his argument. "I suppose we wouldn't want her carried out to the ocean and over to the Eastern Continent, would we?"

"Na," Higuero replied bluntly, "she would die long before gettin' to da East."

"Hey, Goo-arrow?" Patas called. "Do you know any songs we can use for flying over the sea? It's getting kinda hard to see. And the fog is thickening."

"Songs are pointless over da sea if you na know what you are lookin' for."

Chitolla, shivering from the cold, had been listening to the conversation. She didn't understand Patas' question about songs, but she had long been curious about why Higuero focused so intently on the frothy waves below. "What *do* you look for, Higuero?"

The Stripe-Faced bat's eyes remained fixed on the tossing sea. He appeared to be reading the blue-green waters like a book. "I am lookin' at da waves, da colour. It changes when you are closer to land. There are rocks and forests under da water, just like on da land. I am lookin' for signs of that."

"Forests under the sea?" Chinaca laughed. "It just looks like water to me!"

"Then clearly," Higuero replied briskly, "you na know what to look for."

"Okay, okay." Chinaca turned away, feeling more like arguing with Higuero than looking at him. Patas was getting harder to see through the thickening fog, but she could tell the young Vampire was watching her.

Starstruck creep, she thought.

Suddenly, Secha sensed an abrupt change in Higuero's attitude. He had been flying calmly, his wings beating lazily against the winds, his eyes scanning the waters in front of him while his ears listened intently. Now, he raised his head, as if detecting a change in the atmosphere. He let the winds take him behind his followers.

"Da bad winds are comin' up," he bellowed. "This es na good formation for them. We need to make da—"

"Can you speak more clearly, Higuero?" Chinaca yelled. "I can't follow orders I can't understand."

"Form a line!" Higuero roared, tired of her insolence. His tone was urgent, demanding complete obedience.

All except Chinaca became a little frightened, wondering what was going on that would make him suddenly so authoritative, and quickly did as he said. Chitolla, the fastest flier in this weather, ended up in front, with Patas behind her, and Chinaca, slower to follow orders, falling into the back. Higuero hovered above them, Secha holding on tight.

"Now," Higuero continued, "lean left into da winds."

All tilted left.

"Harder! Further into da winds!"

All pushed themselves into the howling winds, leaning as far left as they could possibly go.

"Good," Higuero said, moving back to his position in front, his own wings beating faster than before. He leaned hard to the left, doing exactly as he had commanded the rest to do.

The fogs thickened at an alarming rate. Chinaca, in the back, could no longer see their leader through the haze. All she could see was Patas in front of her, flying almost sideways. Chinaca, too, flew nearly vertically, questioning why in the world they would be asked to do this.

"You better not be just trying to make us look like fools," she snapped, only afterwards realizing that Higuero probably couldn't hear. As the fogs thickened, the roaring winds became more violent.

A thunderous crack boomed through the mist-shrouded sky, and Chinaca thought she saw a flash of light in the heavens above. Her heart rate increased suddenly.

Hating the cold feeling that gripped her, she tried to replace fear with frustration, forcing the trembles going through her to stop. *Well, harem leader, if we die, it'll be your fault for asking us to go this way. Why couldn't we just take the Northern Passage? We wouldn't be wet and cold and smelling like salt and fish.*

She detested flying like this. It was such an awkward position to remain in for so long. Yet Higuero had given no command to return to a normal position. If he had, she hadn't heard it.

By now, the mist was so thick she could barely make out the form of Patas in front of her. Was he still flying sideways? A breeze tugged at Chinaca's right wing, attempting to spin her further left.

Chinaca, feeling she had done enough awkward flying, decided she wasn't going to let this breeze force her upside-down. She pulled her wings into her body for just a second to escape that draft, allowing herself to fall back into a horizontal position.

The moment she spread her wings, a powerful gust grabbed her, catching in her wings like wind in an open sail, flinging her backwards, pulling her away from the group with a loud shriek.

Hearing her scream, Patas glanced backwards just in time to see Chinaca vanish into the fog. "Chinaca!"

"Something's wrong!" Chitolla yelled forwards to Higuero.

The next moment, Patas found the Stripe-Faced bat flying next to him, wings beating furiously.

"Take Secha!" Higuero commanded, hurriedly transferring the little Tent-Maker to Patas. "Let the wind continue to guide you forward!"

Without another word, he disappeared into the mists.

* * *

Higuero threw himself into the wind, hoping it would take him wherever it had taken Chinaca. His eyes and ears turned in all directions, frantically searching the sky and sea for signs of his lost companion.

For a moment, he saw the grey outline of a bat being tossed about in the furious winds. He pulled away from the gale that carried him and headed towards the shape. His heart pounded faster as Chinaca faded from sight, and he called out in a strong voice,

> Winds an' waves, sky o' grey,
> Turn gold as if seein' light o' day,
> Winds an' waves, sky o' grey,
> Fa' da fog be fadin' away

As the song came back to reach him, his vision blurred; the moment was gone in a split second, and the greys and greens and blues that once covered his vision were replaced by a powerful golden light. It pierced the fog and turned the sky into a pale yellow, the waves to a dark orange.

Higuero, now able to see a few meters in all directions, scanned the area, singing as loudly as he could, trying again to grasp sight of the grey shape that had disappeared into the fog. But his song had come too late. He found nothing but crashing waves below and empty air above.

He flew in the direction he thought he had seen her going, but knew from the signs that the situation was hopeless. He could see by the patterns of the waves that he was heading into deeper waters, out into the ocean.

Even I can na take da open waters, he knew. But he pushed himself as far as he dared, continuing his song. *Chinaca, where ya be?*

Suddenly, Higuero felt his wing catch, and a terrible blast tossed him through the air like a scrap of paper. He righted himself and pulled his body out of the gust. Reluctantly, he turned back, forcing himself back to the others.

> Winds an' waves, sky o' grey,
> Turn gold as if seein' light o' day,
> Winds an' waves, sky o' grey,
> Fa' da fog be fadin' away

When he caught sight of the group, he allowed his song to fade. The sky became grey again and the sea returned to its blue-green hue.

Patas turned to him with a terrified look on his face. "Where's Chinaca?"

Higuero looked away so the Vampire wouldn't see the tears in his eyes. "Keep flyin'. It na too far to da Desert Mountains."

"You brought her back, right?" Secha cried, but the sound was too soft for Higuero to hear. He had already pulled himself forward through the wind, leaving her clinging to Patas. A slow tear dropped from the white bat's eye.

Higuero silently took his place in front of Chitolla. No one spoke another word as he guided them through the mists.

* * *

Land appeared as the sun broke over the horizon. Everyone was relieved to feel the sea winds fade into a gentle breeze. The shore was dotted with tall palm trees, and the bats and swallow rested gratefully in their large fronds. Despite their all-night flight, not one of the travelers had any desire to sleep.

After a few moments of silence, Secha turned her eyes to Higuero. His own gaze was directed to the ground, and even when she addressed him, he would not look up. "It's not your fault we lost Chinaca."

"Yes, it was," Higuero replied in his strong voice. "Should na have happened."

But Secha was convinced otherwise. "What would you have done differently?"

Higuero didn't respond.

Chitolla, perched near Patas, whispered quietly to the Vampire, "What now?"

Patas sighed deeply, his face falling. "Nothing. I learn to live as an ex-Vampire, and you stay here with us." He turned to her, his black eyes vague. "We're not going back to Spectral's Temple. Ever. We can't go back. I'll never see my mother again, or my friends…"

"You're giving up on the war?"

"The war can't happen without Chinaca."

"Why not?"

"No one else is silly enough to believe Spectral can be defeated, swallow."

"You don't believe it?"

"I did…" Patas shook his head. "I'm sorry, Chitolla. I wish you could see your mate again. Really."

"Who be goen dair?" A strong female voice echoed through the palms, and all four travelers turned their attention to its source. A reddish bat with a similar appearance to Higuero and the same white stripes on her face flew towards them.

"Gadon," Higuero called out to her. "Mes doolan an mes bein desra shelta fora na da."

The other three gave each other puzzled looks. "What's he saying?" Chitolla asked. It was obvious from their faces that neither Secha nor Patas knew the answer.

"Gadoo," the female bat responded. "Ovey mes." She left her roost and flew away again.

"Come," Higuero said, motioning to the others. "She will show us da place to rest for da day."

The female bat led them through a thick, palm-dominated forest. It wasn't long before they began encountering other bats, some reddish, but most of them grey or brown. Many had white markings on their face, although in a few the markings were faded and almost indiscernible.

"Some of these bats look more like Nectar-Drinkers than Stripe-Faces," Patas noted quietly.

"They are of mixed blood," Higuero explained. "Hybrids. Though Chinaca would probably be offended to hear that her race be mixin' with mine."

"She didn't really like your race, did she?" Secha said.

"She be uncomfortable with anyone not like her."

"That's what it seemed like," Patas said. "Although I've always been taught that all Nectar-Drinkers are like that."

"They na like to depend on anybody else," Higuero agreed.

"Well, it makes sense why they wouldn't like us Vampires. We haven't exactly treated them very well."

"I still don't like how she acted towards you," Chitolla spoke up. "What if the Nectar-Drinkers *do* need help someday?"

"They already need it," Secha pointed out. "The Vampires are pushing them out of their homelands. Do they *ask* other races to help them?"

Higuero shook his head. "A few have. Some are learnin' that they need help from outsiders to escape. But more are like Chinaca: they na truly learn."

The group became silent with this final thought.

"Ova 'ere." The female bat now spoke to them in their tongue. "Ya can rest unda dis leaf."

The four travelers peered under the giant, drooping leaf to find a small group of Stripe-Faced bats huddled underneath, all clinging to the leaf's midrib with their back feet.

"We're not sleeping in a cave?" Patas asked uncertainly.

"We Stripa-Faces oftan sleepen unda leaf tents, lika disa one. It bein a safe place."

"My race does that, too!" Secha said enthusiastically. "That's why we're called 'Tent-Makers.' We all curl together under banana leaves and palm fronds, and sleep side by side to keep each other warm…" An odd tone entered her voice. "I miss my family."

With sympathetic looks and encouraging nods, the half-sleeping bats under the leaf welcomed Secha. She, Higuero, and their guide joined them.

But Patas, hesitating, landed just outside their tent. "I, uh, don't know if I feel comfortable with this…"

"You need to sleep, don't you?" Secha pointed out. "It's safer under here than out there. Much nicer, too."

Patas glanced around for a moment, contemplating. Slowly, he forced himself under the leaf tent and found his place next to Higuero.

Only Chitolla now remained outside. Being a swallow, she couldn't cling to the leaf's midrib and hang like the bats. She fluttered to a more stable-looking roost and lay down. Glancing at the bat-made tent, she suddenly felt quite alone.

A flash of white escaped from under the leaf and found itself hanging near to her. "Chitolla? Are you okay out here?"

"Well… Secha, could you come over to the top of the branch where I am—instead of hanging underneath it?"

Secha thought it was a strange request, but she did as the swallow suggested and landed on all fours, setting herself just in front of the larger creature. "What?"

Chitolla spread her wing towards Secha and hugged her close. Secha cuddled beneath the bird's soft, warm down. Yawning, the white bat closed her eyes, her breath becoming deeper and slower.

For a moment, Chitolla did nothing but soak in the feeling of the warm creature under her wing. *Is this what it's like to have chicks of your own?* With a pang of pain, she realized, *I may never have the chance to find out.*

Finally, she shut her eyes to the brightening world. For a few hours, at least, she could let her troubles fade from her mind—assuming she could convince herself to fall asleep in broad daylight.

Perhaps, she thought, *tomorrow night will reveal a solution.*

* * *

71

Patas tried hard to sleep, to ignore the strange bats, both male and female, brushing up against him. *This isn't so bad*, he thought to himself. *Not so bad, right?*

But being surrounded by strangers gave him the same sad feeling Secha had expressed after speaking about her fellow Tent-Makers. It wasn't just odd being in a new place with an unfamiliar race and unfamiliar sleeping arrangement. His heart throbbed at the thought of never being able to return to his old life.

I'll never see mom, or Mano, or Ézo... the memory of his little brother's death hit him and tears welled up in his eyes.

One of the bats next to him had begun to snore loudly. Not curious enough to investigate whether it was Higuero or one of his lookalikes, Patas tried unsuccessfully to close his ears to the annoying sound. Hot breath and bony, furry bodies pressed against him on every side. Patas was used to sleeping in close quarters with other bats—the Vampire caves were the same way—but not *this* close, and not with a mixture of males and females, a few of them sleep-talking in their foreign tongue.

A tear escaped his eye, and Patas felt himself elbowing another bat in the ribs as he attempted to rub the drop away with his wing. *This will be a long day.*

* * *

Chinaca was sure she was about to die. The powerful winds beat against her mercilessly, tossing her about, threatening to throw her into the dark blue waters below. The waves had grown taller, and more than a few times the Nectar-Drinker was sure one would arise to pull her down into the deep, swallowing her alive.

Chinaca couldn't tell how long she spun wildly out in the middle of the ocean, but it seemed like a very long time. It was as if the winds toyed with her, waiting for her to gain hope of escape before dashing her hopes, drowning them in salty waters. Dizzy and disorientated, she was weary of being the wind's playtoy. She couldn't take it anymore.

"Are you done yet?" Screaming made her throat burn, but she cried out anyway, hoping the wind and water had ears to hear. "Take me already! I *want* to die!"

Her words were grabbed and pulled away by the wind. She tried calling again, but her voice no longer worked. Closing her eyes, she abandoned all hope, all thought, and all efforts to remain alive.

A blast of seawater smacked against her face and she opened her eyes again, gasping in fright and trying to beat her wings against the violent winds. *So much for just letting myself die.*

Then, through the thick grey fog, she saw a dark shape approaching. Heart pumping, she studied it hopefully. A bat!

As it got closer, she saw it was huge, at least as big as Spectral, with long jaws. Its wide wings carved into the howling winds, fighting against them with powerful strokes. Watching, she realized the giant bat was covered in a coat of coal-black fur, darker even than the surrounding night and dense fogs.

It wasn't Higuero, for sure. It wasn't Spectral or Cattae, either, but as it flew towards her she realized it somehow appeared more terrible than either of them, with a muzzle longer and perhaps more developed than theirs, and wings muscular enough to carry it over the lethal winds and cantankerous waves of the open ocean.

It's Death. The thought came with a wave of fear and relief. *It's over. I'm going.*

The black phantom reached out and grabbed her in its large, clawed feet, gripping her tightly and carrying her away into the unknown.

Chinaca allowed herself to fade into a new dimension. As her vision went dark, the waves stopped speaking, and the world faded from memory.

She faintly heard the voice of the coal-black giant speaking to her.

"No worries, sheila… take you away… all over."

SÉVÉRITAS

7

BUKINERO'S SORE WINGS FLOATED OPEN AND CLOSED AS HE DRIFTED on high-altitude winds, staring down at the bleak desert far, far below. He blinked back tears and shut his eyes to the painfully bright world. Already, he had decided that the warm, humid rainforest was more hospitable than the cloudless, arid desert.

He pulled himself forward to hide under Flammeus' wide shadow. "Are we almost there?" Bukinero asked wearily.

"Are we almost there?" the owl repeated in a chiding manner. "Sir Bukinero, I'll have you know I've been counting how many times you have asked that exact question—and you have just raised the count to five in the last hour."

She looked ahead, apparently unbothered by the bright light or the heat waves rising from the sandy ground. In fact, she seemed quite comfortable in this weather, using the waves of heat to her advantage, soaring on them lazily. The bag containing the map and other supplies floated behind her, tied tightly to her leg.

"Dear me," she continued, "I told you earlier that we should arrive this evening. I've travelled much farther distances than this in search of answers, you know. Also, you can rest assured we have made good time: the sun has yet to set and the Peak of Desperation is just ahead." Flammeus pointed with her wing, drawing Bukinero's attention to a small, sandy mountain not too far away, glowing red in the sunlight. "See that? Sévéritas is just behind it."

"Peak of Desperation, huh? What an appropriate name." Bukinero had tired of keeping his thoughts to himself, and now openly conversed with the owl he had once been so hesitant to trust. "What does Sévéritas look like?"

"Well, you will see when we get over the mountain. Dear swallow, relax! We shall be there soon enough."

Flammeus turned to the west. Bukinero, too, caught what sounded like laughter coming from that direction. In the distance, he saw a small group of birds—four in all—which he soon identified as owls.

Flammeus' feathers bunched out as she watched their approach. "I thought so. Thugs. Ruffians. Keep your wits about you, Bukinero. They look like trouble."

"They look just like you," Bukinero replied.

"Dear me, do all owls look the same to you?"

Bukinero wanted to mention that he was now making a mental note of how many times she used the word "dear," but Flammeus continued before he could speak.

"Stick close," she said, "and try to stay out of sight of them."

Too late for that, Bukinero thought as one of the owls made eye contact and waved at them in greeting. As it came closer, the others followed close behind.

"Lovely day for a flight, isn't it, fellow feathered friends?" the lead one said casually as he pulled up beside Flammeus' left wing. "And where would the two of you be headed to today?"

"Sévéritas," Flammeus replied dryly, not even turning to look at the fellow owl.

Bukinero watched the other three owls nervously. One of them took up its place by Flammeus' right wing while another fell behind. The final one hovered just above Flammeus. Bukinero momentarily caught the eyes of this one. He quickly turned away, chills creeping down his spine from the hungry look he had seen.

"Sévéritas?" the lead ruffian said with a bit of chirring. "What are you going there for?"

"We are visiting the *Maxéra*—the Guardians of Sévéritas." Flammeus' tone was again cold. She continued to stare straight ahead.

"The Maxéra of Sévéritas, huh?" The other owls cowed a bit at the response, but their leader was unfazed. "Okay. So, what will you give us in exchange for letting you get there?" His greedy eyes ventured to the bag.

Bukinero felt his heart rate increase, but Flammeus' voice remained steady. "You are not border control. And the *Maxéra* wouldn't approve of you taking advantage of travellers this way."

"That's what you're going to give us? Attitude?" The lead owl's tone was both mocking and angry. "I don't like that offer. Okay, fellas, do your thing."

The owl hovering above Flammeus suddenly dropped, talons outstretched, and dug her claws into Flammeus' back. Flammeus let out a screech of pain and tried to get free of the owl's grip, but the owls on either side hemmed her in.

"Get the little bird!" the lead one yelled.

The owl to the rear dove at him, but too slowly. Bukinero darted ahead, then turned sharply and headed towards Flammeus, calling out, "What do we do?!"

"Get Maxéra Réa!" Flammeus said urgently, struggling against the other birds. Her talons finally found their place in the back of the leader, but the other two owls continued harassing her. She couldn't break free. "Go and find the Guardian Princess! Now!"

The remaining owl had turned and again came at Bukinero, talons outstretched, but the swallow's adrenaline-pumped wings acted more quickly than the bird of prey. With a few twisting swoops, Bukinero made a full circle around the owl—effectively, even if not intentionally, disorienting it—and locked his eyes on the red mountain. He allowed himself to lose altitude, hoping it would gain him enough speed to make an escape.

The owl, recovering from its dizziness, followed after him, wings pumping furiously. As the owl gained on him, Bukinero realized that though he could outmanoeuvre the larger bird, he probably couldn't outrace it. He focused his eyes on the Peak of Desperation, his heart beating faster as it came closer.

The small mountain was soon just ahead, then underneath him— and at that moment, he saw what he knew, without the slightest doubt, had to be the kingdom of Sévéritas.

Beyond the shadow of the mountain, the brilliant sands of red and yellow briskly gave way to luxurious greens. The stunted, scrubby foliage vanished as tall, stately pines and leafy trees of every conceivable colour swept over the landscape. Even from high above, Bukinero was hit with the strong scent of fragrant flowers rising from the forest. He was sure he saw crimson blossoms the size of Flammeus peeking out from between massive trunks.

Basking in the welcoming sights and smells, he almost forgot about the owl chasing him; he stared at something sparkling not too far ahead.

Water... a lake! This is by far the most beautiful thing I have seen all day...

"Aha!" The frightening voice behind him led Bukinero to duck, suddenly recalling his current situation.

"Mah-haz-a-ray anna!" he called out. Hearing chuckles from above, he decided he had pronounced the title wrong. "Mah-naz—uh, Guardian Princess! Help! Guardian Princess!"

The attacking owl chirred madly, screeching in a scornful tone, "Mah-naza Rana! Mah-naza Rana! She can't hear you, little birdy! And she would think you were mocking her if she did!"

The owl's chirring continued to gain volume, the sound breaking Bukinero's concentration. By now, the two had descended far enough that they began to pass the boughs of ancient pine trees. The ground still lay far below, hidden beneath long, leafy branches.

Bukinero had no time to appreciate the beauty around him. The owl was gaining quickly and he wasn't sure how to lose it in the forest canopy. Fear rose within him as he realized the owl was more confident racing through this old-growth forest than he.

The owl seemed to have come to the same conclusion, and it only made his laughter wilder. "Guardian Princess!" he cried gleefully. "Guardian Princess! She isn't here! You're all mine, little birdy! What do you think... should I eat you now, or after boss gives the order?"

Bukinero was sure the wild laughter would kill him long before its talons sunk into his flesh or its sharp beak divided his spinal cord. He wished the chase would end, praying desperately, *Save me, somebody! Chitolla, where are you? What would happen to you if I died?*

A loud squawk signalled the sudden end of the owl's maddening rant. Shocked, Bukinero slowed, only afterwards regarding the fact that it could be a trick. Yet the dark talons didn't sink into his flesh. The forest behind him was completely silent.

Bukinero came to a stop, landing on an outstretched limb. Hesitantly, he turned. What he saw froze him in place.

The owl was now an unmoving lump of feathers wrapped in the embrace of a long and smooth-scaled body. His eyes followed the shape of the serpentine creature, around each coal-black coil towards the animal's long, muscular neck, until he made it to a rounded head with gold spheres for eyes.

The creature, staring at him, caught his gaze and rose its head elegantly, spreading the unusually long ribs in its neck, as if in greeting.

For a moment, all Bukinero could do was stare in fear. But the giant cobra made no move to attack. In fact, it didn't move at all.

Bukinero glanced back at the owl, its head twisted awkwardly, and managed to say in a small voice, "W–where is the Guardian Princess?"

"I am she," the snake replied in a strong, unwavering voice. It certainly wasn't the hissing sibilant he had expected, which caught him off-guard.

"It's... she's... you?"

"Yes," she said casually, "it's me. Now, where is Flammeus? Hermain and I have been awaiting your arrival."

"You... you've been waiting?"

"Yes, Bukinero, we heard you were coming. Where is she?"

Usually, Bukinero would have been tongue-tied at the sight of such a frightening creature, but her unblinking eyes appeared to demand an answer. "Flammeus—she was attacked by other owls." His eyes drew back to the dead owl in the Guardian Princess' coils.

"Yes, they've been causing problems for a while." The princess regarded the limp body. As if suddenly annoyed by the weight, she unceremoniously shifted to allow the body to fall from her coils and crash to the forest floor below. Bukinero watched it fall with something akin to fear.

Maxéra Réa looked up and moved along the branch, as if searching for a position from which she could get a clear view of something in the sky. She folded and unfolded her hood a few times, waited, then again folded and unfolded her hood.

Her eyes returned to Bukinero.

"I have signalled my warriors," the snake said. "They were aware of the attack. Flammeus has been rescued and is being treated. So please, won't you join me?"

* * *

Bukinero's first three impressions of Sévéritas were that it was beautiful, big, and virtually uninhabited. However, the third impression soon proved to be far from accurate.

"The Festival of Sinocore was begun to commemorate the coming of the very first Maxéra," Flammeus half-yelled as she explained the history behind the festival, hoping Bukinero could hear her voice over the many others who were shouting, chatting, whispering, and hissing all around. "Sinocore was a dear spottleback snake. He and his friend Cuttle, a mouse, went on a quest across the Veil in search of someone who could rescue this valley from the evil mongoose Franisicoph."

The black snake, Maxéra Réa, had led them to the fairgrounds in Robbers Valley, where the festival now took place. After listening to Flammeus briefly summarize their situation and their reason for coming, the cobra instructed that they search for Hermain in the crowds while she discuss their dilemma with her brothers, the other Maxéra of Sévéritas.

Bukinero's eyes darted around in search of the tortoise, his ears straining to hear Flammeus' stories. His mind alternated between working in vain to understand the owl's words and attempting to still the chills that ran down his spine every time his head turned.

The valley's residents were varied and colourful, with everything from scales to feathers to fur to antennae to wings present in at least a dozen creatures. However, the vast majority were brightly-patterned snakes—spottlebacks and stripbacks, as Flammeus had explained—unusually large and hairy spiders, black scorpions with gigantic pincers, and a diverse array of rats, mice, and what Flammeus said were hybrid blends of the two.

"What Sinocore and Cuttle didn't know when they first found him," Flammeus continued, oblivious to the swallow's distress, "was that the black cobra Maxéra was actually a descendant of Alexio, the cobra who had trained the great warrior Nickinino, the mongoose who defeated the evil cobra Mikalo in the Mongoose Battle of—"

"Wait… doesn't 'Maxéra' just mean 'ruler,' or something like that?" Bukinero asked. "Why was there someone *named* Maxéra?"

"No no, Maxéra was the first cobra to rule Sévéritas after Mikalo. Generations after Mikalo, since Sévéritas had no ruler and was divided between the time of the Mongoose Battle and the Maxéra's Coming. The Maxéra of today are descendants of the original Maxéra, the great-grandson of Alexio, whom Sinocore and Cuttle brought back from the distant land of Holezenia. Which, as you may or may not be aware, is very close to where Adila's Tale, your wife's favourite story, took place."

A pang entered Bukinero's heart at the thought of Chitolla. Knowing Flammeus hadn't intended any harm by mentioning her, he remained focused on the owl's story. "So, Maxéra was the hero they brought back to defeat the—what was it?"

"Mongoose. They're descendants of the meerkat, which you should be more familiar with; Adila's Tale talks about them, you may recall. In actuality, Maxéra wasn't much of a hero when he first arrived. It took a bit of time after he betrayed Sinocore and Cuttle to Coltheniac—"

"He betrayed them?"

"—before he was accepted back into Sévéritas."

"Why would they make a double-crossing giant black snake their leader?"

"Now, now, Bukinero, there's more to the story than that."

I know, Bukinero thought to himself. *You've tried explaining this several times. But it's still so confusing.*

Nevertheless, the swallow did feel he was having better success understanding the owl's stories than he was at locating Hermain.

"Where *is* that tortoise?" he asked. "I feel like we've searched everywhere! Where *should* one look for wandering tortoises?"

"Sweet corn!" a vendor's voice boomed over the noisy crowds. "A delightfully tasty treat! Crumbs and other tiny morsels taken in trade! Come and get it! Sweet corn! Your whole gang will love it! Méx'a'dulé! Apréeda né gusté, calmeané cador ni jahbon!"

"Huh?" Bukinero turned to Flammeus with a quizzical look. "Is it me, or did he just start speaking gibberish?"

"That's their native tongue. Many of the creatures in Sévéritas don't speak English."

"Yet you do," a new voice said. Unexpectedly, one of the colourful snakes had stopped, his unblinking yellow eyes fixed on the two birds. "Which means, you must be foreigners. Your accent says you are."

Bukinero took a few apprehensive steps away from the reptile. "And who would you be?"

"Cathaial. I'm one of Sinocore's descendants." He waved his head to the left. "Hermain is this way. Follow me."

"He sent you?" Flammeus' tone was one of curiosity, but Bukinero felt a greater sense of caution.

"Not exactly," the spottleback replied. "He just said to keep an eye out for two birds—an owl and a swallow—who looked like they didn't belong." His gaze travelled over the feathered duo. "You fit the description."

Without another word, Cathaial slithered off in the direction he had motioned. Flammeus and Bukinero exchanged glances, then went after him.

Their serpentine guide glided through the crowds with ease, quickly making it difficult to follow him without pressing against and even shoving aside other fair-goers. Fortunately, the fair-goers were clearly accustomed to the routine.

"We must stand out, as Cathaial said," Flammeus noted as she looked over to Bukinero. "We're probably among the very few here who are actually bothered by the busyness!"

Bukinero briefly considered finding space to spread his wings and follow the snake via air. Just as the thought crossed his mind, his eyes caught a glimpse of a large, stony-looking reptile chatting with a small mouse and a bearded lizard.

"There he is!" the swallow exclaimed.

"Sir Hermain!" Flammeus greeted warmly as she, Bukinero, and Cathaial approached. "My, you have been very difficult to find! I'm grateful you asked the locals to direct us, or we may have been searching quite some time."

"We *did* search quite some time." Bukinero muttered the words, but they were audible enough to receive a snicker from the mouse and a short, coughing hiss from Cathaial.

Hermain's face broke into a wide, wrinkly grin. "Well, I am glad to see you again, Flammeus. And to meet you, young swallow. You are the husband of the one I spoke to when I travelled through the Stone Place, correct?"

"Correct."

"As I said, it's nice to meet you. Have you enjoyed the festival?"

As Bukinero pondered how to reply in as nice a way as possible, Cathaial inserted himself into the conversation. "You are staying for the rest of the festival, right? For the dance?"

Bukinero turned his attention to the snake. "What dance?"

"The fairgrounds will be closing in a short time. After that comes the group dance, where everyone gathers in Christioan's Field. The birds dance together, the snakes do a dance, then the arachnids. But before all that, the Maxéra come out and perform a traditional dance, and everyone watches. You will stay, right? You will be participating?"

"I thought Maxéra Réa and her brothers were busy discussing how to get Chitolla back," Bukinero said.

"They *can't* be busy on the night of the festival," the snake insisted. "*Of course* they'll participate! They have to. It's tradition."

"Well, why did she say—"

"The fairgrounds are beginning to close," Hermain interrupted. "You can join in the dance, if you like. I'm sure Chitolla would want you to enjoy your time here and not be so worried about her."

Well, Bukinero thought, anger creeping into his mind, *I'm sure she would want me to keep looking for her.*

"We can wait until the Maxéra have finished their dance," Flammeus suggested. "I'm sure they'll then discuss with us how to get your wife back."

* * *

To Bukinero, the closing of the fairgrounds and preparation for the dance was an excruciatingly long process. The locals buzzed about, but the excitement in the air made him queasy.

"When will it begin?" he asked Flammeus.

"Soon enough." The owl's voice was reassuring, but inside she felt concerned for Bukinero. It was obvious he was more anxious about when the dance would end than when it would begin. "We'll learn more about Chitolla's situation when the Maxéra are ready to talk with us. In the meantime, try to relax."

Finally, the locals began moving out of the valley and onto a spacious green hill. Short, soft blades of grass covered "the field," as the natives called it, and brightly-coloured clouds marked the sun's departure over the horizon. Bukinero and Flammeus followed the crowds, this time flying alongside the various birds, small bats, enormous butterflies, and other winged creatures who took to the air in hopes of reaching the hill before the land-bound residents of Sévéritas. Strangely, the two groups still arrived at the same time, but there was no jostling for position as there had been in the fairgrounds; everyone was given enough space to allow for free movement.

The very top of the hill, Bukinero noticed, was clear of critters. "Why is nobody going over there?"

"Why, that's where Réa and the other Maxéra will perform their dance. I greatly enjoyed their dance the last time I visited."

Flammeus lifted her wing, revealing a jagged red cut across her side, completely void of feathers.

When she caught Bukinero's stare, the owl responded in annoyance. "It's not as bad as it looks, sir swallow. No need to gape at me!"

As the crowds landed, their voices stilled to whispers. Bukinero and Flammeus alit among a group of birds near the top of the hill.

"A front-row view, we have," Flammeus noted cheerily.

The whispers died suddenly. Bukinero's eyes searched for the cause of the abrupt change. There, in the empty area atop the hill, a creature had appeared, drawing the attention of the waiting audience.

It took a moment for Bukinero to realize that the black cobra was not Maxéra Réa. Its thick, masculine build and faded brown stripes identified him as one of her brothers. Raising his head, he spread his massive hood, stretching the ribs in his neck and arching his head.

He's even bigger than the Princess! Bukinero felt both frightened and unexpectedly awed. He was shocked at how regal the snake appeared, golden eyes focused unswervingly on another creature making its way out of the crowd.

A new dancer entered. One cobra, hood raised, quickly became two, one sliding to the left of the first cobra, another to the right. These two were similar in appearance, lightly built, with intricate patterns decorating their silvery skin. They alternated positions, circling the first snake before taking their places at either side of him and turning to face the direction they had come from.

A brown cobra now made its way out of the crowd. Not as heavy as the first cobra, but still well-built, this one tilted its head as if eyeing a competitor.

Bukinero then heard a deep, rhythmic hiss vibrate through the air, and began searching for a musical instrument. It took a moment for him to realize the sound came from the dancing cobras.

What odd… music, Bukinero thought. Yet he felt a strange pleasure from it. *Odd, but somehow fascinating…*

The brown cobra approached the black one slowly, and the two silvery snakes moved away, their motions calculated as they made room for the new dancer. The black cobra remained stone-still as it watched the brown snake come within inches of him.

Suddenly, the black one struck, and the two snakes became a blur of motion. Bukinero jumped, startled, and his heart beat sped up. The music was fast and furious as the snakes struck, evading each other's knife-like fangs.

"Cobras are usually slow strikers," Flammeus noted matter-of-factly.

"That's why mongooses are able to avoid their strikes and take them down. But Alexio had an unusual agility. His descendants have long trained and enhanced their speed-strikes and fast combat skills."

There was only one matter of history Bukinero cared about at the moment. "Have they ever killed each other doing this dance?"

"Don't be silly, Bukinero. They're immune to each other's venom."

As abruptly as the battle began, it stopped. The cobras turned their attention once again to the spot in the crowd where they had made their entrance, preparing to usher in a new presence.

Maxéra Réa appeared, head bowed towards her brothers. Bukinero wasn't sure what had changed, but somehow, the cobra entering the dance didn't seem like the Princess he had met earlier. She wasn't the same frightening creature who had mercilessly suffocated the troublemaking owl. Tonight, she was enchantingly beautiful.

Perhaps it was the purpling sky, which made her scales shimmer like gems. Or the way she glided across the grass as though floating. Or how her delicately bowed head and radiating eyes expressed a gentleness he had not previously experienced.

The rest of the dance was as smooth and elegant as the previous part had been swift and reckless. Réa danced with each of her brothers, one by one, swaying to unheard music.

Bukinero watched, entranced, until Maxéra Réa closed her dance with the last of her four brothers. She inconspicuously sidled into the crowds, removing herself from their attention as her brothers continued the dance.

The swallow found her disappearance startling. "Where'd she go?"

He turned around to look for the snake, and nearly jumped out of his skin when he caught her golden eyes staring back at him.

"Maxéra!" Flammeus whispered at the Princess, who had silently slithered in next to the two birds. "Well done! That was beautiful!"

"Thank you." Réa nodded in recognition. "But I won't be staying to finish the dance. And neither will you. We have business to attend to. It's time we discuss Chitolla's disappearance."

THE EAST

CHINACA FELT SOMETHING COLD AND SMOOTH PRESSING UP AGAINST her left wing. Her right wing was outstretched, her claw touching a slippery surface. She opened her eyes slowly, allowing in the bright light of early evening.

She studied the world around her, but found it quite confusing. Everything was an odd shade of grey or brown, and the surface she rested on didn't look anything like the bark of a tree. She tried to move her left wing, at the same time attempting to grip the smooth surface with her right claw. The surface was unusually hard and her wing didn't move along it as expected.

Why do I feel like my wing is being squeezed between my body and this… surface?

Suddenly, she realized what was wrong.

I'm on the ground. The thought led to instant panic. *I shouldn't be on the ground. Ever. It's dangerous. How did I get here?*

Chinaca tried to recall her last memory, but everything was foggy and unclear. She remembered that, for some reason, she had been flying over water, and she vaguely recalled seeing something that had convinced her she was either dead or about to die.

Does that mean I'm dead now?

"She's awake!"

Startled by the unexpected voice, Chinaca turned to face the speaker. "What are you?" she yelled in shock. "Where is this?"

She recognized that the girl in front of her was a bat. However, Chinaca couldn't figure out what *kind* of bat. The young female looked a bit like a Mouse-Eared bat, but her face was different, and instead of fine fur she was covered in a layer of fuzz. Her wings were small, even for the size of her body, and didn't appear finely-tuned for flying. Her back legs, however, were strong and well-built.

Chinaca soon realized she was surrounded by two dozen of these little bats: mothers holding young pups, wizened elders, teens, fathers— all suggesting they belonged to either a small colony or a large family. Each of them spoke loudly in eager voices.

"She's awake!"

"She looks hungry."

"She looks thirsty, too."

"Answer her question!"

"She should thank Alécto for rescuing her."

"We are the Akona tribe: the Ground Bats!"

"This is our island."

Trying to listen to the many bats speaking at once made Chinaca's head spin; despite her headache, she wanted to make conversation. *After all, if this is the afterlife, it's best I get along with my new neighbours. And if it isn't, perhaps they can help me understand where I am and how I got here.*

"Okay," she began, "so, why is it you... Akona... are called Ground Bats?"

"We like the ground!"

"We dig!"

"Yep, we dig."

"We don't really like flying that much."

"Or climbing."

"I like climbing!"

"You should thank Alécto. He rescued you."

"Yep. You really should."

"You should get something to drink first."

"Yeah, you look very thirsty!"

Water. Chinaca had never felt so thirsty in her life. "I would really like a drink, yes."

"Makes sense."

"The ocean makes people thirsty!"

"That's why we kept you right next to clean drinking water—so that when you woke up—"

"You'd have something to drink!"

Chinaca looked around, quickly finding the nearby pool. It was a small pond, surrounded by pebbles and filled with crystal-clear water. Forgetting her manners, she stuffed her face into the water and gulped it up gratefully. When she was done, she lifted her head, wiped her face with her wing, and addressed the Akona around her.

"Thank you," she said. "I really needed that."

"Oh, you are more than welcome!"

"Yep, you are very welcome!"

"Are you hungry, too?"

"How about some bugs?"

Chinaca gagged at the revolting thought. "No!" The Akona went silent at her sharp rebuke. Embarrassed, she tried to explain in a gentle voice. "I, uh, only eat fruit and nectar."

"Oh, just like Alécto!"

"Maybe *he* could find you something to eat!"

"You should really thank him for rescuing you."

"Yes, you should."

"He's up that tree over there."

Chinaca turned in the direction the last bat had pointed. Nearby was the massive trunk of an ancient tree. As she followed its growth upwards, she found she could barely see its needle-leafed branches far above.

She rolled off her side and spread her wings. It came to her that, having never been on the ground before, she had no idea how to take off. She mentally calculated the distance between herself and the tree.

She sighed. *I suppose I can crawl...*

"Is something the matter?" one of the Akona asked.

Chinaca shrugged. She didn't want to admit that she wasn't sure how to get around on the ground. She reached out a claw, pulled herself forward, and reached out the other claw.

Huh, this isn't so difficult. Kind of like climbing a tree.

"You can use your feet, too," a boy pup piped up.

Chinaca avoided looking at the Akona, blushing self-consciously as she took the youngster's advice. *I knew that.* She tried to ignore the eyes of the tribe members watching her, taking in her every move.

Eventually, inching forward step by step, Chinaca made it to the trunk. Upon reaching it, she grasped the brownish surface with her thumb-claws. Confidently, she clambered upwards, grateful for the familiar feel of papery bark against her skin.

Before long, she looked down to see the small shapes of the Akona some distance beneath her. This was far enough. Without hesitation, she let go of the tree and allowed herself to freefall a short way before spreading her wings and gaining controlled flight.

Chinaca fluttered her way to where the ancient pine's branches began, then picked out a branch further up and flew to it. She grasped it tightly with her back feet, allowing her body to fall into a hanging position.

Finally—back in the trees!

Chinaca scanned her surroundings with a song, in search of the bat who had apparently rescued her. All she could detect were more branches and clusters of pine needles.

"Hello?" she called out.

There was no answer.

She tried again, her voice a little louder. "Hello? Ah-lake-toe?" She fumbled with the name, attempting to pronounce it in the same way she'd heard it.

Hearing movement behind her, Chinaca turned. At first, all she could see was a strange black shape between the branches. Cocking her ears in curiosity, Chinaca followed along the black form until…

She gasped as two large eyes locked with hers.

The black bat gave her a huge smile and waved with an outstretched wing. "Well, g'day mate! Nice to see you up and hoppin'!"

Chinaca froze. A clear memory came to her: of losing the group, of being tossed by the winds, of seeing a black phantom grab her in its claws. It was immediately obvious to her that this bat *was* the black phantom.

Seeing him up close and with a clear mind, Chinaca realized she had made a mistake in her original estimate of his size. She had assumed this bat was as big as Spectral. Now she could tell he was quite obviously larger—nearly twice the size.

But his size wasn't the only thing that startled her. She had never before seen a bat like him. His face was long and elegant, he had no nose-leaf, and his ears were small for the size of his head. Around his neck was a collar of fiery-orange fur, contrasting sharply with the black that covered the rest of his body. His wings, large and muscular, seemed somehow deformed.

His eyes were remarkable: an expanse of soft brown, tinted with gold, with round pupils in the center. Staring into them, Chinaca felt both entranced and afraid. All the bats she had ever met had small, dark eyes. She'd never imagined that bat eyes could look so... *different.*

Realizing her shock, but unsure how to react to it, the giant bat extended a wing towards her in a friendly manner.

"The name's Alécto," he began in his strange accent. "Glad to see you're alright—wasn't expecting to find someone like you out there, flyin' over the ocean. If you don't mind my asking, what were you doin'?"

Chinaca, distracted by Alécto's astoundingly large wing, didn't answer. She stared at him as a shudder ran down her spine, finally able to see why his wings looked deformed. "You... you have a claw on your first *and* second finger?"

The larger bat chuckled and spread out both wings. "Well, I suppose that would make four clawed fingers, if you're countin' both wings."

His warmness did nothing to relieve the look of disbelief on Chinaca's troubled face. "You have claws on your second fingers? Bats don't have claws on their second fingers..."

Alécto shrugged, noting that his attempts at relaxing her were failing. He pulled his wings back towards his body and wrapped each leathery arm around his shoulder.

Chinaca cocked her head. *That's odd. I've never seen a bat do that before.* She looked at her own comparatively small wings and tried emulating his movements, folding one on top of the other, using them like a blanket to cover herself. Frustrated at the awkwardness of trying to get into that position, she soon gave up.

Instead, she pulled her wings close to her body, folding them at her sides. *Much better.*

Alécto stared at her with a look of amusement. Blushing, she tried to hide her embarrassment by conversing with him.

"So... Alécto... thank you for rescuing me."

"No worries, mate. Now, what was a sheila like you doin' out there as shark bait? Takin' a walkabout of sorts, eh?"

Chinaca blinked back her confused look. "Huh?" *Wow, he's even harder to understand than the Stripe-Faced bats...*

"The ocean. What was a sheila like you doin' out there? I thought only Fox-Faced bats such as myself liked takin' ta the open—"

"Fox-Faced bats? Fox-Faced bats only live on the Eastern Continent!"

Alécto nodded. "Well, I guess that explains it, eh, mate?"

"Yep. That explains everything." Chinaca sighed in resignation. "I'm dead. You're Death. You've taken me away to my eternal residence, where all bats live on the ground and eat insects. Except you." Chinaca eyed him. "Although, honestly, I would have expected you to be a Flesh-Eater. But I guess Fox-Faced bats are intimidating enough."

"Quite the joker, aren't ya?" Alécto chuckled, but Chinaca maintained a straight face. "Seriously, what were ya doin' flyin' out over the ocean?"

"I really made it to the Eastern Continent? Alive?"

"Yep."

Ha. That proves the Stripe-Faced bat wrong.

"'Course, I had to carry ya most of the way."

Oh. "Well, I wasn't planning on getting carried over the ocean," she said. "I was flying over the Sea of Deception."

"On your own?"

"No, I had a guide."

"Disobeyed his orders, eh?"

Why must this bat be so insightful? "Look, Alécto, I really need to get back. I have a war to plan."

"A war against what?"

Chinaca's mind raced. She hadn't actually planned on telling him about the war, but it had slipped out and it was too late now to take it back. "Well, there's this horrible Flesh-Eater—a cannibal named Spectral. He's the master of a kingdom called Thériava, only he thinks he's a god, and everyone is afraid of him. But I think that, if we had warriors, we could defeat him."

Alécto seemed intrigued by this. "Hang on, mate. What if I told you that I know of a warrior who could get rid of this Spectral all by 'imself?"

"I... would say you don't know Spectral. Or Cattae, his helper."

"Well, I would say you don't know Bai'ic."

Bay-what? "Who?"

"It looks like introductions are in order, eh?"

* * *

The next night, Chinaca found herself gazing down at the greyish paper-barked trees and pale blue-green leaves passing below. Her wings flapped steadily as she glided above the unfamiliar forest.

"So, Alécto," she said, "this Bai'ic... you're sure he's up for something like this? It won't be easy."

"I told ya, mate," the giant bat insisted, "Bai'ic is strong an' smart. He can beat off this Spectral." He motioned to the forest. "I brought you 'ere to Scrubla, my 'omeland, so you can meet him. Trust me, I wouldn't recommend him if I didn't think he could do it."

Alécto reached out for a pale tree limb with his back claws and folded his wings into his body as he landed. His eyes scanned the leaf-littered ground below, as if expecting something to be there.

"He's sure to be 'round 'ere somewhere. He usually comes to this neck of the woods when he's 'ungry." Alécto's eyes centered on Chinaca, watching as she landed a few inches from him. "I'll see if I can find him. No wandering off too far while I'm gone, right, mate?"

He spread his large wings again, pumping them up and down a few times before letting go of the branch and gliding off into the surrounding trees. He vanished into the woods.

Chinaca's ears filled with the quiet humming of nearby insects. She took in a deep breath of the moist, leaf-scented air. As she stared at the stars above, sparkling silently, her eyes were once again drawn to the glowing moon.

The rustle of leaves alerted her to something scurrying along the forest floor. Chinaca scanned the dark brown earth with a song as she tried to catch sight of the creature below her. She could still hear it moving about, but couldn't quite figure out exactly where or what it was.

She stared down curiously, contemplating her options. Only days before, she would never have considered approaching the ground for any reason.

But if there are friendly ground-dwelling bats like the Akona in the east, it can't be that inhospitable of a place, can it?

The thought of seeing another friendly face was all the convincing she needed. Letting go of the branch, she drifted down towards the leaf-covered ground, wings fluttering. Still not comfortable landing on the forest floor, she picked out the lowest-hanging branch she could find within close range of the sounds. Landing, she rotated her ears, listening to the other creature moving about in the leaves.

"Hello?" she called out hopefully. "Is someone there?"

Chinaca watched with some disappointment as a long, whiskered face poked out of the leaf litter, sniffing at her before scampering away.

Just a mouse, she thought sadly.

She turned her face to the sky, scanning the pale branches for signs of Alécto. Her "black phantom" was nowhere to be seen. She looked back to the ground to see the mouse, now perched on a dead branch, quietly nibbling away at some scrap of food it had collected.

Well, unintelligent company is better than no company, Chinaca thought. She sighed, watching as the mouse chipped away at the crumb with chisel-like teeth.

Without warning, a strange, unexpected chill trailed down her spine, setting every muscle in her body on edge. Chinaca looked around in fear, suddenly convinced that someone was watching her from the tree limbs above.

Move, please.

The strange voice brought with it a flash of red, momentarily blurring her vision.

She looked around frightfully. *Did I just think that, or is someone talking to me?* She glanced at the mouse, who continued to sit and nibble nonchalantly, unaware of what was going on.

Move, please.

This time, Chinaca could tell that the voice and red flashes were directly linked.

"Is someone using a song to talk to me?" she whispered.

The mouse barely perked its ears at the faint sound. Chinaca's ears, however, raced in all directions possible, trying to pick up even a hint of the stranger's voice.

Could you please move away from the mouse, Silver Leaf?

A sense of urgency now replaced the red colouring, but the sound still made Chinaca uneasy.

"Silver Leaf?" Chinaca glanced down and examined her own grizzled fur for a moment.

Slowly, hesitantly, she spread her wings and released her tight grip on the low-hanging limb. She took one last glance at the mouse, watching as it sniffed around for a new morsel. Finally, she flew in the opposite direction of the small rodent.

A powerful blast of air and high-pitched, blood-curling scream hit Chinaca at the same moment. Without thinking, she turned back to face the stick where the mouse had been.

At first, all she saw was a flash of white as a huge wing blocked her vision. The wing then rose above her; her heart froze as she caught the round, black eyes of another bat, situated in a ghostly face. His powerful jaws were clamped tightly around the mouse's dead body, his sharp teeth sinking into the creature's furry neck. The bat watched her for only a moment, then rose silently from the ground, pumping the air with his wide wings.

Chinaca watched the giant white spectre as he selected a branch high above her and grasped it with his back feet, the mouse still hanging limply from his jaws. He covered his face with his wings, hiding the mouse's body from her view.

She could hear his jaws working their way through the mouse's flesh.

"Bai'ic! There you are, mate! I've been lookin' all 'round for you!"

The giant white bat glanced up from his meal as the speaker approached. He twitched one long ear as if waving hello, his jaws still busy with the mouse and his wings carefully shielding his meal from Chinaca's eyes.

"Mate, spit that out," Alécto demanded. He hung beside the white stranger, whacking him with a powerful wing. "You have a guest, and she ain't inta seein' your table manners quite yet."

Bai'ic coughed as Alécto slapped him, the furry mouse falling from his grasp. Turning an annoyed glare towards Alécto, he dropped from his perch to the ground below, soon returning with the mouse held tightly in his teeth. He looked again at Alécto, eyes glowing dangerously, as if daring the other bat to take his meal a second time.

"Chinaca," Alécto called, catching sight of her in the branches below, "come up 'ere." Wrapping a black wing around Bai'ic's shoulders, he continued, "Chinaca, meet Bai'ic. Bai'ic, that lil' bat over there is Chinaca. She's from the Western Continent."

Chinaca's eyes widened in disbelief. *You have got to be kidding me...*

Hesitantly, she flapped her way over to the two larger bats, carefully selecting a roost that positioned Alécto between her and the ghost-like Bai'ic.

She tried to keep her voice low enough that only Alécto could hear. "Are you insane? He's a carnivore!"

Bai'ic rolled his eyes, taking in a big gulp of mouse flesh before letting the rest of his meal fall to the ground. This time, he made no movement to pick it up again. He wiped the blood from his mouth. "Alécto, what did you volunteer me for this time?"

"I know what you're thinkin', mate," Alécto said gently, touching Chinaca's shoulder, "but he's no cannibal. No worries."

Chinaca watched Bai'ic cautiously. He had the same bony, powerful jaws as the Flesh-Eaters, the same predatory form, and he was about the same size as Cattae. But perhaps, she considered, perhaps his nearly completely white body, only tinted in places with faded grey fur and yellowish skin, made him more frightening than either.

"How do I know I can trust you, Bai'ic?" Chinaca asked.

Bai'ic managed a sigh and a chuckle in the same breath. "Why do people ask that strange question? If you knew me, you'd know if I was worth trusting." Bai'ic's gaze journeyed to Alécto. "Whatever this is, buddy, I don't think it's going to work."

"Just listen to what she has ta say," Alécto implored. "Chinaca, tell 'im what you told me, 'bout needin' a warrior to defeat that wicked warlord o' yours."

"Warlord?" Bai'ic now sounded curious.

Chinaca considered how to respond. "As a warrior, you have fought battles before, right?"

"Warrior, that's cute. Actually, I'm a storyteller." Bai'ic's casual tone completely lacked sarcasm.

"A storyteller?" Chinaca replied disbelievingly. She turned back to Alécto with a look of frustration. "You said—"

"He's bein' cheeky." Alécto slapped his friend once again. "Answer her question."

"Answer one: I have never fought battles as a warrior," Bai'ic said. "Answer two: I have fought battles."

"And won them?"

"Yes, I suppose that's an important detail."

"He's a storyteller by trade," Alecto said, "but a warrior at 'eart. Just tell him what you told me. Trust me. If you're gonna go to war, he's someone ta 'ave on your side."

THE DESERT MOUNTAINS

"CHITOLLA! COME ON, SLEEPYHEAD, WAKE UP!"

For a moment, forgetting where she was, Chitolla thought the voice must be that of Bukinero, teasing her for sleeping in so long after a late night's visit to Flammeus' library.

However, as she opened her eyes, she realized it was neither noon nor morning, but still the middle of the night. A few stars pricked through the dark clouds and sky above.

Finally, she recognized Secha in front of her, tugging on her feathers with her little thumb-claw.

"I found something amazing!" the tiny bat said excitedly. "Come see!"

Chitolla slowly stood, recalling the events of the last several days and nights: touching the sapphire web, escaping Spectral's Temple with Patas, and meeting Secha and the other bats in the strange cavern. She recalled their journey across the Sea of Deception, and sleeping the day away on an island full of Stripe-Faced bats. They then completed their journey to the Desert Mountains, where they had camped for the last few nights.

Chitolla could barely see her surroundings in the dark of night. The moon, though round and glowing, was hidden behind clouds, its light muted by their cover.

What could Secha possibly expect me to see in this darkness?

The swallow took off, allowing the little bat to lead her.

* * *

"We're here!" Secha announced eagerly, diving down.

To the swallow's surprise, Secha landed on the ground. Chitolla descended as well. Soon, her claws were digging into what felt like pebble-filled sand. Chitolla couldn't see her surroundings clearly, but the ground fit with what she imagined desert ground would feel like.

"Okay," Secha said, the pleasure in her voice rising, "now, sing this song—it's for seeing flowers in the night."

Chitolla listened carefully, but the bat had gone silent. The swallow turned to face Secha, wondering what was going on. Secha was breathing through her nose, every now and then moving her lips, but Chitolla heard nothing.

Secha turned to her. Seeing the expression on the bird's face, she laughed. "Chitolla, you have to sing it, too, if you want to see!"

"Pardon?"

"You have to sing the song if you want to see all the beautiful desert flowers and cacti! Come on!"

Chitolla turned forwards, looking where Secha had directed her attention. Yes, she could see vaguely white petals, but the darkness hid their shape.

"Secha, I can't see in the dark. How is singing going to help?"

Secha seemed puzzled and a little irritated. "You know, by lighting the world. My eyesight isn't amazing, either, but the songs make up for that."

"So, what you're saying is that singing helps you see?"

"No, silly, listening to the song return helps me see."

Chitolla pondered this for a moment, thinking back to what she knew of the bats in her world. "Oh, I get it! You're speaking about echolocation—using sound to help you see in the darkness!"

"Eko-lok-ashun? What a strange word! We just call it singing."

"Well, I'm sorry, Secha, but swallows like me can't do it."

Secha was shocked. "You can't?" She paused for a moment. "Well, I'll just have to teach you!"

"No, Secha, it's not that simple. I can't even hear when you sing. It's out of my hearing range—"

"Then I'll start by just giving you the words. I can teach you the tune later." Clearly, she didn't understand.

"No, no, Secha, I *can't* do it."

"That's what learning is supposed to fix. Do you want to know the words or not?"

Chitolla stopped insisting, and Secha spoke the words to the song in a soft, rhythmic tone.

> Stars of the land, white moonbeams that stand,
> Glow in the night, let your light shine bright;
> Your beauty is strong, honour us with your song,
> Songs of dancing light, of sunshine in the night

Chitolla listened closely.

"That's a pretty song, Secha," she said when the bad finished. "I wish I could hear it sung."

Suddenly, bright beams of light cascaded from the sky, as the moon peered out from the clouds. Its pale light lit the desert, and Chitolla, eyes wide, could see clearly the assemblage of towering cacti and delicate flowers that Secha had been so excited about.

But as beautiful as the sight was, Chitolla hardly paid any attention to it. She instead watched her companion with a frightened look in her eyes. "Secha, there's something behind you!"

Secha turned around. Something was coming towards her, a slithering creature with over a hundred pairs of legs and long, thick antennae sprouting from a red head. It watched Secha with a hungry look in its little black eyes, flexing and stretching its wide, pincer-like jaws, each tipped with black fangs.

Secha froze with fear. The centipede was easily five times her size, big enough to grab her in its jaws and devour her. She tried to take off, spreading her wings, but they just smacked about uselessly.

Chitolla's instinct was to attack the giant bug and protect her friend. She spread her wings, prepared to rush towards it, but the centipede had already lunged at the small white bat. The world seemed to shift into slow motion. Chitolla watched helplessly as the centipede's jaws rushed towards Secha.

Chitolla's heart dropped. *I won't reach her in time...*

In that split second, a pale bat appeared behind the centipede. The world broke out of slow motion, and all Chitolla managed to catch was a flurry of wings and the sound of a loud *crunch*.

Chitolla and Secha stared in shock at the sight of a larger, yellow bat with big ears. The bat blinked a few times, long lashes fluttering, as she smiled at Secha. In the stranger's mouth was the centipede's squashed head.

"You know, pups shouldn't be trying to take down game this big, darling. You could have been hurt." The yellow bat munched happily on the giant bug.

Secha remained silent for a few moments, recovering from her shock as she watched the strange bat down a crunchy chunk of the disassembled centipede.

"Um, thank you," she replied cautiously. "But I'm not a pup. I'm full grown."

"Really?" The yellow bat didn't seem to mind speaking with her mouth full. "Then you're a Mouse-Eared bat?"

"A what?"

"You know, one of the little bats from further north."

"Oh, no, I'm... a foreigner. My companions and I just came from the south, across the sea."

"Really?" The yellow bat's voice rose in excitement, and she immediately abandoned her partially-eaten centipede. "Have you been hosted yet?"

"Hosted?"

"Oh, you simply must be hosted, darling! All the bats who migrate here from the south are treated to a meal by us, the locals: Big-Eared bats. We spend time socializing, getting to know you, teaching you about the Desert Mountains, the local seasons, hibernation, things you southerners don't seem to know anything about. You simply must be hosted with my family, darling, and bring all your friends with you!"

Secha smiled, enjoying the other bat's friendliness. At the same time, she felt a little overwhelmed. "Well, Chitolla and I would love to come, I'm sure, but I don't even know where the other members of our group are."

"Well, you must find them, darling! I'll ask around to see if anyone else has met them. Oh, I'll have to tell my mother and sisters and aunts to begin preparations! I'm guessing you don't eat scorpions or centipedes, do you?"

Secha grimaced. "Uh, aren't they poisonous?"

"Oh, we're immune. What do you and your friends prefer to eat?"

"Nectar and fruit is good..."

"Got it! Nectar and fruit!" The Big-Eared bat pushed herself off the ground and hovered above it, her wings creating a slight breeze as they fluttered. "Where can I find you? Here?"

"Um... we don't have anywhere else to go..."

"Perfect! I'll meet you here tomorrow night before dinnertime!" She winked at Secha. "My name's Savannah, by the way. And you can bring your pretty pet bird with you, too!"

Secha turned to Chitolla as if expecting her to say something, but Chitolla remained silent. Savannah left without another word, flying off over the distant desert sands.

"Why didn't you say something?" Secha asked after Savannah had left.

Chitolla shrugged. "It seems strange talking to bats who think a talking bird is... well, strange. But I'll speak if the need arises."

* * *

I wonder where Patas is, Secha thought as she lapped up nectar from the white, cup-like flower lying before her. *Higuero did tell him where to meet us. Why hasn't he shown up yet?*

Secha sighed as her eyes came to rest on Chitolla, who perched beside her on the wooden floor. The Tent-Maker grinned as she watched the swallow excitedly leaf through an old, red-covered book. She had never before seen Chitolla in such a joyous mood.

"I'm guessing you really like that book, huh?" Secha asked.

Chitolla looked up from her reading, a smile lighting up her face. "I haven't read from *Creator's Book* since I left the Veil. I'm surprised how much I remember."

Secha's eyes went back to the well-worn volume. "I wish I could read." Her voice was filled with longing. "I bet it's so… amazing."

"You never learned to read?" Chitolla's voice lowered to a hushed whisper as Savannah's mother approached with a plateful of chubby, bell-shaped flowers.

"Refills, anyone?" Savannah's mother asked in her characteristic singsong voice. Her warm and welcoming attitude had quickly made Secha one of her biggest fans.

"No, I'm full, thank you," the little bat replied, her face aglow. She looked across the wooden floor to Higuero, who sat quietly nearby.

The Stripe-Faced bat reached out for another cup of nectar. "Thank you," he said gratefully, allowing Savannah's mother to take the empty flower in front of him.

Secha leaned over to Chitolla, a grin engulfing her face. "Have you been counting how many cups of nectar and plates of fruit he's had? Where does he put it all?"

Chitolla giggled, eyes glancing at the half-full wooden bowl containing the remains of her meal—dead grasshoppers, crickets, and a few squirming worms. Although she had gotten Secha to tell Savannah that she preferred flying insects to the ground-dwelling kind, the swallow was still grateful for the family's hospitality.

Savannah had been excited to bring her new friends to the ancient hollowed-out tree in which her family lived. Upon arrival, the group had learned that all the Big-Eared bats lived in a small grove of hollow trees, and within the cracks in a cliff wall bordering the grove. The "tribe," as they called themselves, was divided into families, and each family inhabited a different tree or rock crevice. Stony desert surrounded the grove on all sides, and it seemed as if someone was always going this way or that in search of desert-dwelling prey.

The Big-Eared bats had little consistency in appearance: they all had enormous ears and none had nose-leafs, but Chitolla had already seen tiny bats not much larger than Secha, bats as big as Higuero, yellow bats, brown and grey bats, and even one with pink ears and a pattern of white spots on otherwise black fur.

The hollow tree in which Savannah's family lived reminded Chitolla of Flammeus' library. Both had an array of shelves and a collection of books. Savannah's home, of course, also had a kitchen, sleeping rooms, and other accommodations that seemed strange to Chitolla, but Savannah insisted were quite standard in a "house."

Chitolla sighed, her mind going back to the simple crevice and mud nest she and Bukinero called home. She considered the Stone Place and her conversation with Hermain. More and more, she had begun to draw connections between the story she'd heard from the traveling tortoise and the adventure she now found herself on.

Chitolla had already decided that this "Spectral," who all the bats were so afraid of, was one and the same as the horrible god who had once inhabited the Stone Place. The timeline made sense. From what she could gather, he had vanished from her world within the last hundred and fifty years, and had been terrorizing the bats of the Echo ever since. He had even ensured that his temples were built over the only entrances to the Bridge—which the bats here called the Underworld—meaning that he more or less controlled access between the worlds.

But why did he leave the Veil? she wondered. *He was becoming more and more powerful there. Why abandon that kingdom to start over here? And what happened to all the bats who were part of his kingdom in the Veil?*

"You again?! Get out of here this instant!"

Savannah's angry cries snapped Chitolla out of her thoughts. She turned to see the Big-Eared bat at the entrance of the tree hollow, holding herself above Patas.

"Uh... I think there's been a mistake..." Patas attempted hesitantly.

But Savannah quickly drowned him our. "How dare you come back! How many times do we have to tell you? The Big-Eared bats are *not* becoming servants of your egotistical king! We don't care about your silly little threats! Back off and leave us alone!"

"Patas, you're here!" Secha's happy voice floated across the room. She dashed over the floor and positioned herself between Patas and Savannah.

The tiny white bat wrapped her delicate wings around Patas' startled and confused form. "Where were you? Please don't leave like that again. We're a group now. We should all stick together, okay?"

Her pretty eyes stared up into his. Patas, blown away by her unexpected hug, turned a bit red. He sputtered out a few incoherent words before nodding.

"Hold on! This is your pal?" Savannah shook her head as if trying to shake the confused expression off her face. "Why, he looks just like a Vampire…"

"He is—ahem, I am—but we're—um—it's kind of a long story—"

"Well," Savannah continued, her stern tone remaining, "before you tell me, you can go tell your fellow Vampires that I don't care if their friend Cattae comes to drag us off or not. We're not going all the way to Thériava to serve their maniacal king!"

Everyone in the room fell quiet. Savannah stared at Patas expectantly, as if prepared for him to fly off and deliver her message immediately.

Clearing his throat, Patas ventured, "Uh, I'm sorry… can you repeat that? Only, not as loudly—please—and with a little more explanation…"

"I want you to tell whoever is in charge that there's been a mistake," Savannah said. "The Big-Eared bats aren't interested in becoming Vampires. We aren't scared of this Cattae, whoever or whatever he is, and honestly, I'm looking forward to meeting him tomorrow night so I can finally tell him to get lost and stop sending messengers to us, telling us to go to Thériava and become servants to Spectral 'or else.' Do you understand?"

Again, everyone fell silent. Savannah glanced at each of her guests with a look of exasperation, trying to figure out why they weren't responding to her. Her family members also looked baffled, searching the faces of their guests for answers.

Finally, Higuero's clear voice broke the silence. "This es na good."

"What is 'na good' about it?" Savannah demanded.

Patas explained, "Spectral sent Cattae to demand something from you, and you're refusing to give it. That is 'na good.'"

"Cattae and Spectral are flesh-eating cannibals." Secha's voice was fearful. "They're huge, powerful, and have an army of Vampires. They destroy colonies that don't agree to Spectral's demands."

Savannah's tone turned wary. "Is that why all the Nectar-Drinkers have been leaving Thériava? None of them would tell us why. The most we ever got out of them was that they didn't feel safe anymore, and it had something to do with their greedy warlord."

"This es na good," Higuero repeated, his voice hardening. "If Spectral es na afraid to come into da Desert Mountains, than we are na safe here."

Savannah, turning her eyes from her guests, looked over her family. "But we Big-Eared bats are strong. And the Vampires told us when Cattae would be coming. We kill scorpions and centipedes—can we not fight off this Cattae?"

Patas shook his head. "I'm not saying you aren't a strong race, but there's not very many of you, and Cattae won't come alone. He'll have an army with him." He watched Savannah's eyes fill with fear. "I'm sorry. I don't know what to do."

"Well, we have to do *something*!" Secha said. "We can't let you face Cattae alone. I may not know how to plan a war or anything like that, but I don't want to leave the Big-Eared bats to Cattae and the Vampires. I want to help, somehow."

After a short pause, a grin overtook Higuero's face. "I spent enough time with Chinaca to know somethin' about her plans. Besides, Cattae knows me well enough by now. Maybe he'd like a visit from an ol' friend?"

Patas grabbed his chance to speak up. "I'm not going anywhere! Hey, maybe I *could* send a message to my pals. It's better than not trying anything, right?"

Chitolla made an excited chattering sound, and Secha knew the swallow had made her own decision clear.

Savannah smiled at her new friends, a look of gratitude taking over her face. "Thank you—all of you. We'll let the rest of the tribe know what's going on, and that you want to be with us in whatever happens." Her eyes journeyed to Chitolla, then down to the book sitting at the swallow's feet. "If nothing else, you can pray that Creator shows Himself to be the true God, proving that Spectral's nothing but a fraud. Who knows? Perhaps He's already working out a plan in our favour."

ANSWERS

10

"SO YOU SEE, DEAR PRINCESS, THE SWALLOW BUKINERO AND I HAVE found ourselves in quite a predicament. We have no idea how to make the door to the Echo reappear, and no idea how to bring back Bukinero's dear sweet wife, Chitolla. I insisted we come here, to you, as I believed you may have the answers we need."

Maxéra Réa and Hermain listened intently as Flammeus explained to them the reason for her visit. Réa's golden eyes remained fixed on the fiery-feathered owl as she spoke, her regal hood extended, her lithe form swaying only slightly. Hermain watched with a small frown creasing his wrinkly face, nodding slowly.

Bukinero, meanwhile, had long ago turned his attention elsewhere. He tried to wait patiently for Flammeus to complete her explanation, his eyes tracing the patterns of burnt sienna and light mahogany that meandered through this circular room.

He sighed for what may have been the hundredth time that day. He had already noticed that Flammeus could be quite wordy, but it seemed to him that she was outdoing herself on this occasion.

How long does it take to tell our story?

Réa had called this place the "Maxéra Castle." Although it was technically a tree hollow, not a real castle, it was far more magnificent than anything Bukinero had ever seen before, certainly nothing like the tree hollow where Flammeus kept her library. The tree itself was enormous: this room was just one of many, yet it easily accommodated the giant snake, rotund tortoise, large owl, swallow, and an array of shelves, desks, displays, and two stairways.

Carved into the walls and along the roof were crevices where multi-coloured gems had been inserted, each polished to perfectly fit its particular nook. The strange gems glowed with a pure yet unnatural light, the rays of colour within them constantly shifting and changing. A column of the same glowing rock rose within the center of the room, and all the rocks together produced enough light to rival the sun.

Along the walls were elaborate tapestries of black cobras, colourful rat snakes, sapphire-winged birds, long-eared bats, and many other creatures, some which Bukinero had never seen before. When he'd asked, Maxéra Réa had told him they depicted stories from the history of Sévéritas. Stories weren't quite his thing, though, so as beautiful as the tapestries were, they weren't the element of the room that intrigued him most.

His eyes continually returned to one particular display—a tall wooden board. On it were little shelves, each containing some small stick, leaf, potted plant, stone, shell, or other such object. Some of the items were odd to look at while others seemed completely ordinary.

Beside each object was a description of the purposes for which it was used. There was a long-leafed white plant whose inner juices, when simply touched, could make one fall asleep almost immediately; there were small, brown sticks that when ground up and mixed with water could cure poisonous bites and stings; and there was a clear, sharp stone that could cut through almost anything, including other stones.

Each of the objects fascinated Bukinero—all the more when the object itself looked like a normal, everyday object. He thought back to his home in the outer wall of the Stone Place, and which of these objects could be useful to him there. The most practical were a paste made from ground shells, for cleaning; a sticky plant juice for repairing items; a grey powder for making mud nests last longer; and a dried seaweed that could keep youngsters healthy and disease-free.

"Enjoying my castle, Bukinero?"

Startled, Bukinero turned to see Maxéra Réa, Hermain, and Flammeus watching him.

"You're finished?" he asked.

"Yes," the Princess answered. "I believe Flammeus has finished filling us in. Come join us."

Bukinero hopped over to the trio.

When he had joined the group, Maxéra Réa addressed them in her powerful voice. "Your story, Flammeus and Bukinero, shows there are some things about the history of the Stone Place, as you call it, that need to be discussed among all of us." She tipped her head slightly in reference to Hermain. "How about you explain to the swallow what led you here, traveller? Flammeus, I believe, is already familiar with the tale, but Bukinero may not understand why he's been brought to this kingdom."

Hermain cleared his throat. "Well, as you know, Bukinero, I visited the mountain where you reside because of rumours I heard. A friend told me that the kingdom of bats that once covered your mountain had vanished, along with their evil warlord, and that swallows had taken up residence in what had been the warlord's temple. As your mate may have told you, the warlord considered himself a god, and his subjects worshiped him by bringing him sacrifices of blood and flesh."

Bukinero nodded, and Hermain continued. "My friend could not say why the kingdom had vanished, nor what had become of the evil warlord, or even when exactly his kingdom came to an end. From my conversation with Chitolla and other swallows on your mountain, I found that they had no knowledge of the temple's prior inhabitants. Neither could they recall at what point their race had begun to live on the walls of the building."

The tortoise now turned his eyes towards Flammeus. "I then went to Flammeus' library looking for answers. Although she couldn't find the information I sought, she said something that got me thinking. A bat from Rénodédosé had visited her recently, and the two had discussed local history."

Bukinero's eyebrows lowered in puzzlement. "Ré-what?"

"Rénodédosé is a sister kingdom to Sévéritas, and not far from your mountain. It's a kingdom of bats, but they're under the authority of a governor and council. They've never been under the leadership of Spectral."

"Wait," Bukinero interrupted. "Who's Spectral?"

"Spectral," Hermain explained, "as Flammeus learned from the bat, was the name of the evil warlord. He insisted that his kingdom be called Thériava, which in his native tongue meant 'Empire of the god of shadows.'"

Bukinero nodded again and Hermain continued his story. "At one point, the leaders of Rénodédosé were so afraid of Spectral overtaking them that they sent messengers to Sévéritas, asking for help in case of attack. But for some reason the threat never materialized, and Spectral's empire, Thériava, simply ceased to be a problem."

He acknowledged Maxéra Réa with a glance. "When I was done visiting Flammeus, I told her I was going to Sévéritas and planned to stay there a while in hopes of learning what had happened to Thériava. I had my suspicions that the Maxéra were somehow involved in the kingdom's disappearance."

Maxéra Réa nodded in agreement, continuing on the tortoise's behalf. "When Hermain came to me, asking about the disappearance of the warlord and whether our ancestors were involved, my brothers and I spent some time discussing whether it would be appropriate to give him answers. Generally, Sévéritas prefers to keep a low profile. We don't see a need to get involved in other kingdoms' affairs and some of our ancestors' actions are kept secret, as it would do no good for outsiders to know."

The cobra's eyes locked onto Bukinero as she spoke. "I have told him little. However, it is your own story, Bukinero, and that of your wife, Chitolla, that has convinced all the Maxéra of the need to reveal the truth about the disappearance of the warlord and his kingdom. Keep in mind that this information is to be shared with no one outside this group, unless necessary, until this whole matter has ended. Understand?"

Bukinero trembled under the regal cobra's stare. "I understand."

Maxéra bobbed her head in acknowledgement. "To make the story short, about a hundred fifty years ago, my ancestors received messengers from Rénodédosé. The Maxéra had already heard of Spectral's Empire—I choose not to call it by any other name—but they hadn't known how serious the situation was. After some deliberation, they decided to act quickly in order to protect their sister kingdom from invasion. Sévéritas sent messengers to Spectral, warning him to take back his threats against Rénodédosé. He laughed, claiming that, as a god, he had complete power and there was nothing we could do to him or his kingdom."

Maxéra Réa paused a moment, her voice becoming almost scornful. "My ancestors proved him wrong."

"How?" Bukinero questioned.

"Poison. A viral potion that my ancestors designed. Bats are social creatures. They are very touchy-feely and like to be near each other. All we needed to do was infect a few with the poison, letting them spread it to others—and to Spectral. The kingdom was wiped out almost overnight."

Bukinero was shocked. "But isn't that a bit… extreme?"

"My ancestors did as they thought best," the Princess replied. "They would not let Spectral destroy Rénodédosé, nor did they want to risk the lives of the members of that kingdom in a war."

Hermain nodded, his face gradually lighting. "I see… I see. Then, Spectral is dead?"

Maxéra Réa hissed loudly, startling everyone. "If that were the case, friend tortoise, I would not be telling this story. Spectral survived the poison."

Flammeus' eyes widened and her feathers fluffed out. "Did he not receive a lethal dose?"

"My ancestors ensured that he received a higher dose than the other bats. The fact that he ate bats that had been poisoned should have killed him." The cobra shook her head in frustration. "When he saw his kingdom dying around him, he fled, and my ancestors could not locate him, no matter how hard they searched." Réa's eyes drew back to Flammeus and Bukinero. "Thanks to Chitolla's discovery, I now know where he's hiding, and why the poison had no effect on him."

She turned away from the group, slithering across the room until she reached a small, dark bookshelf. Using her head, she tipped a thick volume off the lower shelf and onto the floor. She flipped it open with her tail, motioning for the others to come and look.

"For generations," she said, "the Maxéra have known almost everything there is to know about the Bridge that connects the two worlds. Everything, that is, except its location."

She drew their attention to an image in the book. It appeared to Bukinero to be a map of sorts, although many of its features looked similar. Most of the symbols seemed to represent flames, the only exceptions being a spiderweb in each top corner and a long line that linked the center of one spiderweb to the center of the other.

"The Bridge itself is nothing more than a strand of spider silk," the Princess explained. "There is, however, a land located below and around the strand. Long, long ago, the Bridge was a trading kingdom, a place where the two worlds could intermingle. But when the Traitor covered the Bridge with fire, the kingdom was destroyed. It became a terrible place. Trace elements of the previous kingdom remained, but they were distorted, twisted by the Traitor's flames. And they—these trace elements—are the reason Spectral is not dead. Though, if he truly has been living in that kingdom, it may be safe to call him one of the living dead."

"What?" Bukinero asked, now completely puzzled. "What do you mean, 'trace elements'? What do they have to do with Spectral surviving the poison? And what does any of this have to do with Chitolla? How do we get her back?"

"Patience, swallow." Maxéra Réa allowed a hint of sibilance to creep into her voice. "Let me explain. These trace elements are like the items you've been studying in that display. Only, they are more powerful. Being exposed to some cancel the effects of aging, making it impossible for one to die of natural causes. Another makes one immune to poison of every kind. Spectral probably believes himself to be a god because he has been exposed to these elements. However, the Traitor's fire causes some negative side effects—such as the need to consume flesh and blood, unending hunger, and the inability to tolerate outside conditions, like sunlight, moonlight, and rain. Which is why he had a temple built for himself. Without it he wouldn't be able to leave the Bridge."

The cobra princess lowered herself to Bukinero's level, her majestic hood folding back. "Swallow," she said gravely, "we need to return to the

Stone Place immediately and bring Chitolla back. If she's stuck in the in-between kingdom surrounding the Bridge and doesn't know how to get out, she's probably suffering horribly right now. And whether or not she has crossed the Bridge, she is likely to be in danger of Spectral. He could easily kill her, and it's doubtful he himself has been killed."

Bukinero stared into Maxéra Réa's eyes, heart pounding. Desperation and anger rose inside him at the thought of Chitolla trapped in a horrible, flame-filled place, chased by an undying monster.

"Well, what do we do?" Bukinero asked. "The door to the other world vanished! How can we get her back?"

The Princess flicked her tongue, touching it gently to his forehead as if to soothe him. "I know how to reopen the door. I will have my servants carry us to your mountain as quickly as possible. You must return and rescue Chitolla."

* * *

"The final preparations have been made." Maxéra Réa slithered over the desert sands, a large black bird following at her side.

Bukinero, Flammeus, and Hermain now found themselves sitting just outside the tall shadows of Séveritas' majestic trees. Before them was the kingdom, and behind them stood the Peak of Desperation.

As they watched the Princess and her companion approach, Bukinero crouched nervously. "Uh, Guardian Princess... who is this?"

"This is Dreamer," the cobra replied, motioning to the bird beside her. "He's my personal assistant and most trusted warrior. I've asked him to escort you and Flammeus as you travel ahead of Hermain."

The black bird spread his wings and bobbed his bald grey head in greeting. "Pleased to meet you both."

"How do you do," Flammeus said cheerfully as she reached out a clawed foot. Dreamer took it and shook it warmly. "With your companionship, dear Dreamer, I trust this will be a very pleasant journey, indeed."

"Hey," was all Bukinero could manage. Then, as he leaned over to Hermain, he whispered softly, "That's a vulture, isn't it?"

"What of it?" Hermain responded with a tone of curiosity and befuddlement.

Dreamer turned to the swallow and extended his leg. "Greetings, songbird."

Bukinero stared blankly at the vulture's enormous talons before hesitantly reaching out his own leg and shaking one of Dreamer's lengthy toes. *I could fit my whole body inside his claws...*

"As I said," Maxéra Rea stated, "he will escort you." Then, with a sideways glance at Bukinero, she added, "He is my most trusted servant. You have nothing to fear. Bukinero, you remember what I showed you about how to reopen the Door Between Worlds?"

The swallow nodded. "Yes. I remember."

"And you recall my instructions on how to travel safely through the Underworld?"

"Yes."

"Good. Hermain will meet you at the Stone Place. Blessings and safety on your journey. Begana le mé saa."

"Beganan né," Flammeus responded. "We shall see you again shortly."

* * *

"What a lovely morning for a journey!" Flammeus sighed for what Bukinero believed to be the millionth time since they left Séveritas.

"It is nice," Dreamer agreed, gently flapping his wings. The vulture's wide wingspan and high tolerance to desert conditions meant he provided the perfect shade for the two smaller birds, who flew just beneath him.

"I'm glad it's still early morning," Flammeus continued. "The sun isn't quite so intense." She turned to Bukinero with a look of curiosity. "You haven't said much, sir swallow. Is something the matter?"

"Hmm? No. I've just been going over what the Princess told me about the Door and the Bridge and how to cross it. I don't want to forget anything."

Dreamer nodded. "Réa also told me all you need to know about crossing to the Echo. If you forget anything, just ask."

"Will you be coming with me?"

"No. No, songbird, the journey across the Underworld is one you must take alone."

Alone. Bukinero's stomach lurched. *I have to journey across a strange, dangerous world, then somehow find my mate between there and another world that's like no place I've ever been before.*

The very idea of going anywhere foreign made him nervous—in fact, he wasn't sure how Flammeus had convinced him to take this trip to Séveritas.

It's for Chitolla, remember? All for Chitolla.

"Do you smell that?" Dreamer asked suddenly, his head turning this way and that.

Flammeus sniffed the air. "Smells like something's burning. Dreamer, do you—"

"Agh!" the vulture screamed unexpectedly. "I was a fool, watching only the ground. Look up!"

It took a moment for Bukinero to spot a group of fiery-feathered creatures heading towards the trio, their talons grasping blazing torches as they raced across the morning sky.

Flammeus gasped. "The ruffians!"

"Where did they get so many friends?" Bukinero cried in shock.

The once-small group of ragtag owls was now at least a dozen strong. But the same leader remained out front, his eyes glowing dangerously and a malicious smile on his face. "They won't escape this time!" he encouraged his followers. "Attack!"

Flammeus was the first to brace herself as the lead owl charged, flaming stick leading the way. But it was Dreamer's massive wing that first made contact with the attacking bird. As he hit the leader, the vulture simultaneously snatched another owl from the air with a clawed foot.

Bukinero watched, his mind numb with panic, as both Flammeus and Dreamer fought. Dreamer was clearly a trained warrior, his beak flashing out to sever enemy necks and wings, his body wheeling as he maneuvered himself away from the burning torches and sharp beaks of the assailants. But what Flammeus lacked in skill, she made up for in ferocity.

All the swallow could do, meanwhile, was watch in distress. He stared helplessly as Flammeus struggled free of another owl's dagger-like claws.

I have to help them.

"Songbird!" Dreamer cried out, racing towards Bukinero. "You must leave! Now!"

"Leave? What—"

"You have to go, now!" Dreamer yelled. "There's no time to lose! Your mate needs you!"

Chitolla…

"Do songbirds not have a great sense of direction?" Dreamer asked.

Bukinero took a moment to respond. "If you're asking whether I know the way back, I do, but—"

"Then go! Now! Flammeus and I will catch up when we get the chance! We'll meet you at the Stone Place!"

The vulture turned towards an oncoming owl, and Bukinero briefly watched the ensuing battle. His eyes journeyed back to Flammeus, fighting another set of deadly foes.

Chitolla. Bukinero turned, his eyes blind to the course ahead, his instincts working independently of his emotions to lead him on a straight path. Afraid that one of the ruffians would come after him, he dove, increasing his speed until he felt like a small blur racing across an endless world of sand.

WAR

CHITOLLA LOOKED OUT AT THE DOZENS OF BIG-EARED BATS crisscrossing her vision, going to and fro. Perched at the entrance to Savannah's tree hollow, she picked up bits and pieces of conversation from the passing bats. Her heart pounded at the anxiety that hung in the air, leaking into the voice of every individual.

Since Savannah had explained to them the full extent of the danger they were about to face, the bats had been a restless mass of activity. They'd stopped to sleep in the overwhelming midday heat, then resumed their tasks as soon as the desert sun's intensity lessened. Some of them acted as spies or messengers, scanning the desert sands for signs of the approaching army. Secha and some of the other girls were asked to stay with the youngest bats, who were now safely hidden in the most protected rock crevices and tree hollows.

Still others, as Chitolla was surprised to learn, were busy cleaning and making repairs to the bats' armour. Higuero and Secha exchanged glances when Savannah told them this. Patas had responded with a doubtful, "You... make armour?"

"Southerners," Savannah had replied with a roll of her eyes. "So un-advanced. But actually, we don't make it ourselves. We get it from the Mouse-Eared bats who live further north."

Chitolla, for one, was curious to take a peek at this bat-made armour, but felt that poking around might distract the bats from their important work. She chose to remain where she was.

A few trees to the left of Chitolla's roost, Higuero hung from a thick branch, his sturdy chest heaving as he drew deep, heavy breaths. Around him were warriors, the strongest of the local bats, both male and female. They awaited their next instructions.

Hanging above Chitolla was Patas, his ears twitching nervously, his breath coming in large, controlled sighs.

"You should get some sleep," Chitolla suggested. "The army isn't coming until tonight."

The Vampire bat chuckled. "How am I supposed to sleep? When the army comes, I'll be the first one sent out. I'll have to try to make a deal with them. And if I can't, there will be a battle, loss of lives, bloodshed. Besides, I haven't slept well since the night I left my family. But I'd rather not talk about that." He paused and released a sigh of resignation. "How about sending me some good vibes? I could use the confidence right now."

Chitolla regarded the bat for a moment. "How about I pray that Creator grants you courage for this task?"

"Sounds good."

"Everyone needs to be in position upon the army's arrival." Catching Savannah's voice, Chitolla turned her head towards it, soon spotting the large, yellow-furred bat. Savannah flew alongside her mother, who nodded and listened carefully to her daughter's requests.

Glancing up, Savannah spotted the swallow in the corner of her eye. Her face twisted into a slight grimace. "Now, why didn't Secha take care of her bird? She's not supposed to be out here."

Chitolla, taken aback, opened her mouth to speak.

"S'vawna!" Higuero's powerful voice rang out through the grove of trees. "You have orders for us?"

"Yes," Savannah replied as she landed near Higuero and the warriors. "The leaders decided on a special task for you. All of you are to come with me on a trip up north. The Mouse-Ears have a small outpost not too far from here, and we need more armour. We're going to take some goods with us to trade, then bring the new armour back and get it ready for battle. I chose you because you're able to carry more than the others."

"Can we take Chitolla along?" Higuero gave a confident smile in the swallow's direction.

"Secha's bird? Sure. It would be even better if you could somehow train her to carry stuff for us."

"What do you say, Chitolla?" Higuero asked.

Chitolla chirped in agreement, darting down to join the bats.

Patas, watching her journey with the others into the desert sky, sighed regretfully. "So much for sending me good vibes. Please return soon, swallow."

* * *

Chitolla, Higuero, and the rest of the group loaded themselves with brown burlap sacks, filled with valuable trade items. When asked, Savannah listed a few of the treasures the bags contained. "Gems, clay dishes, fresh scorpions—the Mouse-Ears consider it a delicacy. Probably because they can't catch them like we can."

After gathering their cargo, the bats and swallow followed Savannah into the desert. As they traveled, the pale sands gave way to tall, rocky outcroppings, coloured in alternating layers of red, grey, pink, and lavender. Chitolla marveled at its beauty, but Savannah and the others appeared not to notice.

They soon arrived at what looked to be the entrance to a sinkhole. Stopping at the cavernous opening, Savannah called out a few words in greeting, to which a voice inside responded. After a few moments of chatting, the voice gave them permission to enter.

When Chitolla entered the cave and saw a Mouse-Eared bat for the first time, she gasped. *They're soooo cute!*

Of course, she realized, these full-grown furballs with very serious expressions on their faces probably would be offended at being described as "cute." But Chitolla still couldn't help but find them adorable.

The squeaky sound of hundreds of tiny talkative bats drowned out almost every other noise in the cave. Savannah had to shout in order to be heard.

"I need to see Eddie about trading," Savannah explained to a small grey escort. "Could you please take us to him, darling? We're in a hurry."

"Ya ya, I take you," the tiny escort replied. "This way, this way!"

As the group followed behind their little guide, Chitolla marvelled at what lay around her. Much of it was hidden because of the darkness of the cave, but not all.

Glowing droplets of liquid hung in various places, sparkling like stars against the hoary limestone walls and ceiling. The lights had clearly been placed by the bats, as their arrangement was geometrical, rather than scattered.

That wasn't the only element of this underground world that was clearly unnatural. In fact, to Chitolla, the entire cave appeared artificial. Every inch of stone had been carved, chipped away at, or smoothed down. Perfectly shaped columns, decorated sparsely with pictographs of bushes, leaves, and more natural caverns, rose from the floor like trees made of stone. These columns contained evenly-spaced holes, through which tiny bats came and went. They reminded Chitolla of tree hollows—but unlike natural hollows, everything was built to a clear, specific design.

Cone-shaped structures that could have once been stalagmites littered the floor, following a zig-zag pattern. The constructions closest to the wall were taller and wider than the ones nearer to the cave's center. Like the columns, they were dotted with small holes. Filling the spaces on the floor left open by the zig-zagging cones were pools of clear water, sparkling in the light of the glowing droplets, each pond a perfect triangle.

"How could Savannah have called this a 'small outpost?'" Chitolla leaned in close to Higuero as she spoke. "This place is incredible! Everything here was made by the bats?"

He nodded. "S'vawna calls it a city."

"She called it an outpost earlier."

"This es one of their smaller cities."

This is small?! Chitolla's eyes followed along the form of the cave as she attempted to calculate its size. "This is wider than the Stone Place. Wider than that secret cavern the Vampires created. And there's got to be at least a couple hundred bats."

"Apparently, da bigger cities have thousands, even millions."

"If there's so many of them, why can't they help us fight the Vampires?"

"S'vawna says they are too scared," Higuero continued. "They invented armour to combat da fact that they are small and delicate. A long, long time back, da Mouse-Ears had a war with da Big-Ears. Da Big-Ears were less than a hundred strong, da Mouse-Ears in da thousands, but da Big-Ears won easily. Later, da two made a treaty, and da Mouse-Ears built tradin' cities like this one."

"We're here! We're here!" The grey-furred guide was easily able to make himself heard over the ruckus of city residents. Pulling up beside the entrance to one of the many large cone structures, his attention turned back to Savannah. "Pay me well! Pay me well!"

The little bat's eyes were wide and expectant as Savannah pulled something out of the sack she carried and passed it to him. Grinning happily, he flapped a few times, then darted away into the recesses of the cave.

Guess we won't be seeing him again, Chitolla thought.

The group of bats followed Savannah through the cone's entrance. This hole was wider than most of the city's passages, but everyone in the group, including Chitolla, had to fold their wings as they passed through to avoid getting stuck.

On the other side of the entrance, Chitolla saw the others gathered in a semi-circle near the center of a round room. Taking her cue, she dashed to Higuero's side, then gazed around at the building's tan-coloured interior. The room was lit by several glowing, teardrop-shaped objects; Chitolla couldn't decide if they were gems or some hardened, previously liquid substance. Tucked into the corner of the room was a small hole, clearly leading to a lower floor.

It was only a moment later that a small, black female came through the hole and greeted the visitors. "Eddie will be with you shortly." She darted back down the hole.

As promised, another bat soon appeared, waving with one wing before taking his spot on the floor. "Savannah! Savannah! Haven't seen you for a while! You have things for me? Something you need? Tell all, tell all!"

Chitolla looked over the bat curiously. As with all the Mouse-Eared bats, he was small, covered in fine fur, and had dark, attentive eyes. His nearly black face contrasted sharply with his silvery body.

Savannah motioned for the others to place their loads in front of them. "We brought all this in trade for new armour. Unfortunately, some of the southerners—the Vampires—have set their sights on us. It looks like we'll need to go to war to fend them off."

"Ooh." Eddie shivered. "Not good. Not good. Vampires are very scary. And their leader is very smart. Most bats don't invent or build things, but we Mouse-Ears do, and the Vampires do because their leader tells them to." He hesitated. "Have you heard the rumours about their leader being... a... a monster... who eats other bats?"

"Not until recently," Savannah responded, "but it's been confirmed by the southerners."

Eddie shivered again.

Savannah continued, "We need a dozen sets of new armour, with some adjustments made, within the next hour."

Eddie looked over the bags they had brought, counting them. "Then I will need a bigger payment, friend."

Savannah was clearly thrown off. "What do you mean, a bigger payment? This is what we gave you last time."

"It's not enough!" Then, in a gentler, almost pitiful tone, he added, "Times are hard, my friend. Besides, you want the adjustments made within the hour—that's very hard to do, very hard! You ask a lot, my friend, you must pay more!"

"Eddie, I'm not asking much of you. We'll make most of the adjustments back at our settlement. We only need minor adjustments, slight size changes, razoring, and elasticizing. That's all."

"These things you call *minor* changes are far more difficult than you realize, Big-Ear! And it takes a lot to convince my workers to do something so quickly and still do it well!" He looked over the bags again. "If you want it done quickly, I need seven more loads."

Seven? Chitolla thought in shock. *That's nearly twice as much!*

It was clear from Savannah's pained expression that she hadn't expected such a high price. But she didn't have time to argue. "Alright, fine. We'll bring you the rest once the battle is over. Deal?"

"I need the extra seven loads now."

"Now? We don't have time! We need the armour within the hour! We'll pay, just give us until after the battle. We've never backed out of an agreement before, have we?"

"No. No." Still, Eddie shook his head. "It is not a matter of trust, friend. It's a matter of principle."

"Eddie, we're about to go to war! We *need* the armour *now*! Do you understand?"

The Mouse-Ear remained frozen, clearly unconvinced. Savannah sighed in frustration.

"Fine. Then understand this: we Big-Ears are just a small group of hunters living in the middle of the wilderness. But you Mouse-Ears are advanced, you have technology most other bats can only dream of—and you have little ability to defend yourselves. We Big-Ears have protected you for generations. As you said, the leader of the Vampires is smart. Don't you think it's possible that he's going through *us* so that he can more easily get to *you?*"

Eddie became agitated. "It… it's very hard work… my workers need good pay…"

"I know you love your fellow Mouse-Ears very much, and you wouldn't want them to be killed by the Vampires. And we'll do our best to keep their army from getting to you. But we don't have the knowledge or expertise to make the adjustments we're asking for, and our battle plan requires that we return with the armour quickly. We'll give you the extra seven loads—even though both of us know you're overcharging—because we're desperate! These Vampires could wipe out the Big-Ears *and* the Mouse-Ears if we aren't ready by the time they arrive!"

Everyone waited in expectation.

Finally, with another glance over the burlap bags, Eddie ventured, "Ahem… twelve full sets of armour?"

"Yes."

"Minor size adjustments, razoring, and elasticizing—done within the hour?"

"Preferably."

"And I'll make it six extra loads… you know, since we are friends and all."

"That's very generous of you."

Eddie nodded. "Deal. I'll get my workers started immediately." With that, he crawled to the small hole in the floor and disappeared down it.

All eyes turned to Savannah as she sighed loudly and shook her head. "Mouse-Ears. They seem so soft, so small, so delicate—but you have to be harsh in order to get through to them!"

* * *

Patas hung in Savannah's tree hollow, trying to calm his nerves. As he attempted to keep his thoughts from drifting to his Vampire friends and his dear mother Péla, he heard the sound of another bat approaching. He looked up just in time to see a small, brown-furred Big-Ear enter the hollow.

"Have Savannah and the others returned with the armour?" the other bat asked expectantly.

"Not that I know of," Patas replied.

"They would have come this way—you would have seen them."

"In that case, no, they're not here."

The other bat's face clearly displayed his worry. "We have a problem, then."

"Problem?"

"Yes." The Big-Ear's eyes met the Vampire's. "The army is here. Much sooner than expected. We haven't caught sight of the army itself, but the big one, Cattae, captured one of our spies and sent them back with a message: he wants us to send a delegate to meet their messenger in a small grove not too far from here." The bat's eyes became pleading. "What do we do, Vampire?"

Why are you asking me? Patas thought. But he bit his tongue and waited until a more encouraging thought came to him. "I—I can try to buy us some time…"

"Good. Please hurry. I was supposed to send the delegate immediately, but I had hoped to find Savannah …" Then, stopping, he gave a weak smile Patas' way and patted him on the shoulder. "I'm glad you're here to help us, Patas. Really."

Patas tried to smile back, but couldn't force it. The Big-Ear spread his wings and Patas did the same. The two took off across the ever-darkening sky.

* * *

"We're here!" Savannah exclaimed. She shifted her claws, causing the bulbous grey bag she held to release a clanging sound. Just ahead, their home was close enough that all in the group could make out the shapes of other bats weaving amongst the trees.

When they had made it to the grove and put down their heavy loads, one of the many fluttering bats rushed over to them. "Savannah, you're back! We're in trouble. The army has arrived!"

Higuero's ears perked up.

"Cattae asked that we send a delegate to meet his messenger," the bat explained. "Gary has already left with the Vampire, and is escorting him to the meeting place Cattae chose."

"Where's the army?" Savannah asked.

Her face fell in dismay as the other bat shook his head.

"We don't know. Our spies haven't caught sight of them."

Chitolla, spreading her wings and puffing out her feathers in agitation, leaned closer to Higuero. After a moment of listening to her, he asked Savannah, "What will be done if Cattae na accept Patas as a messenger, since he es banished?"

"We haven't planned for that," Savannah responded. "Of course, we didn't plan for the trading to take so long, either, or for the army to arrive so soon." She turned back to the messenger. "What do the other leaders have in mind?"

"They were waiting for you to arrive with the new armour."

"That's the other problem. I only asked the Mouse-Ears to do initial adjustments, like we had planned. None of the armour is ready yet—neither the sets we just brought, nor, I assume, the ones we already have."

"Some of it is done, but not enough."

Chitolla whispered in Higuero's ear again. "Which way to da meetin' place Cattae picked?"

The messenger pointed with his wing. "There's a small grove of trees that way."

"I recall the place," Savannah said. "Is it possible the army is hiding there?"

"We just don't know."

"Well, let's act on what we do know." Savannah turned back to the group that had travelled with her. "We can give these guys the armour we've finished. They'll be the first out in battle. As for the unfinished stuff, we'll just wear it as is."

"Perhaps the other leaders will have another suggestion," the messenger put in.

"Well, let's get to them quick!" Savannah looked over to Higuero. "You're willing to do what we ask of you, southerner?"

Higuero nodded, but he appeared distracted, his ears and eyes darting around as if looking for something.

"What?" Savannah asked.

"Chitolla," Higuero said slowly. "Where es she?"

* * *

Patas' escort spread his wings and came to a sudden stop. "Alright, Vampire, you're on your own from here." At Patas' confused look, he explained, "Cattae made it clear that he only wanted the delegate to meet his messenger. That no one would get hurt if we simply let our messenger and theirs chat before either side made a move."

"You're sure you want to trust him?"

The escort shrugged, but it was clear he didn't intend to stick around. "I'll tell Savannah where you are." With that, he turned and left.

* * *

Ignoring the darkness around her and the feeling of panic that attempted to overwhelm her, Chitolla dashed through the evening sky, encouraged by her own thoughts.

I'm invisible to the bats, she realized. *They see me as a lesser animal, nothing more. They don't know I can think like them. They don't know I can carry messages back to the others. I'm the perfect spy. I can do something the others can't.*

An unusually strong fear for Patas came over her, convincing her that this "something" only she could contribute was vital to his safety.

Creator, I hope this is You directing me. Because something tells me it's quite possible I'm heading to my death.

THE CHALLENGE

12

AS PATAS' WINGS CARRIED HIM ACROSS THE DEEP BLUE SKY, HE desperately hoped Cattae's messenger would be someone he knew. He'd have a better chance of making a deal with a friend than a stranger. Scanning the ground, it wasn't long before he saw a thick but small grove of scraggy trees, their limbs harsh and twisted in the radiant moonlight.

Patas approached with caution. As he came closer, he caught sight of a bat standing in front of the grove. A recollecting smile crept across Patas' lips.

"Mano, buddy!" Patas landed, his wing wrapping around Mano's shoulder in a friendly manner. "I haven't seen you since… well, you know. It's great to see you again!"

Mano, startled speechless, stood stiff with shock, allowing Patas to embrace him. His lips moved silently until he managed to form the beginning of a word. "Patas…?" His face hardened and he roughly pushed Patas away. "Traitor!" he spat venomously, his eyes cold.

Patas released a nervous chuckle. "Uh, well… when did you become a soldier?"

"Recently."

"Oh." Patas looked over his friend. "You're not wearing any armour."

"Won't need it." Mano continued to stare at him with eyes that bled hatred.

Patas took a deep breath. Wiping the uneasy grin from his face, his voice became sombre. "How is my mother?"

"You expect us to be on friendly terms again, after what you did?"

"I…" Patas watched his companion longingly. "Mano, tell the truth. Didn't you ever hope there may be a way to stop living under Spectral's shadow?"

"Are you going to keep blabbering, or is there a reason you're here?"

In the corner of his vision, Patas noticed a shadowed form hanging in the trees behind Mano. His heart caught in his throat as he detected two dark eyes staring at him, both belonging to—

Cattae.

Patas cleared his throat. "The Big-Ears want to avoid bloodshed."

"Good. Then they'll give themselves to us?"

"No. They don't want to become Vampires."

"Well, they can't exactly get what they want then, can they? Either they become Vampires or they die."

Patas spoke slowly, attempting to keep his voice steady. "They're willing to make a deal."

"What deal?" Mano snorted, his stony face giving way to a vicious grin. "The one thing we want, they refuse to give. Do you think Cattae's afraid of a tiny group of hunters? They can do nothing to stand against our armies—or our god! Face it, traitor, you picked the wrong side." Mano looked up into the branches of the trees behind him. "You heard their answer, Cattae. We, your soldiers, will follow behind you and deal with these pagans in any way you please."

"Thank you, servant." Cattae floated out of the grove, landing on the ground next to Patas.

Patas' heart throbbed as he watched Cattae's sharp teeth peek out from behind a ravenous smile. The monster seemed to enjoy Patas' fear, his smile widening as the Vampire trembled.

"The thing that would give me the greatest *pleasure*…" Cattae drew out the word as he spoke in a soft voice, "would be to have you hold the traitor in place while I remove his wings." His eyes bored into Patas. "After all, we don't want him putting up a fight when we take him back to face Spectral, do we?"

Patas felt Mano grab him roughly. He tried to pull away, gazing at his former friend with horror and disbelief. The moment Mano looked into Patas' eyes, he averted his own, hiding from the other Vampire the flash of guilt that filled them.

Cattae ran his tongue across his lower lip, his jaws widening as he reached out a claw towards one of Patas' wings.

"*No!*"

The abrupt yell was followed by a rustle of feathers as a Vampire-sized bird darted in front of Patas. She landed between him and the gruesome cannibal, spreading her wings as if to shield Patas from Cattae's hungry jaws.

Mano jumped back in surprise. Cattae's eyes betrayed his own shock, and for a second or two he stared at the swallow.

"Chitolla, what are you doing here?" Patas placed his claws on the bird's shoulders and gently pushed her away. "Go, now."

Cattae's eyebrows lowered in frustration. "Shoo birdy, shoo." He swatted at her as if she were a pesky fly. "Shoo. Get out of here."

Chitolla fluffed out her feathers, digging her claws deeper into the sandy earth. Her eyes remained on Cattae. "*No!*"

Cattae gasped, his eyes widening. "You," he whispered faintly, as if to himself, "you are from the Veil?"

Chitolla lowered her wings when she heard him say it. "Wait— Spectral told you about my world?"

Cattae didn't appear to have caught her question. He whispered to himself again, "How did you get out of the temple without me knowing…?"

"Hey!" Higuero's brown form appeared, seemingly out of nowhere. "What es goin' down here? You are frightenin' my friends, Cattae?"

Cattae gave the Stripe-Faced bat a look of annoyance. "Ah, I get it. You, Higuero, were the one who helped the traitor escape north. And you," his eyes drew back to Chitolla, "you somehow escaped with him, am I right?"

"That's about right, Cattae," a new voice added. "Only, you've managed to leave out a few of the characters involved."

All eyes drew to a tree just outside the small grove. Hanging from a thin branch, a silver bat stared out at the group, sending a confident smile in their direction.

Chitolla, Higuero, and Patas gasped in unified astonishment.

Cattae, however, chuckled as if this were a new joke being added to the comedy materializing before him. "Oh, dear Chinaca, you came, too?"

"Didn't you miss me and the fun little traps I set for you?" Chinaca's tone was light-hearted. "Please tell me you missed my company. I would be *so* hurt if you told me you had forgotten about me."

"The game is over, Chinaca." The merriment vanished from Cattae's voice. "And it won't end painlessly, either. I'll make sure of that, *fleshling*."

"Over? We haven't even made it to the best part!" Chinaca said playfully. "You mean, I flew all the way across the ocean to find you a more challenging foe, and you want to end the game before I even have a chance to introduce him?"

Cattae's face turned puzzled, one ear cocking back as he considered her words. "What?"

"A challenger, Cattae. You like a challenge, right? Well, here's the game: you fight him. If you win, you get to eat him, and us. If you lose, you and your army leave the Big-Eared bats and my friends alone. Is that worth playing for?"

Cattae appeared dumbfounded. After a moment, his face twisted back to its normal position. He eyed Chinaca suspiciously. "Liar. What challenger could you bring against *me*?"

Chinaca smiled. "His name is Bai'ic. Bay-eek. Strange, I know, but he's from across the ocean, so that can be excused. Don't you want to meet him?"

Cattae's expression didn't change. He did, however, spread his monstrous wings and, with an ease that could only be gained from experience, lifted his body away from the ground. "I pity you, Chinaca, if this is all you can think up. Your time is over. You might as well accept your fate. No living creature you can bring against me—"

"Hey, if I look like a pathetic opponent to you, say so to my face!"

Cattae gasped as a ghostly white bat arose to block his view. The eerily pale creature, nearly glowing in the moonlight, gazed at him through dark eyes set in a snowy face. The other creature smiled, showing off sharp teeth and strong jaws, his massive wings beating quietly against the night air.

Cattae stared back disbelievingly. "You... you... are like... us...?"

"Ouch." Bai'ic's answer was given in a tone of annoyance. "I wouldn't say that. I don't eat other bats or chase them out of their homeland or trick them into thinking I'm a god."

"Are you really here to challenge me?"

"Among other things, yes."

Cattae growled, looking away. "This isn't your fight."

"Does that mean you're afraid?"

The Flesh-Eater's eyes shot back to Bai'ic, a defensive snarl twisting his face. "Don't be so quick to insult a servant of Spectral!"

"Well, I can insult him instead, if you prefer."

"Back up your arrogant words with proof of your strength!"

"I'd love to. I'm ready. Are you, dear Cattae?"

"*Hold it!*" Savannah appeared, materializing out of the sandy desert world. "If there's going to be a duel, it has to be done right!" At Cattae's annoyed glare and Bai'ic's inquisitive glance, she continued. "When we Big-Ears duel, it's done officially: a set time and place is determined, and everyone is invited to watch. That would include your Vampires, Cattae. And both the competitors *must* be arrayed properly for battle!"

"And what would be a battle's proper arrayment?" Bai'ic questioned.

"Armour, of course! We'll set the duel for some time late tonight, so we'll have the time we need to make the necessary adjustments... I suppose I'll be visiting our dear friend Eddie again."

"I don't have to play your silly games," Cattae said harshly. "With one word, I could have the Vampires destroy your puny tribe." He paused. "But Chinaca's right—I like a challenge. Be ready, Easterner, to meet your defeat. Where will the battle take place?"

Savannah thought for a moment. "We have a stadium, but it may not be big enough for a battle between the two of you. How about here, in say, four hours?"

"Good." Cattae turned to Mano. "Servant?"

Mano was in a daze, staring at Bai'ic with incredulity, shocked that there could be anyone as intimidating as—or perhaps even more intimidating than—the two he had worshiped since childhood.

Cattae growled angrily. "Servant!"

Mano withdrew his gaze from Bai'ic, trembling all the more when Cattae's eyes locked with his. "Yes, priest?"

"We need a moment alone." Cattae looked back at Savannah, hovering alongside Bai'ic. "How long will it be until my armour fitting?"

"A few hours, at least. I'll let you know."

"Good. I'll see you soon, then." Cattae turned and flew into the trees, motioning with his wing for Mano to follow.

Watching as the two vanished into the grove, Savannah released a relieved breath. "Glad to not have his eyes on me anymore. I have to confess, he scares me. Just a little." She turned to Bai'ic with a welcoming smile. "Thank you for coming, and for being willing to do this. I'm not sure what the Nectar-Drinker said to convince you—"

"Think nothing of it."

With a final nod at Bai'ic, Savannah directed her smile to Chitolla. "Now, Miss Swallow-from-the-Veil-who-somehow-thought-she-could-get-away-without-telling-us-she's-a-talking-animal, I wouldn't mind your assistance, if you please."

At Savannah's waiting stare, Chitolla spoke up. "Um, yes, I'd love to help. We'll go back to Eddie and trade for new, bigger armour?"

"Uh-huh. And meanwhile, your friend Chinaca will have a chance to catch up with the others… and perhaps explain where she found this giant ghost."

* * *

Mano clung tightly to a thin branch as he watched his master apprehensively. "What?"

Cattae, hanging from a thick bough, appeared distracted, his eyes directed to the ground as he contemplated something. Mano waited with bated breath until the dark grey bat lifted his gaze towards him. "There are matters here I was… unaware of."

Mano was silent in response, but his face betrayed his confusion.

"I need you to take the army and return to Spectral," Cattae said.

"Go back to Thériava?" Mano envisioned the ghostly white bat that had come to challenge his leader. "What about the other Flesh-Eater? Don't you need help—"

"No, dear fleshling, I do not need your help! Question Spectral about the existence of other Flesh-Eaters. I had been led to believe… never mind. Consult with him. Understand?"

Mano nodded as Cattae began beating his wings against the air, soon racing off and out of the Vampire's sight.

* * *

"Alright, I think that's it," Savannah said. Chitolla, Chinaca, Higuero, Secha, and Patas watched as she took one final scrupulous gaze over Bai'ic. "Wing-shields are good. Mask fits perfectly. Knife-claws are sharp and tight-fitting. I'd say you're ready for battle."

Bai'ic nodded, looking around at the group that had gathered in this near-empty tree hollow to watch him get fitted. "Well, how do I look?"

"Intimidating," Savannah responded. "You look incredible, darling."

A mischievous smirk overcame Bai'ic's face, his eyebrows rose, and his voice became playful. "Darling, eh? My, I didn't realize you felt that way about me, *sweetheart*."

Patas burst into uncontrollable laughter. Secha and Higuero stifled their chuckles.

"And what is it you find so funny?" Savannah demanded.

Patas tried to stop laughing long enough to explain. "It's just… ha… like, how you call *everyone* darling… which is not… he… ah… never mind."

Chinaca rolled her eyes. "It's okay, Savannah. Bai'ic's sense of humour gets old very quickly. Trust me. I had to put up with it the *entire* journey back across the ocean."

"Ouch. Don't be so harsh, Silver Leaf." Bai'ic's smile remained as he reprimanded her.

"Well," Savannah said briskly, "sorry to fly away from your joke, Bai'ic, but I believe I should be checking on Cattae and his armour. I'll be back shortly, dar—ahem, *friend*." With that, she flew off.

Patas was still trying to calm his laughter when Bai'ic turned his suspicious-looking smile in the Vampire's direction. "Well, now that my armour-bearer has been sufficiently embarrassed… Chocolate."

It took a moment for Patas' eyes to lock with the Flesh-Eater's. "You mean me?"

"Yes. What's the story with you and White Moth?"

"Who?"

"White Moth." The larger bat motioned towards Secha, a confident smirk on his face. "What's the story?"

Patas turned red, sputtering, "Uh—story? There is no story…"

"But you both like each other."

Patas began chuckling and coughing at the same time. "Ha ha… you say that like it's an obvious fact."

"It's *painfully* obvious."

Patas' ears retreated at the ghostly bat's blatant response, his eyes turning over towards Secha. He smiled at her.

The Tent-Maker replied with a cute grin. "You like me?"

"What?!" Chinaca's response was unexpected, and came in a tone of disgust. "You *can't* like each other! Secha, he'll contaminate you!"

Bai'ic's look became quizzical. "How so?"

All eyes were on Chinaca as she attempted to explain herself. "Well… he can't pursue a relationship with her. That would be demeaning, because he's a Vampire."

"Isn't he on our side?"

"Yeah, but he's still a Vampire. There's a hierarchy. I… my race… the Nectar-Drinkers… and the Tent-Makers, too, I think… we're higher than the Vampires and Stripe-Faced bats. You see, the bats that belong to races that drink nectar or eat fruit, and do other civilized things, they are… more civilized. Purer. And other races are placed on different points on the… the list… depending on their… habits."

"Really?" Bai'ic gazed at Chinaca unblinkingly. "So, where are Flesh-Eaters on that list?"

Chinaca averted her eyes.

"That low, eh? Well, if you really think I'll contaminate you, why did you ask for my help?"

"…because…" The one word seemed to be the most she could get out.

Bai'ic nodded, but didn't comment. An uncomfortable silence followed.

Chitolla returned her attention to Bai'ic's armour. She found the design to be quite fascinating. There was no breastplate or swordbelt—nothing she recognized from the many stories she had read—but each piece clearly filled a bat-relevant role in protection or attack.

The most recognizable aspect was the mask, which had a similar function to a helmet. A tight-fitting fabric, the wing-shield, protected each of Bai'ic's wings. As a weapon, both of his thumb-claws were gloved in sharp blades.

Savannah had had some unusual difficulties in fitting Bai'ic. For one, his large nose-leaf meant that his mask couldn't slide off and on, which was how the masks had been designed to work for the plain-faced Big-Ears and Mouse-Ears. In order to fit his face, it had been necessary to saw it into two parts and carve interlocking formations into each piece. Because of the change, Bai'ic couldn't remove the mask by himself—another bat had to gently undo the fittings.

The colour had also bothered Savannah. It was clear that the armour's appearance was nearly as important, if not as important, as its proper fit. And Bai'ic's ghostly colour was his most striking feature—the fact that there was no complementing set of white or light silver armour presented her with a dilemma. So, settled on a compromise. Instead of choosing for Bai'ic the palest armour they could find, she went with the opposite: black. For the mask, she bought from Eddie a rather expensive piece made from a dark metal with a bluish shine to it.

The long, talon-like knife-claws, fashioned from the same metal, curved slightly to mimic the true shape of their wearer's claws. The difference was that the knives were flatter, allowing for two razor-sharp edges, connecting at a needle-like point.

"You keep staring at me," Bai'ic noted. "Which is encouraging. But it's still uncomfortable."

"You? Uncomfortable?" Secha was surprised. "You seem like the type to enjoy attention."

Bai'ic's face again lit up into a smile. "As true as that is, I'm still uncomfortable. Not because of the attention. The little things that poke me every time I move, they're the issue."

He must mean the bindings for his wing-shields, Chitolla thought. As intimidating as the mask and knife-claws made him, the wing-shields interested her the most. They were made from a fabric designed by the Mouse-Eared bats. In Bai'ic's case, it had been dyed jet black, as dark as a starless sky. The fabric was elastic, stretching and condensing perfectly to fit Bai'ic's wings however much he spread or folded them, as long as he didn't close them entirely. The fabric was lightweight but tough. All in all, it was the perfect way for bats to protect their delicate wing membranes, their most vulnerable feature, from injury.

The fabric was held in place by metal clasps and small wires. Both were so tiny that, even though Chitolla knew where each was located, she couldn't spot them visually.

"I can't see the holdings," she remarked. "Are they really that noticeable?"

Bai'ic spread a wing towards his face and examined it carefully. "The wires are hard to see, but they're pretty easy to feel." He turned to Patas. "Is Vampire armoury anything like this, Chocolate?"

Patas cocked his head a little, unsure how to answer. "I suppose. It's simpler, though. We don't wear wing-shields, and the knife-claws aren't so… what's the word… delicately fashioned. Honestly, I'd say our simpler armour works just as well."

"I think function is only half the concern," Bai'ic pointed out. "I wonder if the Mouse-Ears are as crazy about getting the perfect look as dear Miss Darling is."

"Well," Secha said, "perhaps you males think the design has been overthought, but I think it's impressive and… enchanting."

"Truly? I look that good?"

"Well, we've been staring at you for some time, and I haven't gotten bored of it yet." A grin slipped over Secha's face. "You look very handsome—darling."

THE DUEL

BUKINERO PERCHED ON THE FLOOR OF THE STONE PLACE, PANTING heavily.

Before him was the circular hole that housed the Door Between Worlds. As he caught his breath, he tried to recall the Princess' instructions on reopening it.

It takes four stones, she had said. *Place them inside the hole in this order: triangular, white, round, tiny.*

He looked around. There were bits of rock scattered on the floor, broken off the roof and walls during earthquakes. But he wasn't going to find a white rock in here. He darted out of the Stone Place, soon returning with his chosen pebble. He collected the rest inside, holding them in his feet and beak.

When all four were found, he returned to the hole in the floor. Flying above it, he stared down—and gasped in shock.

The wavy blue lights were already there, weaving their spiderweb pattern.

But how was that possible? The Door couldn't open by itself, could it? The Princess hadn't suggested that possibility. So how was it that the Door was open now?

Unless, he realized, heart racing, *someone opened it from the other side…*

* * *

Savannah's eyes and ears scanned the makeshift stadium. All the Big-Eared bats, a few Mouse-Eared bats, and her new friends from the south were gathered, eagerly anticipating the upcoming duel.

At Savannah's instruction, the once-empty desert area had been made to look like a proper stadium, with portable roosts as stands for the audience and poles marking the boundaries of the "arena."

Only one thing was missing.

Savannah rescanned the audience, then sighed. The only Vampire present for the event was Patas.

Why didn't Cattae ask his army to witness the duel? she wondered. *Something is definitely up.*

Catching sight of Chinaca in the stands, she flew to the silvery Nectar-Drinker and hovered near her.

"Well, darling," Savannah said, "you look about ready for this to begin."

Chinaca greeted her with a smile. "I've been waiting a long time to see Cattae's defeat. A very long time. I just wish the Vampires were here to see it."

"Yes. Their absence troubles me. I wonder where they are?"

"Don't worry about them," Chinaca replied. "I took the liberty of having one of my bats do some detective work. Apparently, Cattae sent the army back to Thériava."

Savannah cocked a long ear to show her curiosity. "One of *your* bats?"

"Bai'ic isn't the only Easterner I brought over. I have five Fox-Faced bats also, and a few smaller companions. After all, you can't have a war without soldiers."

"True enough. Your friends mentioned that you were the one with war plans." Savannah moved closer to Chinaca. "What are your plans now?"

"Once the duel is over, we'll send our army after the Vampires. We'll meet them in battle in Thériava."

"Assuming Bai'ic wins the duel."

"Well, yeah," Chinaca agreed. "Assuming we win." The faintest hint of uncertainty crept into her voice.

"So," Savannah continued, "you've witnessed this Bai'ic's battle prowess?"

Chinaca hesitated. "Only once."

"It was an impressive display?"

Chinaca visualized her first encounter with Bai'ic. The sound of the mouse's bloodcurling scream echoed in her mind.

"Actually," she confessed, "the opponent I saw him take down was… quite a bit smaller than Cattae."

* * *

The grey interior of the Stone Place was still and silent. Faint bits of light seeped through tiny cracks in the stonework. Inside the circular hole, the wavy blue lights continued their dance.

Suddenly, the blue lights fizzled, breaking their pattern. A large bat broke through them and appeared in the Stone Place.

Spectral's hazy eyes soaked in the dim world. He landed on the ground, breathing heavily, closing his eyes. His body became still, his breathing relaxed. Only his large ears moved, twisting this way and that, picking up every little noise.

His ears stilled as they focused on one sound. His eyes opened, his gaze travelling to a pile of rocks not too far from him.

Bukinero heard the giant bat release a mirthless chuckle. Shivering in fear, the swallow crouched down. The rocks didn't offer the sense of security he desired.

"Come out, little one." Spectral's voice was almost friendly. "No point in hiding. Tell me, what creatures inhabit this mountain?"

Bukinero didn't answer.

"Swallows?" Spectral tried.

Silence.

"Ah, yes," Spectral said, inhaling deeply. "Swallows. I can hear them outside. Very recognizable. Tell me something else, do you have a king to look after you?"

Bukinero dared a peek around the rock that hid him. To his surprise, he saw no sign of Spectral near the circular hole.

A gentle grunt brought his eyes upward to the ceiling, where Spectral hung, watching him with a grin. "Do you have a king, swallow?"

Bukinero backed away. Spectral's eyes followed him across the floor, ears honed in as he waited for an answer.

"No," Bukinero finally said. He tried to make his tone harsh and unwelcoming.

"No king? Well, aren't you in luck. I've recently been looking to expand my empire." Spectral's smile widened, sharp teeth appearing. "Surely you can see the benefits that would bring you. You'd have someone to look after you. Someone to guide you. Someone to lead you into a golden age."

His eyes bored into Bukinero. The swallow trembled. It felt like the bat was looking into his soul.

"Someone to worship," Spectral added. He spread his large, dark wings. "I would make the world stand in awe of you."

Bukinero was terrified, but his face displayed only anger and distrust.

Spectral eyed him silently. His next words came out in a whisper. "Of course… it's not like you have much of a choice."

* * *

The sound of a trumpet, blown by one of the Big-Eared bats, announced the end of the long wait. Savannah and Chitolla listened keenly as the trumpeter called out to the audience.

"I now introduce the two duelers who will compete for control of the Desert Mountains." The speaker motioned with his wing to a stand within the borders of the arena. "In this corner, we have Bai'ic, fighting on behalf of the Big-Eared bats and their allies."

Bai'ic's bluish mask glittered in the moonlight. His black wing-shields melded with the darkness, but they didn't hide the ghostliness of his white fur and long, pale ears. Cheers erupted from the crowd.

"And in this corner, we have Cattae, representative of Spectral and the Vampires."

Cattae hung on his roost, silent. He made no move to acknowledge the audience. No one cheered for him.

A chill ran down Chinaca's spine as she watched him. Savannah had shown no favouritism when selecting the armour for each contestant. The same care she had taken in making Bai'ic appear intimidating she had taken in designing Cattae's look.

Horn-like spines protruded from the front and sides of Cattae's copper-coloured mask. His wing-shields were blood-red.

"Did you have to make him look so menacing?" Chinaca asked Savannah. "I think he could pull it off without the armour."

"The more impressive the enemy, the more people will awe at the victor," Savannah answered. "Bai'ic has the chance to show us how skilled a warrior he is."

Storyteller, Chinaca thought. *He insists he's just a storyteller.* Her heart raced as the trumpeter nodded at the two duelers.

"The battle begins… now."

* * *

Bukinero almost didn't jump in time to avoid Spectral's sudden strike. The monster's jaws clamped shut around air, just millimeters from Bukinero's face. He spread his wings, darting away from Spectral as he forced himself into flight.

Spectral laughed as if his near-killing bite had merely been a joke. "I like you, swallow. You're fast." For the first time, the bat noticed a pile of four stones sitting by the hole. "Hmm. Triangular. White. Round. Small. I see you know something about crossing between worlds. Who taught you how to open the Door?"

Bukinero turned to face Spectral in mid-air, bracing himself for another attack.

"I could teach you more," Spectral offered invitingly. "I could teach you so many things."

"The Maxéra."

Spectral watched Bukinero curiously. "What?"

"The Maxéra of Séveritas—the kingdom that killed your followers—they taught me to open the Door."

"Ah. I get the sense you're familiar with me. I suppose you know my name…"

"Spectral."

"Yet I haven't had the pleasure of learning yours."

Bukinero considered for a moment. "Have you met my mate in the other world?"

"Yes." Spectral's answer came without hesitation. "I met her."

The bat watched Bukinero's eyes widen. The swallow briefly let down his guard.

Spectral's face broke into a toothy grin. "She died quickly."

He launched himself at Bukinero.

* * *

At first, neither Bai'ic nor Cattae made a move. Both eyed each other, analyzing their opponent. Bai'ic faced Cattae, while Cattae pretended to watch the ground.

Bai'ic shifted in place, flexing his wings.

Cattae remained still for a moment longer. Then, slowly, his head lifted—but not towards Bai'ic. His gaze turned to someone in the crowd. A smile slipped onto his face as he locked eyes with Chinaca.

"Thank you," he said in his hoarse voice. His words were loud enough for all to hear. "Thank you, Chinaca, for giving me this chance to show off my strength."

He laughed as a tremor ran through her.

"Don't worry," he continued. "I think I'll let *you* live. After all—"

Bai'ic's strike came as a shock to all, particularly Cattae. Bai'ic's jaws were locked around Cattae's shoulder, his fangs ripping into the other bat's flesh.

Cattae, screaming, aimed his teeth at Bai'ic's face. When Bai'ic's mask proved too great a hindrance, he went for his opponent's long ears.

Bai'ic backed off before Cattae could reach him. A smile broke out on his face, revealing blood stains on his lips. "Okay—now am I worthy enough to insult your leader? Or should I wait until your ego has been wounded a bit more?"

* * *

Spectral's jaws were closed as he flung himself at Bukinero. The swallow was driven through the air and pinned between the wall and Spectral's lengthy maw.

Spectral still smiled as he pushed his lips against Bukinero's chest. "You're fun. Much more fun than the Vampires. Their wings just flutter all over the place. You are far more... sleek."

Bukinero tried pushing Spectral's jaws away with his feet. But Spectral's face seemed to be all bone, and nothing he did caused the bat any pain.

Bukinero hurt all over from hitting the wall. His head, in particular, now pulsating with pain, couldn't come up with a plan of survival.

A trickle of dust settled on his shoulders. Looking up, he saw shards of rock falling from the ceiling, shaken loose by his impact. Perhaps the deteriorating Stone Place wasn't strong enough for such a ferocious battle.

A glint of sunlight caught his eye. A new hole had appeared above, letting in a small ray of light.

Bukinero had an idea.

* * *

Cattae growled angrily at Bai'ic, who hovered nearby, nodding as if inviting an assault.

Cattae rushed at Bai'ic. Bai'ic braced himself, raising his clawed feet. At the last moment, Cattae swerved, rushing back to attack from behind. Bai'ic manoeuvered out of reach just in time, with Cattae's teeth barely grazing his wing-shields.

"Still feeling confident?" Cattae quipped, breathing heavily as he brought himself to hover.

"Alright," Bai'ic said. "I confess, I wasn't expecting that."

Chinaca hoped it wasn't nervousness she heard in his voice. *Come on, storyteller, give it to him.*

Cattae watched Bai'ic smugly.

Bai'ic responded with a smile. "Don't let your ego swell too big. I honestly didn't think you could fight." He briefly showed off his large teeth. "Now I don't have to go easy on you."

Cattae appeared no less smug. "Nor I you, Easterner."

* * *

Bukinero's eyes scanned for a weakened section of wall. In the opposite corner, he noticed a few particularly unstable-looking rocks. Already, several tiny gaps allowed in light from the outside, and jagged lines and cracks predicted there would soon be more.

All that's needed are a few small earthquakes, he thought. *Or one or two well-placed hits.*

He considered his words carefully. "Alright," he told Spectral, "I can see this is pretty much hopeless for me. So… could you grant me one last request?"

Spectral's hazy eyes looked into his.

Bukinero forced his voice to remain steady. "Could you… could you not kill me too quickly? I'd like to feel that I put up a fight."

"I make no promises," Spectral replied. Nevertheless, he pulled his jaws back, freeing Bukinero.

Bukinero caught the air with his wings. "Okay," he said. "I'll try to make this fun for you."

He dashed past the giant bat towards the far corner of the Stone Place. Spectral followed the swallow with his eyes and ears, but didn't appear eager to attack again.

Bukinero flew back and forth near the weakened section of wall. *Come on,* he thought, heart pounding as he watched Spectral's serene reaction. *This won't work if you don't follow me.*

* * *

Bai'ic hurled himself at Cattae, grabbing his opponent's wing in his jaws. Cattae fought, his mouth searching for a hold.

Cattae's teeth finally found their place in Bai'ic's forearm. With each bat grasping the other's wing, both tumbled through the air. Bai'ic, releasing his grip, felt flesh rip as he pulled himself free. He hovered for a moment, watching as Cattae continued to fall.

Seconds before hitting the ground, Cattae managed to regain flight. He stared grimly at Bai'ic, watching as small rivers of blood stained the ghostly bat's white fur.

"So," Bai'ic asked, appearing unfazed by his wound, "how long does this battle go on? Until one of us is maimed?"

"Until you are dead," Cattae hissed back.

"What about if you die? Can we call it quits then?"

"*I* have a claim to immortality," Cattae said, grinning.

"No more than I do."

A glint of fear showed from behind Cattae's eyes. His grin faded.

Bai'ic's expression displayed compassion. "You're young. You only became a Flesh-Eater recently. You still have a lot to learn. And the lies of your leader certainly don't help."

"How dare you call Spectral a liar! Do you not realize who and what he is?"

"He's not the first fully immortal Flesh-Eater, Cattae. And he won't be the last." Bai'ic moved closer and whispered to keep his next words from the audience's ears. "And even we so-called immortals aren't invincible."

* * *

Bukinero quickly learned that Spectral wasn't in a hurry to eat. The giant bat continued to eye him silently, seeming almost bored.

Bukinero's eyes locked onto the entrance. *Perhaps if I try leaving—*

Suddenly, Spectral's jaws were there again. Bukinero cried out in pain as they yanked a mouthful of feathers off him.

Spectral hit the weakened section of wall, then used his claws to grasp it. To Bukinero's dismay, barely a chip fell from the stonework.

Okay, he considered, *that wasn't quite where I needed the impact.*

Bukinero hurried to the other side of the room. Spectral didn't follow.

Clearly, he doesn't want to chase me. Bukinero processed this. *What does he want? And how can I use what he wants to put him where I need him?*

"Getting tired, swallow?" Spectral asked.

Bukinero turned to face him. "No, I'm fine. You?"

"I could go on forever."

Bukinero examined the wall again. *Perhaps I can't rely on Spectral to do it for me.*

"Something wrong, swallow?" Spectral questioned.

"Well," Bukinero replied, "if you could go on forever, why do you save your energy?"

"Do you want me to chase you?"

"I don't know… what do you want?"

Spectral cocked his head. "You are one of the most compliant meals I've ever had."

Bukinero raised an eyebrow. "One of?"

"Yes." Spectral paused. "Your mate… she was more compliant." He chuckled. "That, swallow. That look on your face. That is what I want. What I enjoy most."

A pang entered Bukinero's heart, and he tried to swallow back his fear. "M–my mate. How… how did it happen?"

"Oh, dear swallow," Spectral said piteously. "Do you really want the pain of knowing?"

Bukinero nodded. Spectral flew over to hover beside him.

"Well," Spectral began slowly. "It went something like…"

His teeth flashed out and Bukinero dashed away. The bat twisted around to follow, sprinting after him.

Not even his race with the ruffian owl had been this close. Bukinero's tail was within reach of Spectral's jaws, but the bat kept his mouth wide, intent on waiting until it could close around flesh.

Bukinero spotted the weak section of wall and sped towards it. This time, he wasn't planning to save himself. He threw all his focus into hitting the wall with as much force as possible.

* * *

Cattae swiped at Bai'ic with a knife-claw. Bai'ic backed out of reach, but as he did so, he left his belly exposed. Cattae rushed forward, ramming his mask's spines into Bai'ic's stomach. He drove Bai'ic backwards, pinning the white bat against one of the boundary poles.

Bai'ic gasped as the wind was knocked out of him.

Chinaca's eyes widened in horror.

Suddenly, Bai'ic's knife-claw came out to slash Cattae's forearm, severing an artery. Blood spurted from the wound. With his other claw, Bai'ic dug into Cattae's back.

As Bai'ic removed the knife, Cattae drew back, stunned.

Bai'ic dove at Cattae's throat, his teeth clamping around it. A loud crunch was heard as Cattae's neck was crushed in Bai'ic's jaws.

Bai'ic released his hold, and Cattae fell—never to rise again.

* * *

Bukinero was knocked out the moment he hit the wall. He didn't see the stonework collapse around him, nor did he hear Spectral's agonized cries as sunlight rained down into the Stone Place.

When he awoke, he blinked, gazing at the broken rocks around him. By some miracle, he had managed to avoid being crushed by one of the larger pieces. He stood up, shaking debris off his feathers.

His eyes caught Spectral's dark body lying nearby. The bat was still. Bukinero hopped over to examine him.

When he came within a few inches of the giant monster, a claw suddenly reached out to grab him. Hazy eyes watched as he tried to struggle free.

"So… you thought you could kill me?" Spectral's chuckle turned into a cough as he choked on fresh air. "You thought I would die if I left my temple? Is that what the Maxéra told you?"

Spectral paused, his breathing heavy. Tears fell from his eyes, but his words, though slow, came fearlessly. "They were wrong. I can handle a little pain, swallow. Most assuredly, I am not so weak that I can't end your life."

Bukinero's clawing was in vain. Spectral dragged the helpless swallow closer to his jaws.

Spectral released a weak cry as Flammeus' talons dug into his back. He fought to remain alive just a moment longer, to reach out at her… then collapsed, dead.

Flammeus sighed in relief as Spectral took his last breath. "Bukinero?" she called. "Bukinero, are you alright?"

Bukinero now pulled free. His eyes welled with tears when they met Flammeus'. "Was he lying?"

"About what?"

"He said he killed Chitolla. Do you think…"

Flammeus watched Bukinero silently. When she finally spoke, her words were gentle. "Well, dear swallow, there's only one way to find out."

* * *

The audience erupted into cheers as Cattae's dead body hit the ground. Bai'ic landed on his perch, grimacing. A group of nurses hurried over.

Bai'ic brushed them aside. "I'm fine. I heal quickly."

Blood soaked out of the wounds in his belly and on his arm. Neither appeared to bother him, but the nurses were insistent. He finally gave in and let them treat him.

The announcer was all smiles as he called to the crowd. "And the winner is Bai'ic! The ally of the Big-Ears is victorious!"

Chinaca nudged Savannah. "We better make our own announcement, before everyone gets too caught up in the celebration."

Savannah nodded, flying over to the announcer. "This war isn't over yet," she told the audience. "The Vampire army has gone to Thériava. All the Big-Eared bats capable of fighting, together with the dozen or so warriors Chinaca has brought us, will meet them there in battle. We will ensure that Spectral meets the same fate as his priest."

One of the Big-Eared bats spoke up questioningly. "With such a small number of soldiers, do you really think it wise to take on the Vampires—and Spectral—in their home territory?"

"If it es helpful," Higuero said, "I can gather reinforcements from da islands. Many Stripe-Faced bats are strong warriors. We could easily double da count."

"That would be very helpful," Bai'ic agreed.

"Meet us on Wanderer's Beach, on the coast of Thériava," Chinaca instructed. When Higuero nodded, she nodded back. "Thank you, Higuero."

His ears perked at the kind tone in her voice.

"Patas," Chinaca added, "I'd like to speak with you on the way to Thériava. I'd appreciate that inside information you offered me once upon a time."

"Yeah, sure," Patas agreed. He glanced at Higuero with a look that said, *Why is she being nice to us?*

Higuero's responding shrug told him, *I na be knowin'.*

Chinaca's final piece of instruction was directed at Chitolla. "Once the battle is over, the temple will be safe for you to enter. We'll find a way to take you back home."

Chitolla smiled gratefully. *Home. Bukinero, I'm coming home.*

* * *

Bukinero glided through the thick, smoky Underworld, trying to ignore his stinging eyes as he navigated the monstrous flames. *You got through the desert with Flammeus,* he told himself. *You can get through this place with the Maxéra's directions.*

Focusing on the thin strand of blue light twinkling above him, he played over the cobra's instructions again and again, careful to recall every word.

"Follow the Bridge through the Underworld, and keep your eye on it," she had told him. "It may appear to vanish temporarily, but as long as you remain traveling in a straight line, you'll catch sight of it again. Continue until you feel something tugging at you, pulling you in. That's the sign that you've come to the Door."

Taking a deep breath, he felt the strange air prick him as it journeyed down his throat.

"The smoke is toxic and causes hallucinations," the Princess had warned. "You may get dizzy and see or hear things that don't match reality. To avoid this, breathe normally. Do not hyperventilate or try to hold your breath. Just fly through the Underworld as fast as possible without overexerting yourself. If you do experience dizziness or hallucinations, rest for a moment and wait for it to pass."

Bukinero's heart raced as he saw a strong blue light up ahead and felt an odd breeze tug on his feathers. He beat his wings once more before allowing the light's pull to carry him.

As soon as he felt his body leave the Underworld, Bukinero's eyes scanned his surroundings. For a moment, everything looked black, but as he adjusted to the dim lighting he recognized the shapes of two bats before him.

The bats were clearly startled, but he ignored them, looking around until he found the entrance to the temple. They watched as he darted past and exited through the hole.

One made a move to follow, but he was held back by his friend.

"Why bother?" the bat said casually. "It's just a dumb bird."

STORYTELLING

14

CHITOLLA SURVEYED THE BATS FLYING WITH HER. BAI'IC WAS STILL IN his armour; his mask glittered in the faint moonlight. Patas flew near Secha, who in turn flew near Chitolla, and Chinaca followed just behind. They soared along the coast of the Northern Passage, in hopes that the sea winds would speed their travel. They hadn't risked open water since parting ways with Higuero.

This has been quite the adventure, Chitolla thought to herself. *Monstrous cannibal bats, secret tunnels, bat-made caverns and cities and armour, new friends of multiple races…* Then a glance at Bai'ic's battle-arrayed figure reminded her of the most important thing: *This adventure isn't over yet.*

Patas was staring at Bai'ic in an odd manner, tilting his head this way and that, singing under his breath, all seemingly in an attempt to get a clearer view. Turning to Secha, Patas spoke as quietly as he could manage without whispering. "You really think Bai'ic looks handsome?"

Secha's face showed surprise. "Hmm?"

"Earlier, you said he looked 'very handsome.'"

"He does. But I'm sure I'm not the only one who thinks so." She directed her voice at Chinaca. "You'd agree. Bai'ic is handsome, right?"

Chinaca slowed down so she was flying just above Secha. "I try to ignore things like that."

"Then you agree. He is handsome—even without his armour on?"

"If one pays attention… and after getting over the shock of him being a Flesh-Eater and all… yes. I have to admit, he's quite attractive."

Patas seemed bothered by their talk.

Secha smiled at him reassuringly. "Don't worry. He knows it's you I like."

Patas didn't seem to have any control over how red his face became.

"And *I* like you, too, Chocolate!" he heard Bai'ic call out.

Patas suddenly found himself engulfed in enormous wings, powerful jaws pressing hard against his back, and a sloppy wet tongue trailing along his spine to the back of his head.

Bai'ic laughed as he spread his wings, revealing Patas' messy, shocked, and somewhat petrified form.

"Don't look so scared," Bai'ic said. "It's not like I was going to eat you or anything, right?"

Patas tried to smile back. "Ehhh…"

"Like I said earlier," Chinaca put in, "his sense of humour gets old quickly." She looked at Patas with an odd mixture of pity and apathy. "And like I didn't warn you earlier, he gets playful sometimes."

Bai'ic took a new position above the rest of the group. "Perhaps I'd calm down some if we told stories."

"Stories?" Patas asked, still shivering from Bai'ic's unexpected "kiss."

"Sure. It'd be a good way to pass the time."

"Chitolla should start!" Secha said excitedly. "She can tell us that story she really likes, the one about the meerkats."

"Adila's Tale?" Chitolla seemed equally enthused by the idea.

"Ah, you like that story, huh?" Bai'ic said, taking interest. "Of Adila and Dumisai and Marjan…"

Chitolla was surprised. "How do you know it? It takes place in the Veil."

"Hey, not all bats are unaware of the existence of the other world. And Adila's Tale took place before the worlds were divided, you know."

"It's a true story?" Secha said with some surprise. "I didn't know that."

"A story sounds alright," Chinaca said. "Tell us, Chitolla."

Chitolla became nervous. "Well, I'm not a professional storyteller, like Bai'ic…"

"We still want to hear you tell it," Bai'ic encouraged. "Go ahead. How does it begin?"

Chitolla considered for a moment. "Okay," she began. "Adila's mob—that's what a group of meerkats is called—lived in a small savannah, bordered by a dark jungle on one side and a vast desert on the other. They were content to remain in their savannah. After all, it provided just enough food and shelter to make it a good home. The jungle wasn't called the Forbidden Jungle for no reason, and the desert, the Domain of Predators, was also aptly named. Besides, not too far into the desert was a rival mob."

The story began on what was, for Adila, an ordinary day. Her father, Ishi, one of the most respected meerkats in their mob, was prattling on about Jada, a handsome and admired hunter. "He is by far the finest meerkat in the mob," Ishi told his daughter. "When you two are finally married, you'll have by your side the best of the best."

Adila always became uncomfortable when her father spoke like this. She desired to honour his wishes, but her heart wasn't on Jada. "He is respected," Adila ventured hesitantly, "but…"

"But nothing. He's the best, and you will have the best, my daughter."

Adila sighed. She knew her father was already aware where she would take this conversation, if she had the chance.

"May I go back underground?" she asked. Above her, the intense sun scorched the sky, turning it a pale blue.

Knowing who she would visit, Ishi ignored her request. "That Dumisai character you fancy is too low-bred for you, my daughter. His ugly fur, that dark mottled mass, is evidence of that."

"I know he isn't a member of the high caste, like us," Adila said, "and perhaps you don't think he's handsome. But he's smart and creative. And he cares about me more than Jada does. Dumisai has asked you several times for permission to marry me. Jada has yet to ask once."

Elsewhere in the mob, another member of the high caste was yelling at his son.

"Kondo! You rebellious and wicked child!" Koz, seeing he had gotten the attention of the many meerkats who stood nearby, motioned for them to come to him. "You know what my son did? He was asked to look after one of the youngsters, but he abandoned them out in the desert!"

Everyone gasped.

"You have shown yourself to be irresponsible and uncaring, my son," Koz said. "And you've made these mistakes one too many times!"

Kondo cowered under his father's anger, but his face betrayed his disrespect. "Yeah? What do you think you're going to do about it, dear daddy?" Then, he whispered, "You always make such a big deal, humiliating me in front of everyone. But I'm used to it now. If this is your punishment—"

"The punishment is that I'm taking away your inheritance!"

Everyone gasped again, louder than before.

Kondo staggered back. "W–what? You can't do that! No good father takes away his son's inheritance!"

"I am, right now. Kondo, you have been disinherited!"

Clearly ashamed, and burning with hatred, Kondo slunk off into the shadows. The crowd that had gathered to watch his public humiliation dispersed.

Kondo was extremely angry, and when he became angry his mind worked in a strange way. He always sought some sort of condolence, something with which he could gain revenge. As he looked into the Forbidden Jungle, he thought, *My father would be so upset if he found out I went there...*

So Kondo snuck into the dark foliage and began wandering amongst the trees, no goal in mind except to do something his father would disapprove of.

But as he wandered the shadowy forest, something strange caught his eye. A monolith had been erected in the middle of the jungle, but it wasn't the giant stone itself that caught Kondo's attention. Rather, placed in a carved crevice was a black gemstone. Streaks of blue within the jewel radiated shimmering light.

Above and below the gem were inscriptions. Kondo leaned in closely to read: "Leave Me In Peace, Onlooker; for this stone holds dangers to which no mortal should be subject, and has the power to change the world as we know it. This stone has the power to..."

As Kondo read on, his eyes widened in amazement. *This can't be true... can it?* He reread the warning, soaking in every detail. *Leave Me In Peace, Onlooker...*

His eyes returned to the gem. His hands reached out to touch it. When no consequences followed, he lifted the stone from its place, bringing it towards his face. Arms shaking, he glanced about to see if anyone was watching—but the forest appeared empty.

Kondo smiled, eyes again turning to the jewel. *Now, beautiful stone, I just need to come up with a way to sneak you back to the mob...*

That same day, as Kondo was in the forest, Jada was out hunting in the desert. He had forced Dumisai to assist him— forced, because Dumisai avoided Jada whenever possible, since the only thing Jada ever did in Dumisai's presence was brag about how Ishi was so insistent that Adila marry him, and not the "poor creature" she loved.

"Someday, she will be my mate," Jada said, flashing a mocking smile in Dumisai's direction. "Once I get bored enough of my current lifestyle to be interested in her."

Dumisai, as usual, remained silent, but his fingers twisted

around the spear he held. Jada, as well, held a spear, which he pointed this way and that to emphasize his words.

"She's practically mine now—you never even had a chance with her." Jada laughed pridefully. "Just think. She'll be living in my home, having my children, giving all her love to me—"

Suddenly, Dumisai flew into a rage, flinging his spear in Jada's direction. "Stop it!" he yelled.

Dumisai's eyes widened in fear as Jada stared back at him unblinkingly, the end of Dumisai's spear sticking out of his chest, blood spurting from the wound. Jada opened his mouth once, closed it, and then fell to the ground, dead.

Dumisai rushed to Jada's body, panicked. "Jada? Jada?" His mind reeled as he thought about the consequences he would face when the other meerkats found out what he had just done—torture, banishment, perhaps even death. "Jada? I didn't mean…"

His mind fumbled about until he found a solution. Taking Jada's spear, he began slashing the other meerkat's dead body, inventing a story as he created the perfect evidence for it.

Jada and I came across a sleeping hyena. Jada wanted to attack it, but I was too afraid, and hid. Jada snuck up on the hyena and struck out at it, but the hyena awoke and put up a fight. Jada battled bravely, but was killed. The hyena didn't bother to take his body, so when it left, I brought it back.

Dumisai took the story to the mob and they wept for their fallen hero. All but Kondo, who, being a liar himself, had a knack for knowing when others were lying.

This fits into my plans perfectly, Kondo thought.

He waited until he could be alone with Dumisai, then approached him.

"Dumisai," Kondo said with reverence in his voice. "I know what you did—but fear not! Earlier today, I had a vision.

At first I thought it was nothing but silly ideas in my head, but the things I witnessed have come true!"

Getting on his knees, Kondo bowed before the shocked and confused Dumisai. "You, Dumisai, are not the lowest of the low, as you have been told all your life. For the others have a fear placed in their hearts; they do not want you to fulfill your true destiny. Behold!"

Kondo revealed the unearthly gem. "This stone," he told Dumisai, "if you keep it in your presence as you wake and as you sleep, will turn you into the Dark One: a powerful being, fast as a snake, fierce as a lion, and clever beyond compare! Take the stone, Dumisai! It is your destiny!"

With such flattering words and the promise of help from his most loyal friends, Kondo won Dumisai's mind.

I... I am not the least. I am the Dark One. He thought. "What must I do, Kondo?"

Kondo had to force himself not to smile gleefully as he explained his plans.

The next day, Dumisai publically approached Ishi with a request: "Give me Adila's hand in marriage."

As usual, he was snubbed by Ishi. "She will never be yours."

"She already is." Adila stood by her father, fearfully watching the gathering eyes, as Dumisai continued. "She has given me her heart—more fully than you realize. Now, you will give me your permission."

"Never, pathetic wretch!"

Ishi's eyes widened in shock as Dumisai flashed out a knife, driving it into the other meerkat's chest.

Someone screamed, and Adila stood frozen.

"That's the signal!" Kondo called out. "Loyal ones, attack!"

Several other meerkats pulled out knives and began stabbing all they set their eyes on. Dumisai as well, ignoring Adila's horror, joined in the massacre.

Kondo searched the fleeing crowds until he found his father. *Finally,* he thought. *Revenge is mine.*

For a moment longer, Adila stood in disbelief. Not one of the bloodthirsty killers came near her, but she watched as they killed everyone in their path. She looked down and stared at the body of her dead father. Finally, panic set in, and she fled.

Ignorant of the direction she was going, she soon found herself in the Forbidden Jungle. Collapsing, tears pouring from her eyes, she passed out from the trauma.

When she came to, she cried and cried. Too terrified to return to Dumisai, she devised a plan. The only solution was to enter the Domain of Predators and find the rival mob. Perhaps they would accept her—or perhaps they would treat her badly and send her away. It was her only hope.

She wandered to the home of the rival mob, only to find the place covered in blood and dead bodies, just as her home was. Dumisai, Kondo, and the others had been here, too. They had set off on a killing spree, destroying all whom they encountered.

Kondo's plan had simply been to avenge himself by killing his father. But once he had started his deception, he saw no reason not to continue it. He would lead Dumisai on as long as it was beneficial to him.

Besides, some of what Kondo had said about the gemstone was true: every morning, the jewel having been by his side the whole night, Dumisai awoke a larger, stronger, and darker meerkat. Everyone could see the changes, and they stood in awe of their new master.

Kondo soon began to feel a little nervous under Dumisai's gaze, but he never felt tempted to take the gem for himself. *I may enjoy its blessings—but I would hate for its curses to hang over me. Better to enjoy my new puppet.*

Adila, meanwhile, walked on and on, her thoughts random and incoherent, her emotions numbed by hopelessness. Eventually, she again became aware of herself and realized she was lost in the vast desert wasteland. She swallowed, trying to get rid of the pain in her dry throat. It was evening, and the sun had begun to fade from the sky. But rather than relief, the removal of the sun's scorching rays only brought to life the desert's freezing winds.

Adila fell to her knees. Somehow, she still had enough water in her for a few drops to escape her eyes.

I'm going to die out here, she thought sadly. *Without Dumisai, or Daddy... without anyone.*

"Wow." Chitolla looked at Chinaca as the bat began to speak. "I'm seeing a new side of you, swallow."

"What do you mean?"

"I mean, I'm surprised this is your favourite story. It's harsh. Everyone is killed. There's some magical rock. Not the type of story I imagined you liking."

"It is harsh," Bai'ic said, his tone unusually serious, "but it's true."

"Yeah, okay, that bothers me, too," Chinaca said. "A magical stone that makes people stronger?"

"It doesn't sound familiar to you?"

Chinaca shook her head. As Bai'ic's eyes met with the others, they all shook their heads as well.

Suddenly, Secha spoke up: "The Underworld! The Flesh-Eaters! Cattae claims that Spectral's power comes from the Underworld. That somehow, though he was once a Nectar-Drinker, being there and being equipped with the right knowledge about how to survive the fires has made him stronger, darker, immortal..."

"Right. But recall, this is before the Bridge was covered in fire," Bai'ic explained. "Prior to his actual attack, Traitor tested his flames on several rocks, turning them into what are now known as the Underworld Coals. Creator had animals guard each of these stones. But Traitor deceived one of the animals into hiding their stones in the world surrounding the Bridge. Traitor used these coals to start his fire."

Chitolla considered this. "I know that story from *Creator's Book*... but I didn't know there were other stones, or that the story had anything to do with Adila's Tale. How do you know? The version I read doesn't say anything about how the jewel got its power."

Bai'ic was silent for a moment. "As a storyteller, there are many little details I'm required to remember."

Chitolla was clearly confused by his answer, but as he nodded at her to go on, she continued the tale.

A ghostly form caught Adila's attention. She looked over to see a large white bat hovering nearby. The bat smiled at her. "Who are you? You look lost."

"My name is Adila," the meerkat explained. "M—my family is dead." She bowed her head, a look of pain coming over her face.

"Well, you're more than welcome to stay with my colony," the bat said. "The wilderness is not a safe place for a lone meerkat."

Adila was hopeful, but her heart soon dropped. "I would be no good to you. I can't see in the dark, and I can't fly. I would be a burden."

"It's a burden we just agreed to take on. Right, everyone?"

Adila looked up in surprise to see a group of bats flying overhead. With chirps and squeals, they announced their consensus. Gliding down, they danced around her, singing a traditional welcome song.

So Adila went to live with the bats. She stayed in their cave, awaking at night as they did, and they taught her how to find food in the desert. If it weren't for her one reminder, Adila was sure that, in the warm presence of her new friends, she would have wiped away the memory of Dumisai, his betrayal, and the death of her mob.

But one thing kept her from forgetting: Adila soon found that she was pregnant with Dumisai's children.

Meanwhile, Dumisai grew stronger, and his mob, under Kondo, continued to destroy everyone they came across. Dumisai allowed only his most trusted followers to have extended contact with the powerful gem—all but Kondo, who always politely refused the offer. It was soon easy to tell from mere physical form whom Dumisai favoured.

One night, Dumisai awoke to hot breath on his face. He found himself looking into the angry eyes of a strange, striped hyena.

The hyena growled, "I believe you have something that doesn't belong to you, meerkat."

Kondo immediately realized who she was. Getting up, he roused the other meerkats. "We have an intruder! Kill her! She stands against the Dark One's destiny!"

Early the next morning, Adila was about finished hunting for the night when she noticed a large, predatory creature limping through the wilderness. At first she hid, watching it from a distance.

She recognized that the animal was female, and a hyena. But she was surprised to see it was covered in stripes, not spots. *I thought striped hyenas only lived north of the Forbidden Forest...*

Seeing that the hyena was badly wounded, she drew nearer to investigate. The hyena caught sight of Adila, but didn't approach her.

"My name is Marjan," the hyena said. "I'm looking for a group of bloodthirsty meerkats who escaped from me earlier tonight. They have stolen a powerful stone I have been assigned to guard."

Marjan's friendly attitude and voice made Adila feel more comfortable approaching her. Soon, the bats arrived, bringing medicines, and they healed the hyena's wounds. As they talked, Adila realized that the meerkat Marjan was after was Dumisai.

Afraid for her friend, Adila begged Marjan to allow her to speak with him. Perhaps she could talk some sense into him. Marjan consented, and the white bat agreed to use his tracking skills to find Dumisai.

"I know of these stones," the bat told Marjan. "I have suffered from their curse myself. The stone must be hidden again, before more creatures are hurt."

Kondo, in the meantime, considered his options. His deception had fulfilled its purpose, and he could see that the end of Dumisai's reign would be a bloody one. They would continue to attack larger and larger creatures, until they found something they couldn't beat, or the curse wore too heavy on their bodies and minds. Besides, Kondo could see that the stone had begun to affect him, and he wanted to get out before lasting damage was done.

The white bat soon learned that Dumisai's mob was living in a maze of tunnels created by some unknown animal.

Adila entered and wandered the tunnels until she found her lover. "Dumisai!"

Seeing her, Dumisai rushed to hug her. Filled with conflicting emotions, Adila couldn't bring herself to embrace him, and Dumisai soon asked what was wrong. Unsure how to help the clearly deceived meerkat understand what he had done wrong, she decided to start with Marjan's words. "The stone is very dangerous, Dumisai. The Dark One isn't someone you want to be, trust me. Give it back to the hyena so she can hide it away."

Dumisai didn't want to listen. Angered by her words, he drew his sword and prepared to kill her.

It was then that he noticed she was pregnant.

A moment later, he looked up to see Kondo, a disarming smile on his face, his hand holding a sharpened spear. "Kill her, Dumisai. There are others outside. She'll lead them to us."

Rather than obey, Dumisai dropped his sword, a terrified and pained expression coming over his face. "What have I done? Kondo... what have we done?" His eyes turned back to Adila. "We had dreams, plans. About us. And I threw them away... for what? Adila... what have I done...?"

Seeing his puppet turn, Kondo raised his spear, prepared to end his deception the bloody way.

But Creator had other plans.

A shocked look came over Kondo's face as long fangs sunk into his flesh. Large brown coils engulfed him. The resident of the tunnels, a giant cobra, set her eyes on Dumisai and Adila. "You all must leave my nest, now. I will not allow you to so much as breathe near my eggs."

Adila and Dumisai rushed out, but most of Dumisai's mob didn't receive the same warning. Only two or three others managed to stagger back out into the light of day, a traumatized look in their eyes.

That is how one of history's greatest ironies came to be. Today, the darkened decedents of the changed meerkats are renowned for their ability to battle and take down cobras. But their ancestors had no such ability—in fact, for generations their fear of snakes kept them far from the nest of the cobra, Nyoka. For a time, the powerful gemstone was hidden in her tunnels, in order to keep these changed meerkats, now called "mongooses," from going after it.

But once Marjan took it back, she and the stone disappeared, and neither has been seen since.

Adila and Dumisai went on to parent their own mob. She never forgot the kindness of the bats, and she and Dumisai lived near the colony, allowing their children to play together.

FALLING STARS

CHITOLLA SHRUGGED. "AND THAT'S THE END."

There was a moment of silence as everyone contemplated the tale.

"The white bat makes me think of Bai'ic," Secha said in a sweet voice. "Doesn't he seem like Bai'ic?"

The others smiled, and Bai'ic in particular seemed entertained by her connection. "Do I, White Moth?"

"Where do you think the stone went to?" Patas asked.

"If I were Creator," Chinaca put in, "I would have had it thrown into the Underworld with all the other bad stones."

"You're definitely not Creator."

"Well, you know what I mean."

"Why do we say that, anyway?" Patas mused. "If I were this person, I would do this. Well, if you were that person, you would have that person's experiences, and that person's personality. You would end up doing the same thing."

"What I meant, Patas," Chinaca said, "is that if I were in His situation, that's what I would have done."

"But you don't know the full extent of His situation, or all the details—"

"You're overthinking this!"

Secha giggled, clearly engaged, as the Nectar-Drinker and Vampire continued to debate linguistics.

Chitolla, however, had something else on her mind. She looked over to Bai'ic, who appeared to be listening half-heartedly to Chinaca and Patas. "Bai'ic?"

Bai'ic's ears turned towards her. "Yes, Clay?"

"I have a question." He eyed her curiously, and she continued. "How old are you?"

"Very. Why?"

"Well… Flesh-Eaters are immortal, right?"

"That's the idea. It's not entirely true, though."

Chitolla briefly glanced at the other three, who were too busy with their conversation to hear them. "Bai'ic, how did you become a Flesh-Eater? Were you in the Underworld?"

Bai'ic turned away. "Some questions are better left unanswered."

Discouraged, she nevertheless decided to reveal what she was thinking. "Bai'ic, *are* you the white bat in Adila's Tale?"

Bai'ic chuckled. "Now that would make me very, very old." He didn't continue, and Chitolla looked away, feeling slightly embarrassed.

The next time she glanced at him, though, she saw him watching her with a mischievous smile. "What?"

"Clay, would you be interested in learning the song the bats sang to Adila?"

Chitolla appeared puzzled. "What song?"

"The traditional welcome song."

"How would *you* know the song they sang…?"

"As a storyteller, there are many details I'm required to remember," Bai'ic said with a twinkle in his eye. "In fact, the song is *very* special. The bats taught it to Adila so she could use it to see through the darkness, like we do. Only a few of our songs can easily be learned by other creatures, and this is one of them."

"Really?" Chitolla still seemed doubtful. "The book doesn't say anything about that…"

"The written story can never be complete. Would you like me to teach you the song so you can see better in the darkness?"

"How?" Chitolla asked. "Secha tried teaching me to sing the way bats do, but it didn't work."

"This song is different. I'll sing it in a lower voice, so you can hear it, and once you know the words, you can sing it with me. I'll start to go higher, bit by bit, and you can follow my lead. Alright?"

The swallow hesitated.

He laughed warmly. "Come on, give it a try. If the song doesn't work, I was wrong. Okay?"

Chitolla considered for a moment longer, staring up at the night sky and then down to the dim world below. To her eyes, both were an indiscernible mass of darkness, and it was her mind rather than her eyes that convinced her there was a division between the world below and the sky above. *It would be nice to see, if possible.*

Consenting, she nodded at Bai'ic. "Alright, teach me."

Bai'ic returned the nod. "Do exactly as I do." Turning his face towards the star-studded sky, he sang out loudly,

Sing until the stars rain down
Sing until it all falls around
Sing until the stars rain
Dance until the beat fades
Sing until the stars rain down

Moving his gaze downwards, he continued in a different tune.

I didn't know if I could fly
Then you looked into my eyes
Now I'm reaching to the sky
Tonight, I thought I could not survive
Then you breathed into my life
Now I'm dancing through the night sky
Because tonight I fly

He sang through the song again before she joined in. She sung quietly at first, stumbling over the words and going silent during the last few lines. Bai'ic, sending her an encouraging glance, continued unwaveringly. In his fourth time through the song, Chitolla joined in confidently, following his lead as she turned her eyes above.

Sing until the stars rain down
Sing until it all falls around
Sing until the stars rain
Dance until the beat fades
Sing until the stars rain down

For a moment, Chitolla forgot the reason they were singing and simply listened with pleasure as their voices carried through the air. A funny sensation tickled her ears and she blinked, suddenly feeling as if her vision had gone wonky.

She watched the stars, wondering why they appeared to grow larger. She gasped as one star, sparkling just above her head, rushed towards her, passing in front of her eyes on its way into the waters below, leaving behind a trail of sparkling dust. Other stars followed suit, falling around her like liquid drops of light, radiant strands of glowing dust marking the path each took.

Chitolla's heart raced, her mind playing back the words to the song: *Sing until the stars rain down…* Feeling something rubbing against her, she turned to see Bai'ic, his white fur aglow with a strange light as he motioned for her to tilt her head downwards. She did as instructed, singing out again.

I didn't know if I could fly
Then you looked into my eyes
Now I'm reaching to the sky

As she sang, the stars continued to fall. When they reached their destination, they shattered into little pieces. Each white drop of starlight changed colour as it made contact with a solid object. Emerald particles fell into the sea below and blended with the waves, turning the waters a luminous green. Drops of sapphire coated the trees. And the shoreline, weaving its way between the forest and the sea, became golden yellow.

Chitolla scanned the world with her eyes, soaking in details she had never seen before. As the lights began to fade, she remembered: *It's the song*. Singing loudly once again, she didn't notice Bai'ic had stopped to observe her. The words clearly ingrained into her mind, Chitolla watched as the features of the world around her became clear and distinct. She laughed joyously. *I can see!*

Turning to Bai'ic, she saw that his previously white fur now glowed violet. He smiled. "So, it's working?"

"Yes!" she sang excitedly. "It's beautiful! No wonder Secha was so excited to teach me!"

Bai'ic nodded. "This song is designed specifically for starry nights. It won't do you any good in another form of darkness. Like other songs, it works best when you're close to the objects you're detecting."

Chitolla nodded vigorously. "Alright. Thank you, Bai'ic! Thank you!"

* * *

Mano's attempts at attracting his god's attention after getting back to Spectral's Temple were all in vain.

He stood on the floor before the Door to the Underworld. Closing his eyes, he tried to decipher what he was doing wrong. Sacrifices of blood and mindless animals, continuous chanting, self-inflicted wounds, visits to the Underworld—no matter what he did, Spectral didn't come to him. But why? Couldn't his god tell how desperate he was?

Another Vampire approached Mano from behind. "Sir?"

Mano's ear cocked back to listen. "Yes, spy? Anything new?"

"The enemy is at Wanderer's Beach, getting ready for battle. They're guarding against intruders."

"And Cattae? Any sign of him?"

The spy hesitated. "Sir... as I told you, the white Flesh-Eater is still alive. And the enemy claims—"

"And as *I* told *you*, Cattae wouldn't send us off if he couldn't deal with the Flesh-Eater." Mano paused. "So, no sign of him?"

"N–no. Have you consulted with Spectral?"

Mano stared down at the wavy lights. Their dance remained slow and relaxed.

"No," he answered. "Our god is apparently busy."

* * *

Even as the sun's rays spilled over the horizon, the Big-Eared bats, Easterners, and newly-arrived Stripe-Faces were wide awake. While some busily made necessary adjustments to the armour, others were coming up with a plan to defeat Spectral.

Chitolla and Secha had been among those strategizing. But they quickly realized they were of no help, as the conversation seemed overwhelmingly disheartening—with almost all suggestions getting turned down. They decided to leave.

Chitolla and Secha flew through the brightening sky, enjoying the familiar scent of rainforest air. Chitolla practiced her singing and Secha taught her new songs.

"In the Iridescent Forests," Secha said, "we Tent-Makers use a song called Kawéa to find our way around the trees."

"Kawéa?" Chitolla asked.

"It's not in our language. A long, long time ago, we Tent-Makers used to speak another language. This is the only song remembered from it. But no one remembers what the words mean." Secha appeared saddened by this. "The elders try hard to remember that language, but it's more or less extinct."

"What's the song sound like?"

Secha sang in a high, melodious voice.

> Kawéa né shéa, kawé, kawé
> Ini'ii rana, kawé, kawé
> Ya mo kili ké,
> Kawé, jandé.

When Secha finished, Chitolla asked her to repeat it.

"I don't have a good memory for lyrics," the swallow explained. "You may have to sing it a few times for me to catch on."

Secha did so willingly, and eventually Chitolla joined in. The swallow was pleasantly surprised to see that this song had a different effect than the one she had sung before. Rather than brightly-coloured drops of liquid light, this song caused the leaves, trees, and other plants to grow luminous veins, spreading out from their stems to the edges of their forms. The veins bled a dim but somehow powerful olive light which intensified whenever Chitolla focused on a particular object. As it became stronger and brighter, she felt the strange sensation that it was touching her.

"Wow… this is cool!" Chitolla focused on different things. The bark of a tree: *rough, uneven, rock-like*. A nearby leaf: *soft, delicate*. A thorn-covered bush: *ouch!*

Secha tried not to laugh as she watched her friend's reaction. "Don't focus on things that hurt to touch!"

Chitolla smiled back. "Got it. What's another song Tent-Makers sing?"

* * *

When Bukinero first exited Spectral's Temple, his primary concern had been finding Chitolla. But two days had come and gone, and still there was no sign of her.

As he perched on a tree limb, the rising sun telling him he had failed to sleep all night, he let his thoughts wander. Nearby, talking bats filled the rainforest trees. His mind had been too numb to pick up on most of their conversation. But now, as he sat contemplating, he realized it may be best to pay attention and learn what he could about this strange world.

He sighed, focusing on the first voice to reach his ears.

"Now, try this one." The voice was happy and cheerful.

A pause followed before another spoke.

"Glum-what?" the second speaker said. "I don't think I've heard that word before."

Bukinero's heart skipped a beat at the sound of the second voice. *I'm going insane,* he thought. *That couldn't be…* Still, his eyes darted around until they found the source of the conversation. *It's… it's her!*

Spreading his wings, he thrust himself into the air. "Chitolla!" he called. "Chitolla!"

Chitolla turned towards him. Her eyes widened.

"Who's that?" Secha asked.

"Bukinero!" Chitolla laughed gleefully as she rushed towards her mate, grasping his feet with her own. She rested her head against his chest. "Bukinero!"

He stared back at her with joyous disbelief, accepting her touch as he soaked in the feeling of her body pressed against his. "Chitolla! It *is* you!" He looked into her eyes, smiling happily as he tightly held her delicate feet.

"Your mate found you!" Secha said excitedly. "We should tell the others!"

Bukinero held Chitolla a moment longer before responding. "The others?"

"Bukinero, you should meet all my new friends," Chitolla agreed. "Patas! And Chinaca! And Higuero! And Savannah! And Bai'ic!"

Bukinero nodded. "Sure! I'd love to. Chitolla, all that really matters is that you're okay. Honestly, I couldn't tell if Spectral was lying when he told me—"

Chitolla was shocked. "You *met* Spectral?"

"I'll tell you the story sometime." Bukinero chuckled. "For now, I'd really like to hear your story."

"We've been preparing for a war against Spectral."

"Well, then I guess I have good news for you. He's dead."

Secha accepted this information with excitement. "Dead? Are you sure?"

"Yep," Bukinero said. "If he wasn't, I'd be dead. Flammeus killed him. Well, after I weakened him by... I'll explain later."

Chitolla smiled joyfully. "You're right, that is good news! The Vampires won't stand against us if their god is dead! We can go back to the others and tell them we've won!"

* * *

"They're lying!" Mano yelled at the spy as he finished delivering his latest report. "All of them!"

"Mano," the spy said hesitantly, "they're all pretty convinced that both Cattae and Spectral are dead, that the battle's won. They're out there celebrating right now."

"They're playing us!" Mano shook his head in anger. "The white Flesh-Eater is a liar. They're not dead."

"Well," the spy asked, "where are they?"

"Mano?" The young Vampire turned to see Péla fluttering beside him. "I gathered the army, like you asked. They're all here."

Mano turned his attention from the spy and looked around at the many faces staring back. "So you have," he told Péla. "Very good. Not as unreliable as your traitorous son, I see."

Péla's eyes shied away at the mention of Patas, but Mano didn't notice.

Flying to the center of the temple, he announced in as loud a voice as possible, "The traitor Patas has deceived the outsiders—Nectar-Drinkers and Stripe-Faces included—into thinking they can defeat our god and our priest and take Thériava for themselves! The deceiving white Flesh-Eater wants us to think he killed both Cattae and Spectral. The enemy wishes to weaken us with fear so they can steal away our kingdom."

Whispers ricocheted around the building.

"Mano," Péla asked, "are you sure Patas is behind this? He isn't the type—"

"He is with the enemy on Wanderer's Beach, planning their attack." Mano's tone became more excited. "But they will not succeed! I'm convinced Cattae and Spectral have gone into hiding, in a desire to see their servants stand in confidence against the enemy, even without their presence. And will we?"

Frenzied squealing echoed back.

"Yes!"

"We will!"

"Loyal to the death!"

Mano smiled at their responses. "Will you follow my lead, and do as I ask? Our priest and our god will reward us when we have feasted on the blood of our enemies."

Again, the responses were positive.

"Then now, fellow servants of Spectral, is the time to prepare for war!"

* * *

It had been a long night. As the sun continued its way over the horizon, many of those gathered on Wanderer's Beach longed for sleep. Not so for Bukinero, whose inward clock told him that morning was a time to be active, nor Chitolla, who was too excited about having her husband back to even think about rest. The two had managed to convince the others to stay up with them and chat, giving Bukinero the chance to get to know his wife's new friends.

It was there, as they gathered together in a palm on the glimmering sea's edge, that they were unexpectedly approached by a Big-Ear warrior.

"Sorry to disturb you, Chinaca," the dark brown soldier said in a gruff voice, "but there's a Vampire here who insisted I take her to 'the one in charge.'"

"A Vampire?" Chinaca was clearly surprised. "Do you know who it is?"

The Big-Ear warrior rolled his eyes. "I don't know, really. She claims to be Patas'—"

"*Mother!*" The instant Péla's form appeared behind the soldier, Patas flung himself off his roost and rushed towards her, engulfing her in his wings. "You're okay!"

"Patas!" She put her face into her son's chest as he held her tight. "Patas, you're in danger!"

Patas chuckled, unconcerned. "Mom, I'm fine. We're safe now. Cattae and Spectral are dead! They can't hurt us anymore."

"No, Patas." She shook her head. "You're all in danger. Mano has gone mad—he believes Cattae and Spectral are still alive. He's convinced the other Vampires to attack Wanderer's Beach!"

* * *

Moments later, Chinaca had gathered the top warriors and explained to them the situation. "We probably don't have more than a few hours to strategize. From what Péla said, the Vampires are in a frenzy. They're likely not in the state of mind to plan their attack, and besides, they expect Spectral to rescue them. So, we can expect their attack to be passionate, but unorganized."

She took a brief moment to consider. "They know we're on Wanderer's Beach, and that our forces are largely made up of armoured Big-Ears and unarmoured Stripe-Faces. And, of course, they know about Bai'ic. But we've done our best to keep their spies from seeing the other Fox-Faces. So let's start by giving them a shock. We'll send out the five Fox-Faced warriors first, along with Bai'ic. They may know about him, but they've spent their entire lives fearing and worshiping Flesh-Eaters—I doubt they'll be ready to fight against him. And the fear inspired by those first six may be enough to weaken their attack."

"If I may," Bai'ic spoke up in a gentle tone. "I understand, Silver Leaf, that you and the Big-Ears alike have been longing for and expecting war against the Vampires. But I've never liked risking lives in battles. I've always preferred simple, clean victory: fast, and with little bloodshed."

"How do you suggest we do that?"

Bai'ic's eyes were on Chinaca. "I believe that if one cuts off the head, the body will fall."

"No offence, Bai'ic," Chinaca responded bluntly, "but we've already tried that."

Bai'ic didn't respond.

"Right," Savannah said after a moment of silence, "so send out Bai'ic and the Fox-Faced warriors. Before or after the Vampires begin their attack, Chinaca?"

"I'd say before. Unless they've noticed Péla's disappearance, they won't know we're on to them. We've also spent longer preparing for battle than they have, so we'll be ready."

"Where will we attack?"

"Patas says their armour is stored in a cave not far from Spectral's Temple. With his directions, we can get there. Bai'ic can lead the Fox-

Faces, and Savannah, Higuero, and I can follow behind. We'll leave a few soldiers here to guard the beach."

"But what is there to guard here, exactly?" Savannah asked.

Chinaca's gaze drew over to Chitolla, Bukinero, and Secha, who were gathered just outside the ring of top warriors. "The non-battling members of our group. Neither of the swallows are prepared to fight, I doubt Secha wants to be involved, and I don't expect Patas or Péla to join us, since we're going up against their friends."

"Why guard them, when we can just send them back across the sea?" Savannah suggested. "It's remarkably calm, and one of the Stripe-Faces can guide them to a nearby island."

"Hmm… that may be a better idea. If we send them off now, we can put our plans into action immediately. What do you all think?"

Chitolla, Secha, Patas, and Péla nodded in agreement.

"If it's any help," Bukinero said unexpectedly, "I—"

"No offence, swallow, but we don't think it best for you to join in the battle."

"I wasn't about to offer. But I have friends waiting for me back in the Veil. They're strong warriors. If you could somehow get to the temple and bring them here…"

"Yes," Bai'ic responded quickly and affirmatively. "With your permission, Silver Leaf, I'd like to make the temple our destination."

"There could be warriors there," Péla offered, "seeking counsel from Spectral before they begin the battle."

"Fine," Chinaca consented. "Bai'ic and the Fox-Faces can cross over to the Veil while the rest of us continue on to the armoury. But before we do plan any further, Higuero, would you like to guide the non-fighters across the sea?"

FINAL WORDS

THE SEA OF DECEPTION WAS GENTLE, AND A LIGHT BREEZE PLAYED OVER its waters. The sun's strengthening light shimmered on the surface as Higuero led Chitolla, Bukinero, Secha, Patas, and Péla to safety. Only a few minutes into the journey, the group was already aware that one of its members was feeling uncomfortable.

Péla was the first to speak up about her son's agitation. "Patas, you're awfully quiet. Is something wrong?"

He hesitated a moment. "Do you remember what Bai'ic said, about cutting off the head?"

"Yes," Secha responded. "What about it?"

"Well… Spectral and Cattae are already dead. What did he mean?"

Péla in particular didn't understand his concern. "Why does it matter?"

"You'd have to know Bai'ic. He wouldn't just throw out a statement like that without meaning something by it. Do you think…"

"Think what, Patas?"

A queasy feeling filled Patas' stomach. "I need to go back."

"Pardon?"

Patas turned and began flying back towards land.

"Hey!" Higuero called over to him. "What be goin' down?"

"I think," Chitolla said, her wings shaky as she slowed to a halt, "that he figured out what Bai'ic meant."

* * *

"This isn't what I had in mind," Chinaca muttered to herself.

Originally, she had believed the army advancing on the Vampires would consist entirely of Nectar-Drinkers. Instead, she was the only member of her race among a collection of Stripe-Faces and foreigners. She had imagined she would be the only one capable of planning the battle. Now, she had the equally strategic Savannah at her side.

And she certainly hadn't planned on it being daytime when her army advanced. Chinaca looked over to her wings, where her red wing-shields and silver knife-claws weighed heavy against her skin.

"Well, this isn't ideal," she said. "It's too bright and too hot, even under the shadows of the canopy."

Savannah, flying by her side, panted as she spoke. "Bats sure aren't built for the daytime. We'll dehydrate long before we get to our destination."

Chinaca gritted her teeth. "Don't say that. And *please* don't mention water."

"You're the one who mentioned it, darling." Savannah half-heartedly attempted to wipe the sweat from the edge of her mask.

Powerful wing-beats, audible only because of the black wing-shields that threw off otherwise perfect strokes, announced the approach of another warrior.

"Silver Leaf."

Chinaca cocked her ears at Bai'ic.

"It's okay if you and the others head back," he told her. "Fox-Faced bats are fine with flying in the daytime. I don't mind it, either."

"We're fine, Bai'ic," Chinaca said. "A little sunlight can't hurt us."

"No. But the weight of your armour, combined with the sunlight, combined with the fact that you haven't slept in a long while, are likely to affect your ability to fight."

Why does he have to make himself sound so smart all of a sudden?
"We're ready for this, Bai'ic. I've been waiting a long time."

"If the Vampires are still thinking somewhat reasonably, they'll wait until dark to attack."

"Bai'ic, I want this war over with today."

"The Fox-Faces and I can fight today. Wars typically aren't won overnight, Silver Leaf. We'll weaken them. The rest of you can get some rest—"

"*Bai'ic!*" Chinaca shouted. "This is *my* war! Stop trying to control it!"

Bai'ic was silent for a moment. "Silver Leaf, I don't like telling others this, but I've lived a very, very long time and have witnessed many, many wars. Let me advise you."

"Get back in line, like I told you!"

"You're not the only one going into battle. Think about your followers."

"I said—" Chinaca gasped as Bai'ic's powerful claws grabbed her, digging into her shoulders. His giant wings blocked the world from view, hiding her in their embrace.

Bai'ic rushed to a nearby branch and landed on it while holding Chinaca in one foot. His wings trapped her. "Chinaca, are you listening?" His voice came out in a vibrating hiss. "If I have to tell you bluntly, here it is: this is a bad idea."

What's he doing? Chinaca's eyes filled with tears, but not just at his reprimand; his claws seemed to cut into her flesh. "Don't... don't hurt me... please..."

Bai'ic's grip loosened, but he didn't let go, even as she closed her eyes and curled up in terror. "Chinaca." His voice was now soft. "Silver Leaf, listen. Tell me, why is this war so important to you?"

Tears spilled from Chinaca's eyes and she gulped, trying to explain. "Their screams..." Banished memories flooded over her. "My family... I couldn't help them..."

She imagined that night, Cattae's eyes glowing with deadly violence as he stared into her own. He had smiled at her. Laughed. The blood of her father had still been on his teeth, spattered on his face. She saw him turn on what remained of her family and her colony. Their cries had been unbearable. His harsh voice echoed in her ears as she relived the scene.

"He let me go. Cattae said, 'You can't do anything about this, can you? You're just a pathetic fleshling. I'll let you live.' He... he killed all of them. I… I couldn't stop him…"

Bai'ic's claws loosened again and his wing stroked her back. "Silver Leaf, Cattae is dead."

"I know." She could still see the horrible creature. The pictures in her mind played as vividly as if they were part of the present. "I know."

"Then say it."

"Say… say what?"

"Cattae is dead. Say it."

Chinaca paused. "Cattae… Cattae is dead." The tears returned. "But they're dead, too. My family. And I wasn't the one to stop him."

"Chinaca," a voice called.

Chinaca looked over to see Savannah hanging next to Bai'ic.

"We love you, whether or not you're the one who defeats the Vampires," Savannah said. "You don't have to prove yourself to us."

"But… but what am I good for?" Chinaca's words now came out in a rush of emotion. "I'm… I'm the brave one who stands against the Flesh-Eaters. That's how others see me. That's what I have to be."

Bai'ic chuckled. "You are so much more than that, Silver Leaf. And Miss Darling is right. You are valuable to us, whether or not the world sees you as the hero who defeated the Vampires. We love you."

Bai'ic released his grasp, spreading his wings so that Savannah could now embrace Chinaca. The Big-Ear carefully removed Chinaca's tear-stained mask, allowing it to drop to the ground.

"We'll go back," Savannah said softly, but with a tone of finality. "Bai'ic and the Fox-Faces have us covered."

It was only then that Chinaca realized a collection of Fox-Faced, Stripe-Faced, and Big-Eared bats were watching her, their looks filled with care and concern.

Wow. Chinaca's strong emotions began to be replaced by embarrassment. *This is awkward.*

She reached out a claw to wipe away her tears, but Savannah tugged it back with her own. The yellow bat held her tightly as she continued to sob. "It's okay."

Silently, Bai'ic motioned to the other Fox-Faces, then led them deeper into the forest.

They'd barely been gone a moment when Patas arrived, out of breath. "Where's Bai'ic?" His heart melted when he saw Chinaca's teary face. "What's wrong?"

Chinaca shied away, blushing in embarrassment.

"We're fine," Savannah replied. "What's the matter, darling?"

"Bai'ic." Patas' voice was now urgent. "I need to speak with him."

Savannah pointed in the direction the troop had gone. Without another word, Patas whizzed after them.

* * *

Now was the part Chinaca had longed for and Bai'ic had dreaded.

I hate this, Bai'ic thought, wiping a blood stain off his lips. The Vampire it came from lay on the ground below, its head severed by Bai'ic's sharp teeth, blood spilling out of the wound on its side.

Killing mindless creatures was one thing. Killing fellow bats made him uneasy. He knew what the non-Flesh-Eaters could never know—how careful he had to be that the taste of bats didn't get to him. He had to be fully aware that he was taking a valuable life, not just hunting for food.

Creator, help me. I don't wish to dishonour You.

His ears pricked at the sound of another Vampire crawling in the foliage above. He sent a quiet song in its direction, careful not to let himself be heard or seen.

If we can sneak into the temple without alerting any of them…

Another sound caught his ears. Heavy panting and hurried flapping was a clear giveaway of yet another Vampire's presence. When Bai'ic realized who it was, irritation filled him.

"Chocolate!" he snapped. "Why are you here?"

Patas wasn't paying enough attention to hear him, so Bai'ic sent a song in his direction:

See what I say,
My words to you only,

My thoughts for your mind alone…Red!

Chocolate! A gasp of surprise let Bai'ic know that Patas had heard him. *Chocolate, leave, now!*

"That is the trippiest thing," Patas mused. "Bai'ic, is that you? How are you making your voice appear in my thoughts? And the red flashes…" Patas gasped again as Bai'ic appeared, hovering behind him. He froze for a moment, his face paling. "Who… blood… Bai'ic?"

An image of the bat he had just killed entered Bai'ic's mind. "Patas, leave."

"What you said…" Patas' voice was shaky. "What did you mean, about cutting off the head?"

The Flesh-Eater stared at him through bleary eyes.

"You're not going to kill Mano, are you?" Patas asked. "I know he's the enemy. But he… he's my best friend. Maybe I can talk some sense into him."

"What were you thinking of saying to me, traitor?" a voice demanded.

Mano's form materialized out of the foliage, flying fearlessly near to Bai'ic and stopping just short of Patas. His face was hidden behind a golden mask. Jagged knife-claws covered each of his thumbs. "You should learn to be more quiet, Patas. I believe Bai'ic's goal was to sneak up on me and remove my head, like he did to Chito. As I've told you before, your stealth mode lacks stealth."

"Mano," Patas pleaded, "you shouldn't do this! We're free! Spectral and Cattae—"

"Are here watching us now. And if you dare blaspheme by saying otherwise…" Mano's eyebrows furrowed and a dark hiss escaped from between his bared teeth.

"Cattae and Spectral are dead, Mano! I—" Patas' expression changed from one of pleading to one of shock, as in a blur of motion Mano's knife-claw rushed out to slice the left side of his face, leaving a gash that stretched from his forehead to his lips.

Patas managed only to watch with horror and confusion as the taste of his own blood snuck into his senses. "M–Mano…?"

Mano's eyes were cold and dark, his gaze merciless and without a trace of regret. There was no hesitation as he reached his other knife-claw towards Patas' unprotected chest.

The next thing Patas heard was Mano's agonized scream and the sound of bones crushing as Bai'ic's jaws clamped hard onto the Vampire's wing.

Mano flailed, his free knife-claw and sharp teeth viciously scratching and biting at any part of Bai'ic they could reach. The attack hardly fazed the Flesh-Eater. In fact, the cuts he did receive only made Bai'ic's jaws and claws work more incessantly on Mano's wing, until finally, Patas heard the sound of Mano's shoulder being removed from its socket.

Bai'ic dropped Mano and the disabled Vampire fell helplessly to the forest floor. He struggled on the ground, his left wing useless as he tried to find his way back into the air.

Bai'ic spoke with an angry, blunt tone. "If you can find a way, you should come to the temple. There's something there I'd like you to see." He turned, beckoning Patas. "Come."

Patas remained frozen, staring at Mano's pitiful, wounded body. But when Mano's vengeful gaze met his, he looked away and followed after Bai'ic.

* * *

Hundreds of little Vampire eyes peered in surprise as a ghostly white presence graced their gloomy, monotone grey temple.

Bai'ic didn't stop to hear their gasps, whispers, squeals, or hisses. He briefly paused to search the temple, but it only took him a second to find what he was looking for: a perfectly circular hole in the rock-strewn floor, dancing blue lights filling it with an unearthly glow. He rushed towards it with Patas cupped under his right wing.

The moment Patas' body hit the blue lights, fright came over him. His mind told him what to expect: a ringing sound in his head; hard, stiff air; burning smoke and sweltering heat; and Cattae leading him to an unknown place where he would witness another death as Spectral claimed a new sacrifice.

But no such thing happened. Instead, he felt Bai'ic's cool touch on him. Blue lights encircled both of them. Their rays played in Bai'ic's pale fur, so that it looked as if he glowed. It wasn't a harsh glow, either. It was powerful, but drawing. Almost enchanting.

Enchanting. He heard the word spoken in Secha's sweet, child-like voice.

"We're here," he heard the Flesh-Eater say.

Patas gasped as he found himself staring into the eyes of a large, fire-coloured owl. The blue lights were gone. Patas and Bai'ic hovered just over the rocky floor of a dimly-lit building.

"Who would you be?" the owl spoke in a friendly voice, her eyes gleaming.

Patas gulped.

"Bai'ic," the white Flesh-Eater said. But there was no time for proper introductions. "I need Spectral's body. Could you carry it back to the Echo?"

"What do you have in mind?" Flammeus asked.

"I want the body to see that it's been decapitated."

* * *

"Is this good, Mano?"

Mano used his feet and remaining thumb-claw to crawl his way off the shoulders of the two bats who now carried him.

"Yes, this is good," Mano said. When one offered a wing in aid, he let out a hiss. "I said, this is good! I'm not completely helpless!"

The two Vampires waited as Mano made his way onto a thick stone ledge. Behind him was the forest, and before him was Spectral's Temple.

Mano congratulated himself on thinking of the perfect vantage point from which to view Bai'ic's mysterious "something." The entrance to the temple provided an unobstructed view of the interior, and he wouldn't have to jostle for position among the many bats who now paced nearby, their ardent prayers to Spectral having been interrupted by Bai'ic's unexpected appearance.

Mano wondered for a moment what the Flesh-Eater had in mind.

I should warn the crowd of his upcoming deception, he mused. He cleared his throat and opened his mouth to speak.

But his words were drowned out by sudden, shrill cries of terror as a giant red-feathered creature appeared from the circular opening below. Its brilliant golden eyes turned up to face the bats, revealing a small, hooked beak.

The Vampires began whizzing back and forth in fear.

"An owl!"

"Monstrous bird!"

"Predator!"

This is part of the white ghost's trick, Mano thought, angry with his fellow bats for panicking so easily. "Cowards! All of you! Hold your ground!"

Bai'ic was the next to appear. When he spoke, his voice carried to every corner of the stone building. "Look down here, all of you, and decide for yourself if it is I or Mano who has lied to you about the condition of your priest and your god!"

It was only a few moments before all mouths were closed and all eyes wide with astonishment. On the floor of the temple, beneath the owl's feet, was a lump of fur, bearing the shape, size, and colour of the fearful god of Thériava.

Not one of the bats inside the temple moved or blinked, each considering what the evidence before them would mean for their future.

"He's dead?" One of the Vampires who had helped Mano to the entrance of the temple now stared into the building with confusion. "But Mano, you said…"

He turned to find that the injured bat had vanished.

Instead, now approaching him were two birds, one brown and one blue, and a silvery female Nectar-Drinker.

"Flammeus!" the brown bird said with joy, flying down to greet the owl. Clearly, the dead body of Spectral didn't catch her interest. "Bukinero, it's Flammeus! She's here in the Echo!"

"Well," the silver bat noted as she hovered just outside the temple, a smile on her face. "Looks like Bai'ic's plan worked after all."

 # EPILOGUE: NEW STORIES

THREE NIGHTS LATER

"ADILA WHIPPED A TARE..." SECHA'S RIGHT THUMB-CLAW JOURNEYED along the page, her mouth forming the words her claw pointed towards.

"Wiped a tear," Chitolla corrected gently.

Nodding, Secha continued. "Adila wiped a tear from her eye. 'Who are you?' she asked the white bat hoover—hovering above her. It smiled at her. 'Who are *you*?' he asked. 'You look lost.'"

Secha glanced over to Chitolla, who stood beside her on the wooden floor of Flammeus' library. She grinned happily. "I think I'm getting better at this!"

Chitolla nodded, beaming at the little bat.

"Can you read the next part?" Secha asked. "I'll follow along."

Chitolla's gaze rested on the book.

"My name is Adila," the meerkat explained. "I–I lost my family." She bowed her head, trying to hide the look of pain that had come over her face.

The white bat eyed her for a moment. "Well, you're more than welcome to stay with us for a time, if you like. The wilderness is not a safe place for a lone meerkat."

The white bat motioned towards the large group of tan and cream-coloured bats around him. "This is my colony. I'm sure they'll be more than happy to take care of you. Isn't that right, everyone?"

With squeals and chirps, the bats announced their consensus.

Adila raised her eyes to the sound but shook her head. "I would be no good to you. I can't see in the dark, and I can't fly. I would be a burden."

"It's a burden we just agreed to take on. Right?" The other bats again showed their approval. They danced around Adila, singing her a welcome song.

That song remained on Adila's mind and heart for the rest of her life. And the white bat took care of Adila as long as she lived with the colony.

Secha giggled. "Bai'ic."

Chitolla smiled in return. "You still think of Bai'ic when you hear about the white bat?"

"Yes! And from that mysterious, evasive answer he gave you, I think it's quite possible the two are one and the same." Secha sighed wistfully. "Wouldn't that be so... amazing?"

"Of course it would!"

Chitolla gazed at the small circle of critters gathered in a corner of the library. Savannah, Higuero, Patas, Chinaca, and even the wrinkly tortoise Hermain relaxed on the floor, smiles covering their faces as they watched Bai'ic and Flammeus chat about history, the worlds, and Creator.

"My my, dear Bai'ic!" Chitolla caught Flammeus' words as they floated across the room. "When I suggested that all of you bats come to the Veil for a visit to my library, you said you would like *me* to teach *you* about the history of the worlds. But it seems to me that *you* have been doing the teaching and *I* am your eager student!"

Bai'ic smirked, and the listening bats all laughed in agreement.

A flutter of wings brought Chitolla's attention to Bukinero, who landed beside her. "Where have you been?" she asked.

"Wandering the library, of course." Bukinero seemed surprised by the question. "Where did you think I was?"

"You? *Reading* books?"

"Yes, *I* was *reading* books." He chuckled, pressing his body up against hers. "I was looking for information on some of the cool things I saw in the Maxéra Castle in Sévéritas. I wanted to know if any of the objects were mentioned in the books here."

"Are they?"

"Quite a few, actually. I'll tell you more about it later." Bukinero eyed the book that lay open in front of Secha. "Were you in the middle of a story?"

"Yes," Chitolla responded, "but it can wait."

"Actually, now seems like a good time. I haven't heard you retell this story to me in… too long."

Bukinero's heart raced as he felt Chitolla's beak rub against his cheek. He gently ran his own beak through her feathers, treasuring the warmth of his wife's presence.

"Alright," Secha said excitedly, "I'm ready when you are!"

* * *

"So," Flammeus began, "we both agree that the first sin was when Zoe and Kyro allowed Traitor to convince them to disobey Creator's orders. But you say the Underworld Coals were actually Traitor's original plan, that he had them in place long before this event?" The owl considered this. "Have you ever heard of this, Hermain?"

"Certainly," Hermain replied. "And I agree with Bai'ic that it fits the timeline of events and the evidence we have from that time."

Flammeus chirred. "We have virtually no evidence left of that time, dear Hermain! How can one even begin to know these things?"

"They can't," Chinaca spoke up, a smile on her face. "Which is part of what makes this conversation so amusing. You three have been talking for at least half an hour about stuff no one could possibly know! Why bother?"

"I want to introduce a topic!" Patas inserted energetically. "Was the ancestor of the Nectar-Drinkers, Vampires, Stripe-Faces, and, I suppose, Tent-Makers white or black in colour?"

Savannah's expression made it clear she considered it an odd question. "Sorry, darling, but I actually believe the question is more random than what they've been discussing."

Higuero chuckled. "How about we just say that da Nectar-Drinkers are wrong, and we Stripe-Faces are right: our ancestor was black."

"I agree," Bai'ic said, winking at Chinaca. "Let's assume the Nectar-Drinkers are wrong."

Chinaca rolled her eyes. "That's not very scientific, Bai'ic."

Bai'ic gasped in mock astonishment. "Wait… you're saying that just because I decide to agree with something… that doesn't make it true?"

Flammeus tried to contain her chirring. "This is a serious conversation, dear Bai'ic! Now, back to our discussion on the Purple Jesters of Mitibiniamanana…"

Patas laughed with the other bats as the entertaining chat between Flammeus and Bai'ic continued, but part of his attention was focused elsewhere. Longing glances were often cast towards Secha, whose grin lit up her white face with a beautiful glow.

As he watched her, Patas began to hum a tune, one he had hummed many, many times before. But now, new lyrics formed in his mind, and he thought about the moment he would share them with her.

Tell me that you love me;
Tell me that it's true.
Tell me, 'cause my love,
I wanna live my life with you.

And as the stars fade into day,
Promise you'll come home to your place,
In my arms, safe in my embrace,
Will you choose my side as your dwelling place?

 # AFTERWORD

I, FLAMMEUS, DECIDED TO UNDERTAKE THIS WRITING SO THAT THE generations to come may have a complete firsthand account of the events that have brought together the Veil and the Echo after a millennium of separation.

What was once Thériava was released back to the colonies that fled Spectral's power. Some of those colonies have begun to reclaim their ancestors' homelands. When finally convinced of Spectral's death, most Vampires scattered—Mano, in particular, has disappeared—but a few, including Patas and his mother Péla, instead joined the Nectar-Drinkers. Although the Nectar-Drinkers were hesitant to accept them, after generations of being abused by their kind, I do have hope that the two races will learn to live together peaceably.

Due to the dangers of the Underworld, it was decided by the bats, and by the leaders of Sévéritas, that there should be doorkeepers to monitor passage between the Echo and the Veil. Bai'ic volunteered almost immediately, and, motioning to me, said something along the lines of, "Fire Flower volunteers, too."

As for Chitolla and Bukinero, the dear swallows still come to the library frequently… and I have been told their next batch of eggs is on the way. Adorable Secha frequently volleys between worlds, spending equal amounts of time with the swallows as she does investigating Patas' activities.

For those who read this in the near or far future, this is truly the first written record from us:

Those who remember when the worlds came to meet,
When the Traitor's terrible fires met their first defeat;
For the Bridge is not lost, and though the flames rage with passion,
Creator's story for the worlds stands against all oppression.
—The Veil, 1796

CPSIA information can be obtained at www.ICGtesting.com
Printed in the USA
LVOW100538110413

328583LV00007B/23/P

essential reading for anyone interested in the lives and times of such leaders as Themistocles, Aristides, Cimon, Pericles, Alcibiades, and Lysander.

Podlecki, Anthony J. *The Life of Themistocles: A Critical Survey of the Literary and Archaeological Evidence.* Montreal: McGill-Queen's University Press, 1975. Not a conventional biography but, as the subtitle states, a systematic review of the evidence, grouped under such headings as "Plutarch," "Coins," and "Buildings and Walls."

Pritchett, W. Kendrick. *Marathon.* Berkeley: University of California Press, 1960. A review of ancient sources, firsthand accounts of the terrain, and detailed reconstructions of the great battle of 490 B.C., in which Athenians defeated a Persian expeditionary force. Written by the most famous military topographer of his generation.

Renault, Mary. *The Nature of Alexander.* London: Allen Lane, 1975. An extended essay on the character of Alexander the Great and the ancient evidence that alternately seems to illuminate and obscure our view of him. This book grew out of the research Renault conducted before writing her Alexander trilogy of historical novels, and she brings a novelist's sensibility to her reconstruction. I have taken from Renault the suggestion that the setting for Alexander's early feat in taming Bucephalus was a public horse fair, not a private royal showing.

Rosenbloom, David. *Aeschylus: Persians.* London: Duckworth, 2006. A superb introduction to the oldest surviving play in the world, to the circumstances of its creation, and to its later performance history.

Seltman, Charles Theodore. *Athens, Its History and Coinage before the Persian Invasion.* Chicago: Ares, 1974. Much broader in scope than the title suggests, this book by numismatist Seltman offers provocative theories about the coins minted from the famous Athenian silver strike and the use of special emblems on Attic coins to encode the city's celebration of its victories over the Persians.

Smith, John Sharwood. *Greece and the Persians.* London: Duckworth, 2002. Written in short sections for easy reading and reference, this is not a comprehensive history but, rather, a compact introduction to three topics: the Persian background, the campaign of Xerxes, and the expedition of the Ten Thousand.

Stark, Freya. *Ionia: A Quest.* London: J. Murray, 1954. In 1952, the author visited 55 archaeological sites in Turkey and the Aegean islands, at a time when the remains of Ionia were so little known that she encountered another tourist at only one (Pergamon). Stark is a master at interweaving the story of her own journey with retellings of Herodotus and other ancient sources. The book is worth seeking out just for the first double-page map, in which modern place names and land contours in black and white are overlaid with the ancient Greek place names in red.

Talbert, Richard J. A., et. al., eds. *The Barrington Atlas of the Greek and Roman World.* Princeton: Princeton University Press, 2000. A monument of scholarship and cartography, this huge atlas includes not only the Mediterranean but ancient sites from Scotland to Sri Lanka. Invaluable for studying the topography of the Persian Empire, as well as the Greek world.

Tatum, James. *Xenophon's Imperial Fiction: On the Education of Cyrus.* Princeton: Princeton University Press, 1989. An important work of scholarship that considers Xenophon's *Cyropaedia* both as a historical source and as a forerunner of the modern novel.

Thucydides. *History of the Peloponnesian War*, rev. ed. Rex Warner, trans. Baltimore: Penguin, 1954. This classic text by Thucydides deals with the Persian influence on Athens and Sparta in Book 8 of the unfinished history, covering the years from 413 B.C. to 410 B.C.

Time-Life Books, ed. *Persians: Masters of Empire.* Alexandria, VA: Time-Life Books, 1995. This *Lost Civilizations* volume shares the virtues of the rest of the series: authoritative authors and contributors, an emphasis on archaeology and important sites, special essays (in this case, on such topics as Persepolis and the royal tribute), an up-to-date presentation of recent research, and of course, dazzling photographs (many of them archival and hard to find elsewhere).

Trundle, Matthew. *Greek Mercenaries: From the Late Archaic Period to Alexander.* London: Routledge, 2004. An up-to-date survey of current scholarship on mercenaries in their social and economic settings, rather than on the battlefield. The book provides a good background for an understanding of Xenophon and the Ten Thousand.

Tuplin, Christopher, ed. *Persian Responses: Political and Cultural Interaction with(in) the Achaemenid Empire.* Swansea: Classical Press of Wales, 2007. As the cute typography of the subtitle suggests, the 14 essays in this book are more revealing of current academic trends than of substantial new insights into Persian history and civilization. You will want it for the sake of half a dozen superb essays, headed by Alan Lloyd on Darius in Egypt, Robin Lane Fox on Alexander as the "last of the Achaemenids," and Lindsay Allen and St. John Simpson with two views of the rediscovery of Persepolis by early travelers.

Warry, John Gibson. *Warfare in the Classical World*. London: Salamander Books, 1980. The subtitle says it all: *An Illustrated Encyclopedia of Weapons, Warriors, and Warfare in the Ancient Civilizations of Greece and Rome*.

Wartenberg, Ute. *After Marathon: War, Society and Money in Fifth-Century Greece*. London: British Museum Press, 1995. An absorbing study of Greek history as seen through the lens of coins minted by Athens and other city-states. The author is a noted numismatist and formerly the assistant keeper of coins and medals in the British Museum.

Waterford, Robin. *Xenophon's Retreat: Greece, Persia, and the End of the Golden Age*. Cambridge: Harvard University Press, 2006. Waterford, a translator of Xenophon's *Anabasis*, covered much of the route of the Ten Thousand in a Land Rover Discovery and actually succeeded in identifying a cairn that may be the monument raised by the Greek mercenaries when they first caught site of the Black Sea. He summarizes Xenophon's account and adds many historical and speculative reflections of his own.

Welsh, Frank. *Building the Trireme*. London: Constable and Company, Ltd., 1988. This account of the design, construction, and sea trials of the ship *Olympias* was written by a member of the Trireme Trust and provides an engaging personal diary of the project.

Wood, Michael. *In the Footsteps of Alexander the Great: A Journey from Greece to Asia*. Berkeley: University of California Press, 1997. A popular account of the author's own trek along Alexander's route, with all the benefits to be derived from an eyewitness description of the terrain. Particularly valuable for tracing the surviving local traditions about the larger-than-life Alexander in art, drama, and song.

Xenophon. *A History of My Times*. Rex Warner, trans. New York: Penguin, 1978. A classic translation (with a provocative introduction) of Xenophon's attempt to conclude Thucydides's history—an attempt that grew into an idiosyncratic chronicle of the entire half-century that followed the end of the Peloponnesian War.

————. *The Persian Expedition*. Rex Warner, trans. Harmondsworth: Penguin, 1972. The translation of the *Anabasis* of Xenophon, the account of the adventures of the Ten Thousand; contains an introduction and notes by George Cawkwell.

Notes